DANIEL CONRAD DESERVES TO DIE

Natasha Alvandi

Daniel Conrad Deserves to Die

ISBN: 978-1-7346855-4-1
Library of Congress Control Number: 2020941648

Cover art by Tyler Goodro

To Mark Stelter

Acknowledgments

Embarrassing fact: Daniel Conrad and I have been together for a long time. Yes, my longest relationship with a man who isn't my father is with a fictional character.

Daniel Conrad popped into my head when I was studying English at Rice University in 2001. He was amorphous, just a man afraid of his own mortality, struggling for relevance in a changing world. During my time pursuing my Ph.D. in English at the University of Southern California, he grew limbs and a voice. When I failed or made a mistake, I'd wonder what Daniel might do or say in those situations. What would happen if he spilled coffee on his laptop during a conference presentation? How would he react if a student or a colleague saw him in line in the drug store purchasing a box of condoms? That time he flirted with his department chair? A misunderstanding, a mistake, nothing real.

I didn't begin writing *Daniel Conrad* until after I was a professor myself at Lone Star College in Houston, Texas. While Daniel might have been with me for nearly twenty years, surviving three cross-country moves and two marriages, the man he is today wouldn't be the same if I hadn't lived my own story during the forming and writing of this book. A former professor of mine, Emily Hodgson Anderson, wrote a beautiful piece about the shadow book, the story of a writer's life that exists behind each published work. There is a shadow book behind this novel too, one that involves real people who inspire and encourage the best of who I am as a woman and a writer. It's time to thank these human beings for showing up for me on this planet.

Mark Stelter, thank you for giving me the time and the confidence to write and finish this book. Thank you for reading my work, then reading it once more, oh, and one more time again. (Maybe you should read the whole book again. What do you think? Now that you're done, I changed a line on page 183. I think it's best if you just start from the beginning.) Thank you for all of the times we discussed my plot and characters while we hiked God's wilderness together. I don't know if we are married, if we are divorced, or if we are living in adjoining tents with coexisting mountain lions and rabbits as our only companions. What I do know is that I became close to you because I wanted to get to know the mind of an older, male professor for this book, and I fell in love with you. Thank you for falling in love with me, too. Thank you for your passion, your drive, and your intensity. Thank you for the music. Thank you for the dreams. Thank you for being my husband. You are extraordinary.

Don Blevins, thank you for reading *Daniel Conrad* twice and not dying—yet. When I met you, I told you I didn't intend on ever publishing my fiction. It satisfied me enough if my stories affected those I loved. You read my work and encouraged me again and again to send out my writing, sometimes driving me crazy with "Why isn't this published yet?" Thank you for finding a place for me among your spinning plates, Old Man. You showed me unconditional love when I didn't deserve it. Thank you for a beautiful friendship even when it isn't and wasn't easy. You are a good man. I am honored to know you.

To my mother and father, Sigrid and Yousef Alvandi, thank you for surrounding me with books and encouraging me to write my own stories. When you took me to the homes of L. M. Montgomery, Louisa May Alcott, and Laura Ingalls Wilder, you showed me that the women writers I loved were real people with clothes to iron, dishes to wash, and meals to cook. You taught me that life doesn't have to be perfect to create, but that living is perfect for creation. Thank you for allowing me to be myself, that different, prairie-bonnet wearing kid who carried around stacks of books with her everywhere she went. Thank you for your vibrancy, your resilience, your intelligence, your support, and your love. Thank you for always believing in me. You are the parents I would choose. I love you more than I can possibly express.

Further, I want to honor David Wickham's memory with this book. He was a true gentleman and an amazing professor. While I miss him, his passion, his exuberance, and his joy still shine on this planet. The little I shared with him of this book made him laugh. If you knew the purity of David's laugh, you know what a gift it was to make him chuckle or guffaw.

Thank you to All Things That Matter Press for believing in this book. Thank you, Deb and Philip Harris, for your hard work and support. You are amazing, caring, compassionate human beings producing great work for those of us love to read.

Thank you, Sigrid Alvandi, Matthew Clakely, Becky Langdon, Jessica Stelter, Stephanie Stelter, and Erika Wenstrom for reading early drafts of this book. I appreciate your honesty and criticism.

Thank you, Tyler Goodro, for your creativity on the cover design. You have a great future ahead of you.

To Daniel Conrad, this book is a love letter to you. I might find you repulsive, I might wish you'd die, but here you are alive for people to read.

"Woe, woe, woe…in a little while we shall all be dead. Therefore let us behave as though we were dead already."

~Raymond Chandler

CHAPTER ONE

Like all great moments of revelation, the truth came to me under extreme stress.

It was my fifty-third birthday, and there I was in my Dean's office, not understanding a word she was saying. What was clear: she was angry. But that wasn't all of it. Oh, no. Right outside her office, feminist protesters chanted their disdain for me and sexist bastards everywhere. "Fire him! Fire him!"

And that's when the truth hit me: All women are insane. Some less so than others. But all—every last one of them, over half of humanity—is certifiably batshit crazy.

Now, hear me out. I'm not a misogynistic monster. When it comes to insanity, I know what I'm talking about. I have a Ph.D. in Psychology and a Master's in Counseling. Deranged people have been my area of expertise for the last twenty-two years. I wrote my dissertation on patients in a psych ward. After that, I worked as a court-appointed psychologist for six years before I got this gig teaching at Evergreen University. Back then, I counseled a guy who used to pull out his hair and eat it for breakfast. Not lunch. Not dinner. Just breakfast. Another guy who thought the government planted a bug in his left nut. He used to play me tape recordings of the interference. I listened.

But nothing prepared me for the truth, which I realized while I sat in my Dean's office as feminist protesters chanted "Fire Daniel Conrad!" Women are irrational and unpredictable. Every last one of them. And they're everywhere.

"You know me. I'm a straight shooter." Dean Dyer leaned across her desk like she was letting me in on a secret.

Did I know her? She had been my dean for the past year and every one of our conversations left me feeling like I had been hit on the head and I had lost at least ten IQ points. So far nothing she said made sense. Just put me out of my misery, lady. Use that straight shooting and shoot me in the head. The feminist protesters won't mind.

But, instead, she continued.

"We've had a monkey on our back for thirty years. A large monkey."

A monkey? What was she talking about? And who was this *we*? The university? Dean Dyer and someone? Dean Dyer and me?

And didn't she hear the female voices outside shouting "Fire Daniel Conrad! Fire him! Fire him!"? Twenty women, maybe more, gathered outside her office in the Free Speech Zone during the one hour a week the administration allowed students to reenact Vietnam-era student activism. The students called it Protest Hour. The administration tolerated it as long as it wasn't about them. If students complained about anything more significant than the sandwich options in the cafeteria, the administration rescheduled that week's Protest Hour to a less convenient time. Although nothing about Monday mornings between nine and ten a.m. was convenient.

I tried to tell myself that twenty-odd students protesting my existence at the university wasn't bad. Last I heard, our university had seventeen thousand students, but the administration always exaggerated our numbers. We counted everyone we could as a student to prove we were growing as an institution so we'd get more money from the state. I'm pretty sure the janitors counted as students. There was no way seventeen thousand people regularly attended classes. It was a small campus, but let's just say they were right: seventeen thousand students. Twenty out of seventeen thousand students wasn't a serious problem. That's sixteen thousand nine hundred and eighty students who weren't shouting for my resignation. Statistics don't lie, except when they do. So ninety-nine point eight eight percent of the student body was satisfied with me and my teaching. Even the university couldn't deny that sounded like I was doing fine work. I deserved an award.

Still, those twenty women outside were reaching a fever pitch. In that moment, I could have sworn they screeched "Daniel Conrad deserves to die!" even though I wasn't so sure of the last part since killing me was a bit of an overreaction. All I did was write a goddamn book. I didn't murder anyone. Maybe they were shouting "Daniel Conrad deserves a tie!" although the idea of any of these women buying me a thoughtful birthday present was about as likely as Dean Dyer making any sense with whatever she was spouting about a monkey.

I tried to concentrate on what the dean was saying even though it was absurd that our meeting just happened to coincide with the one hour a week an animated protest happened right outside her window about me. It was all too convenient. The impromptu meeting, the protest that regularly had been occurring about me since I published my book, and how unfazed she seemed about the fact that they might—or might not—be chanting death threats. "Daniel Conrad deserves to die!" No, they said it that time. Die. That's what they said. Die.

"That monkey ... that very large monkey's got a rope around our necks. And he's tied it tight. And he's pulling. Pulling hard."

I couldn't help myself. "This monkey you speak of, has he been growing? Or was he always large?"

"This is no laughing matter, Doctor Conrad. You need to … do … your students."

Do them? Was she seriously asking me to sleep with my students?

"I'm pretty sure that wouldn't help anything," I said.

The feminist protesters swelled with a new saying: "Daniel Conrad is a user and abuser of women! A user and abuser!" which didn't stick. So they resorted to their old standby "Fire Daniel Conrad! Fire him! Fire him!" You'd think after all the protesting, they'd have this down by now.

Dean Dyer was still going strong. "We need you … to do … something, someone, anything, anyone."

It was as if I was getting bad cellphone reception in a face-to-face conversation.

"Your numbers. They have to go up. And all this—" she waved her hand at me "—all this has to go down."

"My numbers?"

"Your success."

"Personal, professional success? It has to go down?"

"You know I'm talking about your classroom attrition and how those numbers need to go up."

"My numbers are bad?"

"Abysmally low. The worst I've seen."

"And this makes the monkey on your back upset?"

"The monkey isn't on *my* back, Doctor Conrad."

"The monkey on our back?"

"It doesn't make the monkey smile."

Well, that made sense. The mangy monkey who has been mercilessly living on the university's back for thirty years isn't happy. He's probably depressed just being affiliated with Evergreen for that long. I knew I was ready to kill myself listening to whatever Dean Dyer was talking about. Imagine thirty years of it. Not that there was a monkey. But still.

"So what should I do?" I needed guidance. Something that made sense.

"Pass more students. Sooner than later."

"Or?"

"Or you'll have less desirable classes in the future."

My schedule couldn't get any worse. I taught four Psych 101 classes.

"And I'm placing a note in your file."

"What file?"

"Your file with HR."

I didn't know I had a file. "What file? What note?"

"Doctor Conrad, the note's going in your file. I'd watch myself if I were you."

Dean Dyer got up from her seat.

"I'm late for a meeting," she said. "Good talk."

"Fire Daniel Conrad! Fire him! Fire him!" swelled in the background.

Maybe I could mention the protest. Just to soften her heart. Show her that we're all on the same team. Us versus them.

"Must be annoying hearing those protesters every week."

She didn't say a word. She stared at me.

"Well, you must be tired of hearing fire Daniel Conrad outside your office."

She gave me a blank look for a moment and then she said one word, short and sing-songy. "No."

No, she wasn't tired of hearing it? Or, no, she didn't hear it? Before I could ask or figure out a way to ask, Dean Dyer shooed me out of her office.

"Time to run along," she said, closing her door behind me.

I shook my head and looked at my watch. 9:43. The feminist protest was in full swing just outside, but the campus police wouldn't let them continue past ten. It wasn't my proudest moment, but I considered ducking into the men's room to wait out the protest in the back stall. No one would know. The good news is I didn't do it. I wish I could say I had too much self-respect. Sadly, no. The truth? I remembered that if I didn't get back to my office sooner than later, a woman much scarier than twenty coeds asking for my certain resignation—and possible execution—was waiting for me: Jasmine.

Maybe calling Jasmine scary isn't fair to her. She wasn't an axe murderer or a psychopath, even though I have to admit in the upcoming days I began to doubt who she was and if she was telling me the truth, but I'll get to that. No, Jasmine was the twenty-four-year-old woman I'd been sleeping with.

She was one of those women you'd see once—maybe you'd be gutsy enough to say hello or good morning to when she stepped into the elevator—and she'd linger in your fantasies for days, weeks, months. The smell of her long brown hair. Her flawless olive skin. Her dark, fuck-me eyes.

But my relationship with Jasmine wasn't going so well. Lately, she felt the need to remind me of her attractiveness. It started with her clothes and hair. Before I had the chance to compliment her on her outfit, the first words out of her mouth were "I'm looking really cute today, aren't I?" but the *aren't I* wasn't really a question. It was a statement. And I'd smile and nod and say "Yes" or "I was going to say something." Then she'd scrunch up her face and say "Really? Because you never compliment me anymore."

I wanted to tell her I never compliment her because she doesn't give me a chance to, but I shrugged and said some excuse about how she distracted me while I was writing my next book or preparing for a lecture.

Recently, she'd begun to extend the self-compliments on her clothes and hair to directly saying she was hot or beautiful, but each time it felt like a dig. A reminder of just how lucky I was to be with her.

Whenever she saw me, she told me someone had hit on her. Sometimes she told me who. Damon, the work-study mailroom kid who had to be nineteen. My coworker Frank, who I really hated. Smarmy bastard never let me forget that he read my "Pop Psych Puppy Book," as he liked to call it.

There was no way someone like Jasmine could find Frank even the slightest bit attractive. Damon maybe. But not Frank. Frank had a puffy face with at least three chins. He had to be my age.

Frank's quite the flirt, she texted me after we went out with a bunch of my colleagues for drinks.

She was trying to make me jealous, I think. But it didn't matter. If anything, the increasing number of texts made her less attractive and sometimes pathetic. *I don't like anyone else. I like you. Just you,* last night's read.

Jasmine, who had a way of talking that capitalized her words, said she would pop by my office at nine fifteen with my Birthday Surprise—whatever that meant. With Jasmine, surprises were never safe. Perhaps she'd show up at my office in a trench coat with nothing on underneath, and I'd have a second to think if I should risk having sex in my office before ten a.m. on the same day my Dean's already reprimanded me and a horde of students demanded my resignation.

It was my birthday, after all. She wouldn't have to offer if she was mad—I was thirty minutes late—but if she was prepared, I wouldn't refuse. Or maybe I would. My realization in Dean Dyer's office that all women are insane should have confirmed my initial reaction to hide in the restroom until the feminist protesters dispersed and Jasmine inevitably gave up and left, but I knew I needed to get to my office as soon as possible. No point leaving someone that volatile—read: an average woman—in my office with a grudge.

I ventured out into the cold to cross campus just so I could see Jasmine and she could give me my Birthday Surprise, which I was beginning to hope was something worth receiving and nothing that would cause me more of a headache than the sound of "Fire him! Fire him!" radiating out from the Free Speech Zone.

A school called Evergreen should have an abundance of trees I could shimmy behind or, at the very least, tall bushes or plants. No. Apart from its name, Evergreen was on a prairie, flat and not lush or green except when the administration decided to re-sod the grass. Nowhere to hide. Not even a convenient series of lampposts.

I tried to duck my head. Maybe it was my survival instincts or maybe my morbid curiosity, but I couldn't cross the picket line without looking at the feminist protesters. All bundled up in winter coats, gloves, and hats, the girls were devoted. It had to be the coldest day of the year. One of those freak cold fronts that makes you think you're up north, when in reality you're in the middle of Nowhere, America. If they weren't asking for my head on a pike, I would feel sorry for them. They looked pathetic huddled together. A ragtag group of feminist protest warriors in hodgepodge winter gear.

Only three of the women clutched posters, but all three posters were coordinated, quite possibly all made by one person. The posters all had numbers on them, presumably their ages: 19, 20, and 21. Under each number, the sign said: I'm Daniel Conrad's NEXT VICTIM. Which was extreme since no woman has *ever* been my victim, and if I was going to choose three victims out of that crowd, it wouldn't be those three women.

The whole idea was preposterous. I don't sleep with students.

Unlike some rotund professors who say with smug grins, "I would never sleep with a student," I've had opportunities. Especially in my younger days, women used to come in at the end of the semester and say "I want an A. I'm so close. What can I do? There has to be something I can do," and I'd smile and say "No, nothing," because that's the kind of guy I am.

Still, it wasn't as if the protesters got the idea that I slept with young women out of thin air. Sure, there was Jasmine who was twenty-four—and not *my* grad student, mind you—but more tellingly, my book did imply that I only dated women who were under twenty-five.

Okay, my book didn't imply. My book, *Puppy Love: Why Older Men Should Only Date Women Under 25,* said that was what I did. I wrote I will not date you if you're over twenty-five. No matter what. Even if we're in love. I'll sleep with you on the eve of your twenty-fifth birthday, but at midnight, when you're twenty-five, that's it. You're gone. Out of my life. No contact. Why? Because at twenty-five, women become undesirable to men.

Or at least that's what I wrote.

Much like how no one wants to adopt an old dog at the shelter, but everyone wants a puppy, younger women are in high demand. Ask any American man. Everything being equal, a woman in her mid-forties or a woman in her early twenties? The twenty-two-year-old wins every time. That's just a fact. Yes, it could be that evolutionarily we're driven to go for the most fertile young thing who's willing to spend the night with us, but I argue it's more than that. Young women have fun, they enjoy sex, and they see the world as a place of possibility. Under twenty-five, they think they have time to mess around before they meet Prince Charming. Over twenty-five, their frontal lobes are fully developed. Suddenly the girl who enjoyed flashing skin at a party now has impulse control. Instead of buying fishnet stockings and body glitter, she now wonders how her choices will affect her ability to pop out kids with a respectable husband at her side. The puppy has become the old dog.

With that, my philosophy was born: if you can, why not have the frisky puppy forever and not have to deal with the old dog in her later years, when she's slowed down, has arthritis in her back legs, and needs to be put down? I'm just surprised no one wrote the book before I did. And before you judge me, yes, I am aware it's pop psychology, not academic psychological research like any self-respecting university professor should do. None of what I wrote was really based on anything apart from anecdotal evidence. But it did make me famous, so I have that. I had hoped with that notoriety, I would have enough money to retire, but writing nonfiction just doesn't bring in the big bucks. So, twelve thousand four hundred sixty-eight dollars later, I am the biggest sleaze Evergreen University has ever seen.

Logic would have it that if you're a university professor, writing that you only date women less than half your age might make a thinking person question your morality. And if I knew then what I know now, I wouldn't have written the goddamn book in the first place. Even with the twelve thousand four hundred sixty-eight dollars in royalties and the ten thousand advance for *The Older Man's Practical Guide to Dating Women Under 25*, which I still needed to write, my teaching job paid more. Not to mention my sanity had to be worth something. Meeting with Dean Dyer made me think sanity shouldn't be undervalued.

I hunched by the protesters and tried to hide my face in my coat.

Perhaps I didn't move fast enough. I got distracted by one woman with full breasts in a formfitting turtleneck. Where was her coat? She caught my eye and, instead of smiling, she shouted, "There he is! The pervert!"

A few of the girls lunged toward me.

And that's when I started to run.

CHAPTER TWO

Fight or flight. That's what it was. I ran and ran and didn't stop until I passed the Admin Building and entered the psychology wing of Willoughby Hall.

Only then did I realize that the protesters weren't chasing me, and if they really wanted to get me, they could. My office hours were posted online. Between classes and office hours, I was a sitting duck at least fifteen hours a week easy.

So they probably weren't chasing me, which made me feel like a bozo for running. Still, when the villagers shout "Kill the freak!" you run. True, the protesters weren't carrying pitchforks. They were, unfortunately for my reputation, a group of girls, not a biker gang. At least one of them might have been in my eleven a.m. Psych 101 class. It didn't look good to be running from students on campus. Off campus, sure. On campus, that had to be in a faculty handbook somewhere: no running, hiding, any -ing verb that involves dodging students.

I hoped they didn't put two and two together and conclude that I thought they were after me. Maybe they assumed I was late for an appointment. Plausible enough. Professors have lectures, committee meetings, books to read, articles to write, papers to grade.

But I knew they saw me scurrying—no, sprinting—away and they didn't think *He must have a meeting with a textbook rep. Otherwise he'd stop and chat*. No, they saw me hightail it out of there and each one of them thought *There goes Daniel Conrad. What a coward. Running from a bunch of girls.*

So I was feeling sorry for myself, perhaps a little too sorry for myself, trudging down the hall like a death row inmate clean out of appeals, when laughter emanated from my office. Oh no. Did my birthday surprise start without me?

My door was open. Jasmine sat inside. And look who was hanging out in my doorway, leaning his back against my doorjamb, entertaining my girl, but my coworker Frank, the bastard.

"What happened to you?" Frank asked. "You're a mess, buddy."

Fucking Frank.

"Just came from a meeting," I said to him, turning to Jasmine. "Sorry I'm late."

"Some meeting," Frank continued, eying the top of my head. "Were you rolling around on the floor?"

I pushed my hair down with both my hands. Frank was right. I was a mess. I tucked in my shirttail and gave him a look that said, "Don't even try."

But he kept going. "You can't leave a beautiful woman like Jasmine waiting all morning. It's a crime really."

"Stop, Frank!" Jasmine laughed in that way women do when they're saying no but they mean yes, please compliment me; I'm all ears.

Frank chuckled, which only made Jasmine pay more attention to him.

I needed them to shut up. Stop their laughter. There were things to do.

"Well, now I'm here," I said.

"I have your Birthday Surprise," Jasmine said. "When you're ready."

I envisioned my birthday surprise to be a "Happy Birthday, Mr. President" routine given how much Jasmine had talked it up, but she wasn't wearing a trench coat or anything sexy. Just a pair of jeans, an oversized, V-neck sweater, and three scarves. What did I expect on the coldest day of the year?

Frank squirmed. Feeling uncomfortable, buddy? Out of place?

"Birthday surprise, eh? That's my cue. Most likely something you don't want me to see."

Yes, yes, Frank, you better go.

But Jasmine tittered and turned to Frank. She even went as far as to reach out to him as she laughed, lightly brushing against his arm.

"Oh, you'll love it," she said, picking up a wooden picture frame by her feet and clutching it to her chest. She eyed me, then got up from her chair and scurried next to Frank. "Here, look."

Frank glanced down at the frame and at Jasmine's cleavage peeking out from under the mass of scarves around her neck. Great. Check out my girl right in front of me, Frank. Some "buddy" you are.

Jasmine pointed to something on the front side of the frame, which I couldn't see. They both laughed.

"That's great," Frank said. "He'll love it."

"He's right here," I said, but they didn't pay attention.

They were too busy pointing at things and cackling, elbowing each other at the extra funny bits of whatever it was that they were looking at. You'd think they could have done this while I was in my meeting, but, no, they enjoyed doing it right in front of me.

"That's the best part," Frank said.

"I thought about highlighting it," Jasmine replied. "But I wanted to keep it pristine."

"No, that's good," Frank said. "You'd pretty much have to highlight the whole thing. It's just that funny."

Jasmine oh, Franked again. "You're hilarious!"

All that laughing and obvious flirting in front of me brought me to my second realization of the morning: every woman, no matter how beautiful or brilliant, is annoying to some man. And Jasmine was annoying the hell out of me.

Make no mistake, at twenty-four years old, Jasmine was exquisite. She even had that perfect hour-glass shape most young women starve out of their bodies.

And there she was, this fantasy woman to most men, my Jasmine, laughing that girly girl giggle of hers young women think men want, but which only annoyed the hell out of me, especially when it was with Frank and no doubt because she was mad at me for making her wait thirty minutes in my office. See realization number one: all women are insane.

I know. Stop complaining. You're with a beautiful woman almost thirty years your junior and you're annoyed? You're fifty-three. She's probably annoyed by the fact that her girlfriends think you have to pop a pill to keep it up.

That may be. But like I said, every woman, even the most gorgeous woman in the world, is annoying to someone. And Jasmine's tee-hees and oh, Franks were driving me insane, making me wonder how much longer I could put up with her.

My book's thesis and my still-to-be written *Practical Guide*—not to mention the fact that I am a man—explain why I was with Jasmine at that moment.

But as to why she was with me, a couple of months ago, right after my book came out, her faux-journalistic spirit kicked in—she was in the Masters of Professional Writing Program—and she just had to see if I practiced what I preached. She looked up my office hours online, popped by my office at the university, and leaned in my doorway.

Now that I know her, she was in full-on seduction mode, batting her eyelashes, flipping her hair, and rubbing her hands lightly over her upper thighs. Not that Jasmine would have to do a lot of seducing.

"Professor Conrad," she said, "I'd like to talk with you about writing."

"Do I know you?"

"I'm writing a book. A book you might be interested in."

Well, she wasn't writing a book. She *wanted* to write a book. Big difference. I was—and still am—her whole book. It's almost unfair when I think about it.

She gave me her full name: Jasmine Jacobson. I asked her if she wanted to grab a drink. She looked flustered and said, "Sure."

We went to the campus pub and talked about writing over a bottle and a half of wine. Whenever the subject of her book came up, she got shy. "No, no, you'll think it's a dumb idea," she said.

"Try me."

"No," she said over and over.

Finally, three and a half glasses of red wine later, she was ready.

"Do you like spending time with me?" she slurred.

I barely knew her, but I said yes.

"But why?"

"Well, you're a woman."

Drunk Jasmine nodded. True, true.

I continued, "A seemingly smart, attractive woman. Resourceful. Interesting."

Of course, being a woman, she focused on one thing.

"You find me attractive?"

"Yes." I might have said "Definitely." I'm not sure.

"That's my book." She pointed at me. "Right there. That's it."

"Your book is about me finding you attractive?"

"No, I'm twenty-four," she said. "On January eighth, I'll be twenty-five. We can date until you dump me then, in five months. When you do, I'll write a book about dating the guy who dumps women when they turn twenty-five, and I'll be famous, too. Especially if I can convince you to stay."

"I'm telling you now, we'll be over in January."

"Doubtful," she said. "I can be quite persuasive."

"Prove it," I said. "Come closer."

She got up and stumbled.

"Come here." I grabbed her by the arm. "Sit on my lap."

Later, Jasmine gave me an earful about that. When she felt secure enough in our relationship to voice her opinions, she made it clear that she thought sitting on my lap was *pervy* and reinforced our age difference. "I'm not your little girl, Conrad," she said when I asked her to do it a few weeks after that first time.

But in that moment—our first moment together—she did it. And sitting on my lap, she pressed into me and kissed me hard, even nibbling on my lower lip.

That was all we did that night. I drove her home and walked her to her door. She kissed me again. "You're wonderful," she said. It was nice to hear. I remember thinking, This can work, me and this little girl.

The idea of having Jasmine as my girlfriend appealed to me since my publishers would appreciate a woman under twenty-five on my arm for the release of my *Practical Guide*. And if everything went according to plan, I could churn the book out and meet my deadline with room to spare. The book would be on sale by Thanksgiving, mid-December at the latest. Had to beat the Christmas rush. Of course, that didn't happen.

If I had more than spoken with a woman anywhere close to twenty-five since I was forty, I would've remembered just how needy they are. They really are like baby animals. Perhaps that's the problem with my whole puppy theory. No one thinks about how much time and attention those little ones need when they're sitting in a cage all cuddled up under a sign that says Puppies for Sale by the highway. Not until you plunk down the cash and bring one home do you realize the burden you've taken on: if she's not begging or whimpering all night, she's gnawing on your favorite shoe. Even if you give her a squeaky toy, she'll chomp on it over and over until you're about ready to lose your mind from the high-pitched whine.

Jasmine was that puppy. Always calling me or texting me. Whatcha doing? Whatcha up to? Missing you *so* much. I could have just ignored her yelping, but I felt responsible for her. On the rare days I said no, she pouted, which was disturbing, especially when your girlfriend finds it funny that you were in your mid-thirties when she was in Kindergarten.

So really, when I wrote my first book, I hadn't been with a twenty-something woman in years. Little did I know how annoying they could be in real life, especially when they giggle "Oh, Frank" for the umpteenth time and your first name is Daniel.

"I don't have all day." I picked up a book on Skinner and Operant Conditioning and turned to a random page. "Either give me my present or don't. I don't care. Just stop wasting my time while you two do whatever the hell it is you're doing."

"I'm gonna go," Frank said.

"Good," I said. "Close the door behind you."

He did. Then it was just Jasmine and me. And silence.

Jasmine crossed her arms and glared at me.

"What?" I said.

"You know what."

"Listen, Jasmine, I don't have all day to—"

"Here." she flung the frame on my desk. "I got that hilarious article framed. The one asking for the Board of Trustees to evaluate your morality. I thought you'd find it funny, but obviously you don't find anything funny anymore."

I tried not to react to Jasmine's dig.

I glanced down at the article. Sure enough Fire Daniel Conrad! jumped out at me. So this was what Frank and Jasmine were snickering at. The possibility of me losing my job. Nice.

"This is serious," I said. "You don't know the intricacies of the situation—"

"Tell me."

"You wouldn't understand," I said.

Probably because I didn't understand the intricacies of the situation myself. Still, Jasmine and Frank had been laughing, yukking it up right in front of me about an article in the student newspaper asking the board to fire me. Sure, I could have been less harsh, but Jasmine needed to learn how inappropriate it was to joke about serious subjects. This was the real world, not college, even though we were at a college.

I had offended Jasmine before; usually when I ignored one of her many emails or texts. She'd scowl at me as I'd hem and haw. "What text? No, I don't think you sent me one last night." Then I'd glance at my phone and hit a few buttons. "Oh, here it is. Must be my phone acting up again."

She'd glare, maybe even try the silent treatment with me, but she was too attached to the idea of writing her book to break up with me or put up too much of a fight. So in a way, I was in a win-win situation. She couldn't harp too much on my faults or I would dump her. And if I left her before she was twenty-five, she wouldn't have much to write about, would she? So I got good sex when I wanted it from a woman less than half my age. And she'd keep turning up the heat to keep me around after she lost her mind about the way I treated her, which she did more often than not lately.

But this time, she seemed truly upset.

"I've got to go," she said, inching toward the door.

"You're really going to leave me all alone on my birthday?" I tried to convince her to stay. "You know I didn't mean it. It's just that I've been stressed lately. Kind of under the gun."

The sad part was that I *had* been stressed. With Dean Dyer and the feminist protesters on my rear.

"I need to get ready for class," she said.

"Are you mad at me?"

"No."

"Are you lying to me?"

"Maybe."

She edged to the door. I followed her.

"Happy birthday, Conrad."

She hugged me and teetered up like she wanted a kiss, but before I could move, she backed away and pulled open the door to the hall. Tease.

A pink paper the size of one of those While You Were Out message sheets fluttered to the floor. I stooped down and picked it up. It was just a plain piece of pink paper with a note scrawled across one side in red ink.

It didn't have my name on it. Nothing on the back, either, to indicate who it was to or from. Even then, its message was clear: Hey, asshole, I'm on to you. You're a liar and a cheater. You'll pay.

"Wow. That's intense," Jasmine said, reading the note over my shoulder. "You scared?"

I was. Just not as much as I should have been.

CHAPTER THREE

Probably a prank, I know, but I had to get out of there. I had to get off campus. I needed to think. It was almost ten thirty in the morning, Jasmine was long gone, and I'm not proud of this, but I knew that The Palace Cabaret, a strip club that had popped up in one of those old factories in the beaten down part of town, was open. It had a buffet brunch for nine ninety-nine plus tax. And the drive would clear my head. Being around real women who were paid to be accommodating and not crazy couldn't hurt, either. So I got in my Porsche—the car I probably shouldn't have bought after my book came out, but mine thanks to the exorbitant monthly payments and insurance premiums—and I started to drive.

Fuck Evergreen. If I'm going to be hounded by these people, I will be the man they think I am. I might as well enjoy the morning, driving as fast as I can down the highway in a car I really can't afford toward bouncing breasts and a buffet brunch.

It felt good getting away from the planned community of Greenwood where Evergreen University stood like a bastion of intellectual vigor appropriate to a culturally vacant suburban community. As the carefully crafted comforts of Greenwood peeled away and billboards and rundown buildings took their place, I began to breathe again.

Maybe I could figure out who wrote that note.

Oddly enough, it wasn't the first time someone had threatened to make me pay. There were the usual suspects: my coworkers and students who weren't worth the worry. All harmless, really. Some jealous. Others just looking for a laugh or attention. What was the most any of them could do? Try to get me fired, but that was going nowhere.

My moral ground was just as solid as the next guy's. Even if I was a raging asshole, I wasn't going anywhere anytime soon. It took decades for Evergreen's administrators to get anything done. If someone wanted to fire me, they could start on the paperwork. Signatures would be needed, witnesses would have to be called, I would give my statement, more signatures would be needed. That paperwork might be processed in five years. Five years? I might be dead by then.

My colleagues could let it slip to a reporter that I get it on with women in my office. Who cares. I don't. Maybe once. Even if someone published lies, they would only bolster book sales, especially if I ever finished that damn *Practical Guide*. There's such a thing as freedom of speech. Even for academics.

It's true: the feminist protesters on campus were fanatical with impassioned flyers and editorials detailing how sexist I was. There was one woman in particular, Lacey Griffin-Smith, who no doubt wanted to make me the focus of her senior thesis for that useless Women and Gender Studies degree. She led the charge against me with a weekly column in the student newspaper called "Not Your Puppy." I'd have thought it'd be a one-off editorial, but no. She went on and on.

If the article Jasmine framed for me meant anything, Lacey Griffin-Smith wanted to destroy me.

In her latest column, she called for the Board of Trustees to evaluate my morality: Yes, he has tenure, but in admitting to using women and suggesting that other older men should do the same in his book, Professor Daniel Conrad has violated the moral turpitude clause in his contract. A professor is supposed to protect and nurture young minds, not use them and spit them out when he deems them unattractive. He is a disgrace to the public image of Evergreen University.

But that wasn't all. Her column cited other moral turpitude clause firings at other universities. A case where a tenured sociology professor got caught smuggling drugs in Latin America. Fired, obviously. Another where some Nebraskan department chair slept with an adjunct professor and a male student—at the same time. Fired again.

But I wrote a book. I didn't engage in drug smuggling or double penetration. Still, her article ended with: Fire Daniel Conrad. He is a misogynistic monster who has taken advantage of countless women on this campus.

Countless women? Really? Obviously, Lacey Griffin-Smith thought I was quite the Don Juan. How many women did she think I had used? Didn't people know I was with Jasmine? Was it just naturally assumed that I was with Jasmine and fifteen other women who looked just like her? How many annoying, young women could I handle? *Countless*? That seemed like too many. Especially if they were all like Jasmine.

What a nightmare.

I've only been with thirty-six women in my entire life. Even if we account for my faulty memory and add in another woman who should be included, that's thirty-seven women, which most certainly isn't countless. Thirty-seven is a number. Respectable and quite low considering I've been sexually active for over thirty-five years. To be fair, a misogynistic monster should have a number in the hundreds. Not close to one woman a year.

So Lacey Griffin-Smith or any of her lackeys could have written the note. The you'll pay could be a reference to their desire to have me shamed out of the profession.

My coworkers were a real option, too. No matter how much they claimed to look down on my popular success, if you can call it that, and sneer at my book's lack of academic research, they were jealous. Including Frank, the whole Psychology Department hated me, especially the new hire Ph.Double D. I never called her that to her face, mind. Ph.Double D could mentor Lacey Griffin-Smith on how to attack men. From the moment I met her, she was venomous.

I always make a point to attend those dreadful mixers the administration hosts every August during the week faculty return to campus. Normally, I zip in and out. Make small talk with a couple of people, pile my plate high, make sure I'm seen by the president and vice president of the university, exchange a few words with the vice provost and I'm out.

But last August, this woman—young, blonde, slightly pudgy, with ridiculously large breasts—caught my eye. To be perfectly clear, I didn't find her attractive. She wasn't bad looking for a college professor, but she was average for the outside world even with those enormous breasts. So it wasn't her looks. It was what she was saying.

"My dissertation research on rape survivors suffering from PTSD shows just how damaging men like him can be," she said to Dean Dyer and two cronies from the English Department who were nodding their heads. "Daniel Conrad is a criminal for writing that book."

Me? A criminal?

Just plain wrong.

So I sidled up to her, planted a huge grin on my face, extended my hand, and said, "I couldn't help overhearing. I'm Daniel Criminal—I mean, Conrad. Nice to meet you."

She winced. It was obvious she didn't want to shake my hand, but she did because Dean Dyer was watching and Ph.Double D was new and didn't know that it would have been fine with the dean if she threw her drink in my face. Instead, she just let her hand go limp in mine, like she knew she had to take it for a few seconds and it would be over.

Still, the words liar, cheater, and asshole rang out as a clear indicator my coworkers, including Ph.Double D, didn't write that note. Probably not Lacey or the feminist protesters, either. My book had been out for months. Strange that anyone was still protesting it in the first place, but there wasn't much else going on at Evergreen.

No, the note-writer knew something: liar, cheater, asshole.

And it couldn't be good.

He or she was *onto* me, which implied that my deception wasn't working.

Sure there was the fact that I lied about dating young women in my book, but the language—Hey asshole—combined with you're a liar and a cheater, was personal.

And that's when my guilty conscience kicked in.

Because, unknown to Jasmine and everyone else who recognized me as the man who only dated women under twenty-five, I was in contact with a woman I used to know. Sharon. And Sharon was forty-nine.

Sharon and I weren't having sex. Still, Jasmine would be angry.

The last couple of weeks, I'd met Sharon for coffee or I invited her to dinner when I knew Jasmine was in class or at one of those viewing parties Jasmine and her friends threw for every rattleheaded TV show imaginable. I used to encourage her to party alone even before Sharon and I started back up. Jasmine claimed her girlfriends "loooooved" me, but she didn't put up too much of a fight when I told her I was tired or needed to write my *Practical Guide* or a grant proposal that night.

"I just don't have energy like I used to," I said, and she was sympathetic. She understood.

Once she even mentioned that her dad had gone to his yearly physical. He needed testosterone and maybe I did, too. That stung. But most nights she didn't mention her father or any traits we might have in common. In fact, she rarely mentioned him at all. I once asked her how old her father was, but she just said, "Older than you," which could mean he was eighty or maybe fifty-four. Hell, he could be older than me by a month or a week for all I know.

But, every time, she'd leave—eventually. After Jasmine got her fill of kisses and protracted goodbyes, double checking—no, triple checking—that I didn't want to go, that I couldn't go, she would head out, assuming I needed to sleep or work. And then I'd meet up with Sharon.

Sharon and I had a history. A bad history. I'll just leave it at that.

Lately, when I saw Sharon, she was unaffectionate in person. Rude. Like she deserved better than me. I'd start a story, something about my day or maybe something we both should be interested in, a new psychological study, for instance—something Jasmine would listen to; there were times Jasmine would shut up and listen, believe it or not. Sharon would cut me off with an eye roll or a deep, protracted sigh. That was if I was lucky. Most of the time, she just ignored me.

Jasmine, being a Third Wave Feminist or a Post-Third Wave Feminist, whatever they're calling it these days, would insist on splitting the check. Sharon would disdain my every attempt at a conversation during the meal and expect me to pick up the tab.

But when I got home, a picture would be waiting for me in my email. Better than anything Jasmine could text even though Sharon's breasts were lopsided if you really looked at them. Those pictures were staggering in that they followed a night of disparagement and scorn.

"Just trying out my new cam," she titled the last email, almost like she didn't care. No words in the body of the email. But there was an attachment with her smiling, topless.

Maybe that was Jasmine's problem. Jasmine was available—too available for someone like me. I wondered what she saw in me or if she would want me, an old guy long past his sexual peak, if she met me on the street and didn't expect to turn me into a bestseller of her own.

With Sharon, I never felt old. I could be myself. Even if she treated me like shit.

Maybe that was why I was seeing Sharon, meeting her places when I should have been writing my *Practical Guide* or spending time with Jasmine. It wasn't as if I was cheating on Jasmine, not really.

But by the time I arrived at The Palace Cabaret and found a good parking spot away from everyone so my Porsche wouldn't be dinged by some strip club-loving, door-swinging asshole, I was just paranoid enough to wonder if Sharon was the problem. If I was a liar and a cheater, according to the note, because I met with her behind Jasmine's back, however innocently, I might add, or if I was a liar and a cheater because of who Sharon and I were to each other years ago, back when I made more than my fair share of mistakes.

No point thinking about it. Not then. There was a whole warehouse full of women eager to please and a buffet of chicken wings and sliders that weren't half bad if I didn't think too much about the food and I sat back and enjoyed the show. So I pushed all thoughts of Sharon out of my mind, went in, paid my nine ninety-nine plus tax with the intention of seeing some tits on a Monday morning.

That was the plan, anyway: to get away from Evergreen and all the crazy women in my life—Sharon, Jasmine, Dean Dyer, Ph.Double D, Lacey Griffin-Smith, the feminist protesters—by, yes, seeing woman after woman strip naked and writhe on a grungy stage. Not much of an escape, really, but chowing down on a chicken wing, I was at peace for a moment.

But that's the thing about escapes. The ones that cost nine ninety-nine plus tax are only temporary.

CHAPTER FOUR

"Conrad, can you hear me? Where are you?"

Jasmine. Barely audible. I probably shouldn't have answered my phone. I tried to toggle the volume up, but the stripper's "Pour Some Sugar on Me" prevailed.

"Downtown," I said, moving away from the stage and leaving my buffet plate on my tiny table.

"You're not on campus?"

"Nope, left to clear my head."

"Oh."

Jasmine rarely paused in a conversation unless she was upset. I should have been more attentive, but I had enough on my mind between Dean Dyer, the feminist protesters, and the threatening note. Not to mention Jasmine herself.

"There used to be a time when you'd just grab me," she started.

Oh, no. She was going off without any prompting. I should have asked "What's wrong?" Maybe I would have gotten good guy points.

"You used to see me and you'd just grab me," she went on. "I couldn't leave without you groping me. Now it's 'okay, bye.'"

"Can't you give me a mulligan? You know, because it's my birthday? I'm an old man. Over half of a century old."

That worked. She chuckled. Progress.

Then a longer pause. Oh, no.

"But it's more than just today. It's every day lately. Do you even want to be with me?"

"I do," I said. "I really do."

I looked back at my table. A blonde waitress in a nearly see-through shirt picked up my plate. No, wait, I gestured at her. "I'm coming back," I mouthed. She looked at me like I had one too many screws loose, but she left my plate alone.

"Do you still find me attractive?" Jasmine asked.

"I do," I said. "I really do, but—"

She whimpered.

"But you asking these questions is really unattractive," I finished.

Another call. I looked at the caller ID. Some unknown number.

"I have to get this," I said. "It's the dean."

It wasn't.

"Fine," she said. "Bye."

I accepted the next call relieved to be done with Jasmine even for the time being.

"Danny!" a woman's voice boomed on the other end. "Don't you dare hang up."

Shit. I'd recognize that voice and that hideous version of my first name anywhere. No one called me Danny except my agent, Alexandra Morris. I thought I had been successful at screening her calls.

"How's that *Practical Guide* coming?"

"Oh, you know, it's coming."

"Don't bullshit me, Danny."

"You know I'd never do that, Alex."

I could almost hear Alexandra cringing on the other end. That's what you get for calling me Danny, Alex.

"I know you'd take ten from the publisher and another ten from me as a loan and then miss your deadline by two months. I know that."

She was talking in thousands. A ten thousand dollar advance on my *Practical Guide* and a ten thousand dollar loan from Alexandra. There's that phrase "Don't mix business with pleasure." No one mentions the dangers of mixing business with money, however counterintuitive that might sound.

"We're going to squeeze that book out of you whether you like it or not, Danny. Your market exists now. Give it a day, and they'll be on to something else. How to date forty-year-olds probably."

"Maybe I could get a jump on that market and write that book instead."

"Cute," she said, even though her voice indicated that she didn't think I was cute at all. "Seriously, we need your *Practical Guide* before the end of the month."

"No way," I said. "I need at least two months, maybe three."

"Unless you have a good reason that I can use to drum up interest, like maybe you're strung out on heroin or roughing it on a reality TV show. Even then, time's running out. Your book needed to hit shelves last month."

"There's a lot going on. Stressful things."

"Bullshit," Alexandra said. "Other people's lives are stressful. Your life is inspiring. You're the man who dates twenty-year-olds."

Her voice was flat, like she was reading from a script.

"To tell you the truth—"

"Danny," she said, "I don't care what the truth is. The truth won't sell. So even if you got the clap from one of these women, you need to slap a happy grin on your face and write a book that sells sex to older men. How many pages do you have? This moment. No lying."

I had a document titled "Practical Guide" on my computer. I hadn't opened the thing in months. I might have five pages double spaced. Maybe I could copy and paste passages from my original book and add in some tips. That could work. With the copied pages, I'd be close to a quarter of the way done with illustrations, charts, and graphs added in. Huge pie charts. That would help eke out the page numbers the publisher wanted. Still, five pages was discouraging. I couldn't tell Alexandra five pages and expect her to be calm.

"I've got about fifty pages, give or take twenty," I said.

"What's this give or take twenty bullshit?"

"Thirty good pages."

She grunted.

"You know, we have collaborators. No one would know. You'd finish. You could make some money, pay me back, keep the extra."

"You mean a ghostwriter?"

"A collaborator."

"Not going to happen."

For better or worse, that damn book was mine.

"Then stop being a girl, Danny, and get that *Practical Guide—*"

"Give it up!" A male voice reverberated over the loudspeaker. "If you liked Candy, you're going to L.O.V.E. Cindy, who will make all your fantasies come true. Let's give it up for Cindy! Come on out, baby girl!"

"Danny ... are you at a strip club?"

"No," I said. "I'm at school. It's a Monday morning, remember?"

"Sounds like a strip club."

"Just a normal day at Evergreen," I said. "Oh, the dean's waving me over. Got to go."

"Wait. I want to see something tomorrow," she said. "If not, I'm hiring a collaborator or two."

"No collaborators." I clicked my phone off.

I went back to my table, reclaimed my plate, and even got up for seconds from the buffet. Might as well get my money's worth.

I was having a good time. Enjoying my birthday. Even flirting a bit with my waitress. I told her, "It's my birthday," and she said if she had a nickel for every man who told her that, she'd be the Queen of America. I told her, "No, really, you'll see." I pulled out my wallet. She looked at my driver's license and said, "Oh, honey, you don't look a day over forty-five." I know she was hoping for a big tip, but it felt good.

So I was enjoying myself, flirting with my waitress, watching the show, when I looked down at my phone and saw a voice message flashing red.

A message from Dean Dyer's executive assistant, Tim. The dean wanted to see me at four thirty p.m. Again? Hadn't we just met no more than three hours ago?

I asked the waitress if I could take a call outside and come back in.

She shook her head. "Rules are rules, hun."

I left the safety of The Palace Cabaret knowing I'd have to pay another nine ninety-nine plus tax to get back in. I might be cheap, but I'm not an idiot. Even I know it would be pushing it to give my boss a call in earshot of the male announcer asking us to "give it up" for Cindy.

In the parking lot, on my way back to my car, I dialed Tim. Straight to voicemail. Maybe the kid was at lunch. So much for Tim cluing me in to why Dean Dyer wanted to meet two times in one day.

And then I saw it, right across the driver's side of my much too expensive Porsche, not one swipe, but three solid, horizontal gouges over a foot long each. Motherfucker. Those were some deep grooves. Someone put muscle into it.

I looked around. No one. Maybe The Palace Cabaret had cameras or someone saw the bastard hanging around my car. I ran back up to The Palace Cabaret, right up to the big bouncer standing by the door.

"Did you see anyone doing anything to my car?" I gestured to the back of the parking lot.

The bouncer didn't move his eyes but kept his gaze like he was one of the Queen's guards. "Nope," he said.

"Look," I said. "My car's been keyed. That Porsche over there."

"I didn't see nothing."

"That's a double negative."

"Nothing. Single or double, I saw nothing," he repeated.

"You must have cameras, something."

"Nope," he said, still not looking at me or my car, keeping his gaze straight ahead.

"I'm holding The Palace Cabaret liable."

He pointed to a sign: Park At Your Own Risk.

"That's bullshit," I said.

He pointed at the sign again.

"Risk is risk. Move along."

And so I did. But before I left, I made a show of taking down his name. Dwayne was all he would give me. "There's only one Dwayne" he said. "Boss knows who I am."

"Well, Dwayne," I said, "Boss will be hearing from me."

When I got to my car, I tried not to look at the gouged door, and I peeled out of the parking lot. Back to Evergreen.

I sure as hell hoped Dean Dyer didn't want to talk about why I skipped out on my office hours to go to a strip club. If those feminists chanted "Daniel Conrad deserves to die!" when I was minding my own business, living off my measly twelve thousand four hundred sixty-eight dollar success from my first book, imagine what they would say if they saw me kicking back at The Palace Cabaret on a Monday morning. They'd probably advocate for me to be drawn and quartered or burned at the stake.

But knowing how things worked at Evergreen, I never got in trouble for anything I did do. It was always things I didn't do that were the problem.

And there was a lot I wasn't doing.

CHAPTER FIVE

One of the advantages of academia is that there is very little oversight or supervision. I usually went months without having a sit-down meeting with my boss. I suppose it was possible Dean Dyer's monkey was rearing its ugly head. But I knew the truth in my gut: this second meeting had to be about something more heinous than whatever was on the university's to-do list for thirty years: me.

When we'd talked that morning, Dean Dyer mentioned that my attrition rates were abysmally low. Maybe I could impress her by bringing a plan to the table, but I couldn't even remember the difference between success rates and completion rates. Both involved how the state funded Evergreen, but one required us to keep failing students in our classes and give them F's for the good of the university. The other required us to give everyone As, Bs, and Cs, and God forbid we gave them Ds or Fs. We were supposed to do both, have high completion and success rates, but one might have been more important than the other, even though neither were important by any real-world standard.

I wanted to cancel the meeting with Dean Dyer, but it was too late, so I trudged to the Admin Building and waited in a short chair next to her office, across from Tim's receptionist desk.

Tim was typing away on his computer. Then a bleep. Tim looked up. She must have him trained with electronic bells and whistles.

"You can go on in," he said.

"Good mood or bad?" I whispered.

Come on, Tim. Give a guy something, anything.

Tim smiled. Maybe that was a good sign?

"I heard that," Dean Dyer said behind me. "Timmy, hold my calls. You think you can handle that?"

I forced a smile of my own. Dean Dyer continued to glare at me from her doorway until she gave up and waved her hand at me, more like a *shoo* motion, but through her office door. She looked like she was luring vermin—maybe a rat—right into a trap. Even with a plastered on smile, her disgust was evident.

"Just asking Tim about his mood," I said.

Dean Dyer grimaced.

"Close the door behind you and take a seat, Doctor Conrad."

I plopped down in the cushy chair directly across from Dean Dyer for the second time that day. No matter how much I squirmed, I never found a way to sit in that chair comfortably. Even the rinky-dink tables and chairs at The Palace Cabaret were better. Maybe the administration designed the furniture to wage psychological warfare against faculty members. Or maybe it was just like everything else at Evergreen: the veneer of competence was all that mattered.

"Why do you think you're here, Doctor Conrad?"

Great.

"I don't think I'm here to win an award or give my approval on a statue of me for the courtyard, if that's what you're asking."

Her eyes narrowed. "The statue project is no laughing matter."

I didn't even know there was a statue project. Wait, I had heard something about the school spending twenty-eight thousand dollars on a new bronze statue of an eagle, our mascot. I thought people were joking. That was real? So the Liberal Arts travel budget was really slashed in half to make up the difference? I'd thought that was another joke. Were the rumors that Dean Dyer floated the idea of checking out dry erase markers to the faculty true, too? If the statute was real, then maybe.

All that and the chair I was in hurt my back. I tried not to squirm. No point looking untrustworthy, like I had anything to hide.

"No," I said. "I'm sure the new statue will be great. Everything around here is great."

"No need for sarcasm, Doctor Conrad."

"I wasn't being sarcastic. I really do think we need a new statue. It will be good for morale, for students."

"Well, that's why you're here."

"The statue?"

"No, our students."

Great. Maybe she heard from one of the feminist protesters that I ran away from them that morning.

"I always try to put students first. Sometimes I might prioritize my research interests, but when it comes to our students, I care."

"You might care too much."

Wow. Really? Was *she* being sarcastic? No. Her face hadn't moved during our conversation.

"Thank you?"

Was I winning some sort of Most Caring Teacher of the Year award? That's me, the guy who cares too much.

"This is no laughing matter, Doctor Conrad. We are putting up posters."

A new statue *and* posters? What was this woman talking about? Did she think I was the interior decorator?

She didn't make sense and her face wasn't moving normally. Was she having a stroke? Her speech wasn't slurred. Still, something was off. Early stages of dementia?

She had to be around my age. Frightening thought: were people my age going senile already?

"Maintenance will put up the posters tonight. You need to watch yourself, Doctor Conrad. This is the first step. If these posters don't deter … deter what you do, then we will take action."

Okay, so what I did was bad. And there would be posters. Posters going up that night.

"I understand."

Even though I didn't.

"Good talk," she said. "No matter who you are, the university can't have you jumping around like a monkey, throwing your feces everywhere."

And now I'm the monkey? At what point would it be okay to ask for an intervention?

"No more jumping," I said. "And I will stop flinging my feces."

"Good," she said. "I'm glad you're taking this seriously."

Was my face any different now than when she told me "This is no laughing matter?" Maybe the confusion or that uncomfortable chair made me sullen. Or maybe it was the possibility that I could be doddering on senility if people my age were already exhibiting signs of early onset dementia.

She got up and led me out of her office.

"Timmy," she said, "give Doctor Conrad his packet."

Tim jumped up. Poor guy.

"The posters should help," she said again. "But the complaints need to stop."

What complaints? And would this also end up in my file?

Too late. She was gone. Her door shut behind her.

Tim handed me a packet entitled "Evaluating My Behavior: Step One of My New Improvement Plan." Wait. Was I on an Improvement Plan? The packet had a sticky note pointing to one of the subsections with Daniel Conrad written on it. I thumbed to the sticky as I walked back to my office. Did I Just Cross the Line? was in big bold print. Followed by a series of questions I—or anyone wondering if he or she had "crossed the line"—could ask him or herself.

Do you:

- Say "Just joking!" or "Just kidding!" more than necessary?
- Make inappropriate jokes?
- Notice that your coworkers, students, or administrators walk away or back away when you speak

to them?

- Notice people change the subject when you join conversations?
- Ever wish you could take back that comment you made?

This was bad.

It's time to W.O.R.R.Y.

Oh no. Not an acronym.

Work
Over
Relationships while
Respecting
Yourself

There was also a section on what constituted a hostile work environment. Just publishing *Puppy Love* should get me fired since there was bound to be some woman who thought my book referenced her. My *Practical Guide* wouldn't be better. If that thing ever hit shelves, I'd be screwed.

That night, I couldn't sleep, wondering what those posters would say and if I was on an Improvement Plan without knowing it.

I thought the posters might repeat the W.O.R.R.Y. acronym from the packet, which would have been bad enough, but they were worse. Much worse.

Across from my office, where there used to be a Join Psych Club banner with a cartoon Freud giving a cheesy thumbs up, was a new poster with a big picture of a young girl sitting in a classroom. She was wearing a short jean skirt. Not that you could see up her skirt. Oh, no. A male professor—whose face wasn't visible, but whose back took up a great deal of the picture—loomed over her. She looked scared but intrigued at the same time.

In huge neon pink font under the girl, the poster screamed You Don't Have To Trade Sex For Grades!

Sex for grades? That's what Dean Dyer thinks I'm doing? Ridiculous. I don't sleep with my students, lady. It's something I've never done. Okay, maybe once, but that was a long time ago, and she was a returning student, not some eighteen-year-old. She earned her grade, thank you very much. Sex for grades? Preposterous.

Wasn't at least part of Dean Dyer's complaint that I wasn't passing enough students? Did this have to do with the fact that I just didn't have enough eager students willing to spread their legs? If so, good for them. Glad they have integrity. Now take these posters down. Stop wasting taxpayers' money on a non-issue.

But predictably, more wasted money. Along the poster's base: Visit C.A.R.E., the new **C**enter for **A**cademic **R**espect and **E**mpowerment in the basement of Caulfield Hall. You deserve a respectful learning environment. We have confidential counselors ready to help.

A new center? Confidential counselors at the ready? Could there be a clearer warning to women who walk down my end of the hall? Who else was the poster about? My next-door neighbor to my right was Dr. Susie Sousa, a sixty-seven-year-old grandmother of six. To my left was Ph.Double D. I wasn't sure which of them was less likely to find herself in a quid pro quo arrangement. Susie had a certain flair about her.

So the poster wasn't about Ph.Double D or Susie, but me, obviously.

I looked at the poster again. The guy, the professor, in it even looked like me. His back anyway. And the fact that he was wearing a button-down shirt, rolled up at the elbows. No, that could be anyone. Wasn't that how professors dressed?

His shirt looked rumpled and he had brown hair cut just like mine. I squinted at the poster. Was that a picture of me? Could be, but I doubted the school would be bold enough to use my image without my permission. Although one thing I'd learned working at Evergreen was that just when you think you know the depths of their incompetence, you find a new low.

Even if it wasn't me, but some overpaid actor who looked like me, everyone would see the resemblance.

No doubt the poster would cramp my style.

Not that I was trying to sleep with students.

But it would make me look like something I definitely wasn't: a misogynistic asshole.

To everyone except Jasmine. That Jasmine. She probably would laugh and say, "Listen, you don't have to trade sex for daily grades, but you do have to trade sex for an A in the course."

Looking at that damn poster, I actually thought about snapping a picture of it and sending it to her. It would be something she would enjoy, but I knew she'd be by soon enough. She was always stopping by, saying things—inappropriate things—when I should be working.

But she never came by. She usually appeared at school in the morning. Most mornings, she even brought coffee. That day, no Jasmine.

"You have to see this," I wanted to text her throughout the afternoon. "Come by when you have a second."

I didn't.

When Sharon called at six to see if I wanted to grab dinner, which meant did I want to pay for her dinner and get insulted, I hadn't heard from or seen Jasmine in over twenty-four hours. So I packed up and left, hoping Jasmine would show up and I'd be gone.

CHAPTER SIX

Sharon picked the restaurant: Mama Carlita's. She either didn't care that I couldn't stomach most Mexican food or she got a secret thrill from the fact that nachos and enchiladas gave me diarrhea. Whichever, we were back eating at Mama Carlita's, just like we did before everything between us went to hell.

The vibe in that place used to be a bit off, but nothing I could put my finger on. I always attributed the strange feeling I got when I opened the door to the fact that it was in a strip mall. Normally, middle class housewives would distrust a restaurant in a strip mall near the highway, but because it was smack in the center of the suburbs, the residents of the magical Greenwood Planned Community considered it just risky enough to be a comfortable quirky. The place was always packed around lunch and dinner. This time, not a soul.

Since I had been there last, someone had replaced its background loop of tinny ay, yi, yi, yi mariachi music with a mix of late nineties pop music, which should have made suburbanites more, not less, at home.

Our waiter led us to a table in the back, right under a giant mural of the Alamo I didn't remember the restaurant having. Not that there was anything wrong with the Alamo, but wasn't Mexico on the wrong side—or the right side—of that one, depending on one's perspective? The mural wasn't a simple picture of the building, which could be more neutral. No, there were people there, too. A little hand-painted Crockett, Bowie, and Travis leading a bunch of white people in what read like a block party with Santa Anna's troops. Weren't the white people slaughtered, not given wine coolers?

Were they purposefully misremembering the Alamo to sell more tacos?

"That mural," I said, pointing at the wall, "is historically inaccurate."

"Are you really starting up on that again?" Sharon sighed.

"What do you mean?"

"You wouldn't shut up about it before."

"I've never seen that mural before in my life."

"You have. And you wouldn't shut up about it."

"Maybe it was a different mural."

"No. You said the same thing. Historically something. Blah, blah. Remember? It was our last night together. My earring fell in your eye."

"Your earring fell in my eye?"

"Yes."

"You're thinking of someone else, another one of your boyfriends."

"No, it was you. Historically blah, blah, on and on. Maybe you're losing your memory."

"Or maybe it was another guy," I mumbled. "Too many to keep them all straight."

Sharon looked down at the menu. She either didn't hear my comment or she was ignoring me. I stared up at the mural. It's the kind of thing I would remember. In the corner was the artist's name, Ernesto Santiago Cruz, and his phone number. Did he hope that people looking to commission murals would see his work and give him a call? Or did he want women to call him up? "Hey, baby, that's one hot mural." Even though it wasn't. Everyone looked out of proportion. Squat bodies. Swollen heads. Still, maybe it was working for him. Maybe chicks dig historically inaccurate, out-of-proportion murals.

"I'm getting the mozzarella sticks for an appetizer. You want anything?" Sharon asked.

"Mozzarella sticks at a Mexican restaurant?"

"It's right here under Appetizers."

I leaned across the table and looked at Sharon's menu upside down. Sure enough: mozzarella sticks.

"Don't you find that a bit odd? The mural, the music, and now the mozzarella sticks? Doesn't all this feel off to you?"

"The shrimp tacos are ah-mazing here. Expensive, but ah-mazing," she said.

"Ah-mazing?" I said. "Like the poetry teacher?"

"Don't start, Daniel. I don't want to hear it," she said. "You were cheating. I was cheating. Get over it."

Which was just wrong. I never cheated on Sharon. My ex-wife Elle, sure, I'll admit the truth. I did cheat on Elle with Sharon. And during that time Sharon and I had great sex. Sometimes at my place when Elle was out of town. One time on her staircase, although her cat kept pouncing on my feet, which was weird. But let's be clear: I never cheated on Sharon. She cheated on me and broke my heart with Alan the poetry teacher, who she delighted in telling me was "ah-mazing" in bed despite being a sixty-five-year-old loser who spends his time teaching lifelong learning classes at the Greenwood Community Center, hoping to bed middle aged housewives. I know, I know. A cheater getting cheated on. Not a lot of sympathy there. Still, heartbreak's heartbreak.

I glanced at the menu. Shrimp tacos twenty-five bucks? What was this place? Well, don't hold back on my account, Sharon. By all means, why don't you order dessert, too? Maybe something with edible gold leaf. Or maybe spring for every authentic Mexican dessert they have. Couldn't amount to much. Looking at the menu, I saw that they had brownies, apple pies, and milk shakes. Oh, and vegan chocolate chip cookies. Authentic Mexican cuisine is always vegan. And while you're at it, maybe you should give Ernesto Santiago Cruz a call. He's your type of man: an authentic artist and full of bullshit.

When the waiter came by for our drink order, Sharon paused over the wine list and took out a pair of reading glasses.

Sharon had reading glasses? Maybe she had them back when we were together, but used to be shy about whipping them out. Her frames were that old lady pink, shaped in a retro style that crossed the border from funky to eccentric.

"A bottle of this," she said, pointing at the wine list so only the waiter could see. Why was she hiding the purchase from me? I'd see the price on the check. "And a Coors for him."

"I don't drink Coors anymore," I said, hoping it would bother Sharon that she just didn't know things about me or my life.

"Get him a Coors," she said to the waiter. "And we're ready to order our food, too."

I wasn't ready, but Sharon didn't care. I scanned the menu. Fajitas. They couldn't screw that up, could they?

Sharon rattled off her order. Yes, he could substitute the corn tortillas for the flour.

"I'm allergic to gluten," Sharon said to the waiter.

Since when? Sharon ate pizza just last week. I saw her.

"It'll be an extra buck-fifty, but our corn tortillas are handmade in house."

"That's fine," Sharon said.

Thanks, Sharon. Don't even ask the guy who's footing the bill.

"And for you, sir?"

"I'll take the chicken fajitas."

"Oh," Sharon said to the waiter. "No onions for him."

Which was weird because why would she care if I was eating onions unless she wanted to kiss me after dinner.

I gave the guy a sheepish grin. "If she says so."

"Listen to the lady," the waiter said. "Your wife knows best."

After he left, I leaned across the table so I could whisper to Sharon, "Funny he thought we were married."

"Funny how?"

"I don't know, just funny."

And then silence.

"Since when do you have a gluten allergy?"

"I don't."

"But you just—"

"The flour tortillas are always so soggy here. The corn ones are better."

"So you lied?"

"He's just a waiter," she said. "Since when do you care about stuff like that?"

The waiter brought our wine and beer.

Sharon took a few gulps of her Chardonnay.

"You really with this Jasmine person?" she asked.

"Yes."

"You have a picture?"

I did. Too many pictures. For every selfie Jasmine uploaded to her social media accounts, she emailed me four or five. Maybe I could include that in my *Practical Guide.* Prepare to see more than your fair share of pictures of your under-twenty-five gal.

No matter what I criticized about Jasmine, the girl photographed well.

I flipped open my phone. Yes, I have a flip phone.

"Here," I said, showing Sharon one we had taken together with my phone a while back. One of us smiling, even though before that, Jasmine had insisted that we try a more "gangsta" look. I kept saying "gangster." "No, it's gangsta." Jasmine laughed. She couldn't keep a straight face for any of the pictures after that.

"Your little friend is pretty," Sharon said.

"My little friend?"

"How old is she?"

"Twenty-four."

"Cutting it close, eh?"

Was Sharon making a joke? Quite possibly. And she had read my book. That was something.

"Yes, well, we're going to break up in January. Don't have a lot in common," I said.

"We never had a lot in common, either."

"What about psychology?"

"Not the way you talk about it."

"Sex, then."

"We had sex in common?"

"Sure, why not? We were good together."

Sharon grimaced and drank more wine. I drank some of my beer. I was paying for it; I might as well enjoy it. There wasn't much else to do but look at the mural or photos of Jasmine, both of which depressed me.

Our food came.

"Your dish is gluten free. I made sure," the waiter said to Sharon. "I changed your husband's tortillas to corn, too. Just in case you two want to share."

Of course, I wanted the flour tortillas, but I didn't complain.

We ate a while in silence. I stared at the Alamo mural. Had I blocked it out? Maybe Sharon had traumatized me. Perhaps I had blocked out other things from that time, too. What else?

"Let me see the girl up close," she said, gesturing to my phone. I handed it to her, half-worried she might snoop and read some of Jasmine's texts. Then again, if she did, it might make Sharon jealous, which could only be good for me.

"She's gorgeous."

Nicest thing I ever heard Sharon say and it was about Jasmine and not me.

"I bet waiters don't assume the two of you are married," she continued.

"No," I said. "They think she's my daughter."

"Daddy issues," Sharon said, shaking her head. "She must have daddy issues. Or something wrong with her head."

"Couldn't she just like me?"

"Don't think so. She's way out of your league."

"I've been with women like her before," I said. Even though I hadn't. "Besides, her father is older than me. Much older."

Sharon didn't need to know Jasmine was with me hoping to land a book deal.

"Is she an actress?"

"I didn't hire her to play my girlfriend, if that's what you mean."

"I meant she's beautiful and looks like an actress, someone I've seen before. Has she been on TV?"

"No."

Not that I knew of, anyway.

"She looks like one of the girls from that dating show. You know the one with the lisp. Jessica? Jennifer?"

Sharon watches reality TV? Why?

"You must be thinking of someone else. She's smart. She's a writer," I said. "She's writing a book, a memoir, right now."

"Something you have in common," Sharon said. "Writing."

"It's a different kind of writing," I said. "And we're breaking up in January."

Sharon's foot edged against mine. Maybe her leg was asleep. Maybe she didn't know—and then I felt her bare foot on my knee. Oh, yes. She was doing whatever she was doing on purpose.

"You don't want to get together then?" she asked, inching up my inner thigh.

"I'm with Jasmine," I said. "And aren't you still with Brian? Your husband?"

"You didn't answer my question," she pressed. "Do you want to get together … like we used to?"

Of course I did.

"No," I replied.

"You're a horrible liar, Daniel," she said.

I squirmed out from under her foot.

"We can't go back to my place. Jasmine might come by."

"Brian's out of town."

Poor Brian already knew about us. For some reason, he didn't kill me when Sharon went crazy and confessed everything two years ago. That didn't mean he wouldn't kill me if he caught me in bed with his wife now that they'd spent thousands in marriage counseling.

Although if he was going to kill someone, he probably should kill his wife. She was the insatiable—

"How far out of town is he?"

"London."

"You sure?"

"Yes," she said. "He wouldn't say he's going on a transatlantic flight and hide out in the garage. He's a good guy."

"Good guys can be driven to extremes," I said. "And there are private detectives and friends of friends who help people out in these situations."

"Brian's a non-issue, but if you're too chicken, that's fine," she said.

"I'm not scared of Brian. It's just … rude."

"Well, Miss Manners, you're the one who used to call me up begging. And that was after Brian knew, too."

That was one night. Maybe more than that. Right after my divorce, I was drunk more than I was sober. I remember calling Sharon, telling her I missed and needed her. I might have asked her to marry me. The details are fuzzy.

"I'm the one doing you the favor here," she said. "Giving you a courtesy."

Some courtesy. Sharon leaned forward and stretched her arm under the table and grabbed my hand. She squeezed it tight like she needed to communicate something to me, something she couldn't just say out loud, not here, not now.

"Fine," I said. "Let's get out of here."

I asked her for directions to her house even though I knew exactly where she lived: in the most desirable neighborhood on the Westside of Greenwood, Woodslake Grove. I used to drive by to see if her BMW SUV was parked in the driveway just to know if she was home or somewhere else. Because Sharon's "Artistic Free Child" wanted a pottery studio, Brian complied and converted their garage with a kiln worth at least ten grand. He had to get a special permit from the Greenwood Community Standards Committee to begin construction. In his own garage. Probably took the bastard a good six months to convince the Greenwood higher-ups. They no doubt approved because Brian was a tastemaker, whatever the hell that meant. Sharon said it on more than one occasion: "Brian and I are community *tastemakers*." Probably couldn't hurt property values to have a real, authentic artist in your community, especially one who was a suburban mom, not some actual artist who didn't shower or pay his monthly association dues. Since Sharon's pottery studio was harmless and tucked away in the garage, the people of Greenwood could pat themselves on the back. They supported the arts.

Brian did the whole thing, even painted the walls pink for her as a surprise, when she and I were out of town one weekend. I guess the poor guy thought she could use it as a pottery studio but that he could still park his Benz in the garage, off to the side.

I remember her asking, "Does Brian really think I can create art next to a car? The man has no common sense."

So Brian's Mercedes was always on the street and Sharon planted her SUV in the driveway. I did wonder how often she used the studio. She never mentioned firing up the kiln.

"The house is off Greenwood Boulevard," she said. "Turn left at the Shell station. The second street on the right is Woodslake Grove. That's the street. We're at the back of the cul-de-sac. Number fifteen."

"Okay," I said.

She got up. "See you there. Greenwood Boulevard. Left at the Shell station. Second street on the right, Woodslake Grove. Fifteen Woodslake Grove."

"Got it."

"If you decide not to come, let me know so I can make other plans," she said.

"I'll be there," I said.

I thought she might kiss me, even though, yes, she was a married woman and the mother of three kids. Even when we were together two years ago, she wasn't demonstrative. I guess Jasmine's lengthy goodbyes made me completely forget what it was like to be with a normal woman who didn't say "kiss me again" a million times before leaving.

Not that Sharon was normal.

As the waiter ran my credit card, I glanced at my phone. No word from Jasmine. Probably still mad at me for yesterday, off pouting somewhere about how I mistreated her. Or maybe she had enough for her book and she was done.

No texts. No calls. I told myself if she wanted me to remain faithful, she would call me on the way to Sharon's.

And even if Jasmine did call, this was something I had to do. Something I needed to get out of my system.

Although it had been a while, the wounds still smarted. Sharon cheated on me and then proceeded to tell everyone about us, including my then wife. She destroyed my life and kept her perfect little suburban dream with the doting husband and the virtuoso twin daughters and the All-American son in high school. Sharon deserved my scorn, my disdain for what she did.

Then there was the way she grabbed my hand.

So I paid for Sharon's meal and Chardonnay, drove down Greenwood Boulevard and turned left at the Shell station. Lights out, pumps off, closed. Suburban living at its finest. Even the Greenwood gas stations kept everyone in check, telling you no one should be coming or going after nine p.m. Stay safe, snug in your bed, alarm system set, locks triple checked. The rest of you: stay out.

I turned on Woodslake Grove, which, no, didn't have any woods, lakes, or groves on it. Sharon's striking Colonial house was where it always had been. Towering columns, nothing like my cookie-cutter house from the front unless you really looked at it. No question the view from the road was beautiful, unique, but the sides: straight HardiePlank. Just like the cobblestone street that extended a good six feet at the entrance to Woodslake Grove before turning into concrete. Still, amenities made Woodslake Grove better than other Greenwood Community villages. Deeper lots with well-placed, trophy trees surrounded in mulch. A bike trail. Two parks with wooden playground equipment. Not plastic like in my neighborhood.

I parked down the street in a pathetic attempt to divert a private detective from putting two and two together. Not that I needed to protect Sharon. She was cheating on her husband. I wasn't cheating on anyone.

Well, maybe Jasmine.

Woodslake Grove. Sharon's house. Back where I used to be—again.

I thought about leaving. Turning my car back on and pulling out of the cul-de-sac, burning rubber. That would show Sharon.

But I knew she wouldn't care. She'd call up some other guy. Maybe someone she was flirting with online. A man with money this time. Someone who could snatch her away. One of the many Woodslake Grove investment bankers or corporate lawyers with a bigger house with a deeper lawn and the ability to take Sharon and the kids to Jackson

Hole for the summer. Someone who could give Sharon everything she wanted.

Those pictures she took couldn't have been for me and me alone.

So I knocked on her front door and followed her up to the bedroom she shared with Brian, believing the lies I told myself. An everyday occurrence in Greenwood, where we grasp onto everything we have—even when it's bad for us and not what we want—because someone else real or imaginary might want it or deserve it more.

CHAPTER SEVEN

Right after we were done, Sharon picked up her iPhone from her nightstand.

"You're really sweaty," she said, not looking at me. "You need a shower."

She was reading emails, I think. Or texts. I couldn't tell. Even though I was nestled into her, both of her hands were holding her phone.

"A shower might be a good idea," I said.

Especially if I ran into Jasmine later.

"It's just down the hall," she said, not looking up.

I knew where her shower was.

"You want in?"

"No, I'm good."

"Where are the kids?"

"The girls are at a sleepover. Cameron's asleep in his room or watching TV downstairs," she said.

Great mom. Her teenage son was in the house. Hopefully the kid didn't hear his mother having sex with another man while his father was out of town. That's the kind of thing that can scar a boy.

Sharon's phone dinged.

"You okay? Did Brian message you?"

"Not Brian," she said. "Alan."

"The poetry teacher?"

"Yes."

"You've been with him this whole time, too?"

"No," she said. "We've been messaging, going out, grabbing coffee, dinner."

"That's what we were doing up until just now."

Sharon rolled her eyes.

"I thought you knew this wasn't exclusive."

Like she had to tell me.

"I just didn't know you rekindled your relationships with everyone all at once."

"Is that a problem?"

"No," I said. "It's good for me, actually. I wouldn't want anyone to know I slept with a woman over twenty-five anyway. I have my *Practical Guide* coming out any day."

Well, not any day. Not that Sharon was paying any attention.

I needed to move or do something, but I just stood there naked. Luckily, my phone rang.

"Your little friend?" Sharon said, not looking up from her phone.

A goofy picture of Jasmine flashed across the screen. When she took the picture, she said it looked like a llama on crack. She loved to grab my phone and take pictures of herself. Sometimes they were sexy. Most of the time they were just weird. A llama on crack?

I let Jasmine's call go to voicemail.

"You going to shower?"

"No, I think I'll head home," I said. No point running into Sharon's teenage son in the bathroom.

"Go home then. Makes no difference to me."

The phone rang again.

Jasmine's llama-face.

"If you're going to ignore her, turn your ringer down," Sharon griped.

I toggled the volume button on the side of my phone and leaned down to kiss Sharon. She jerked her face away from me. My lips scraped against the side of her jaw.

Sharon winced.

My phone buzzed in my hand. Another call from Jasmine.

I started to get dressed as I pretended to answer my phone, letting it buzz against my cheek. I made a show of telling "Jasmine" that I loved her and I'd be home soon, waving goodbye to Sharon, who didn't look fazed to hear me talking to my girlfriend. And I was out—down the stairs, past Sharon's living room and out the door—without anyone seeing me.

On the drive home, I didn't call Jasmine back. I could call her tomorrow. Tell her I fell asleep at my desk or maybe that I decided to grab a late viewing of one of those Oscar-bait movies. Were they still in the theater? Maybe it was better to tell her a made-up friend of mine—any male name would do—was depressed. He needed to talk about his failed marriage. I took him out for drinks, and you know how Larry is. He just wouldn't go home so I had to stay with him. It was a little after midnight. That wouldn't be too unbelievable. Of course, Jasmine would ask questions. "Why haven't I heard about this Larry before?" Probably because he doesn't exist. Better stick with the movie. I could look up plot summaries, reviews, prepare.

Or maybe Jasmine and I could break up. What did we have, a little over a month left? At least then I'd have time to find someone else before I had to publicize my *Practical Guide*. There was no way Jasmine would last that long. I wasn't even a quarter of the way done with the book. If I broke up with her soon, I'd have enough time to write. Then when I was finished, I could worry about finding someone for publicity. If Alexandra was willing to invest in a ghostwriter or two, I'm sure she could procure the company of an attractive twenty-something woman for a press tour. It was as good an idea as any. Although even the lowest level prostitute was probably more expensive than those down-on-their luck Ph.Ds who plagiarized for a living.

I pulled into my driveway. Someone in a hoodie and jeans was sitting on my stoop. Maybe a woman. Kind of short, but her head was resting on her knees. She looked up.

Jasmine.

Well, that's not creepy at all. By all means, call and call and then just come over and stakeout my place.

She ran up and hugged me.

"So good to see you, Conrad," she said.

"What are you doing here?" I asked, trying to keep my cool. Strange how she thought she had a right to stalk me. Yet another *practical* thing I couldn't include in my *Practical Guide*: young women have no boundaries. Or this one, maybe abnormal woman, doesn't have any boundaries. I really needed to increase my sample size. It's never a good sign when your n equals 1.

"Finally, a friendly face," she said. "I think it's all over."

"What's all over?"

"My parents. Didn't you get my messages?"

Messages? No. I didn't think to check them.

"I've been a wreck all day," she said. "I hate when they do this, but this time I think it's for real."

She whimpered and launched into one of those long, choking sobs that makes you wonder if the woman will make it out alive.

"Come here," I said. She buried her face in my chest. Her tiny shoulders shook her frame and mine as she blubbered something incoherent.

"You say your parents are all over?" I asked, not sure if I should guide her inside and out of the cold or pay attention to her every word.

Jasmine nodded into me. Her face was gooey and hot. My shirt was getting damp.

"What happened?" I finally asked. Did they die?

"Di-vorce," she blubbered.

All that sobbing should be reserved for dead or dying mothers and fathers, not divorcing parents. Especially when you're an adult.

And then I remembered just how annoying Jasmine could be, emoting everywhere when I wouldn't mind a little peace and quiet.

"It'll be okay," I patted her again. Not sure what else there was to say.

More tears and snivels, but Jasmine eventually stopped sobbing. I'd like to think it was because of my attentions, but I think she just ran out of tears.

"Can I stay with you tonight?" She looked up at me. Dark circles under her bloodshot eyes.

"Of course," I said. "If you think it will help."

I leaned in to comfort her.

"It's just so shocking," she said. "You think you know someone, that they're telling you the truth—"

My heart raced. Did she know about Sharon? "It's not what you think."

She looked at me like I was off my rocker.

"My parents. My mother's gone crazy. She had a knife. She just kept waving it around."

I knew there was something off about Jasmine, but was her whole family unhinged? I mean, the girl came to me, pretending to enjoy the company of a man old enough to be her father all for her future success.

Insanity does run in families.

"I don't know if I can sleep. I'm wired and worried and crawling out of my skin," Jasmine said.

I rubbed Jasmine's goose-bumpy arms. I could feel her bones. Had she been losing weight?

"Have you eaten?" I asked.

"I don't remember."

"Well, let's fix that first," I said, feeling a bit hungry myself and wishing I had picked up the rest of the fajitas I didn't get a chance to finish at Mama Carlita's.

I brought Jasmine inside and took her into my kitchen. Together, we whipped up some pancakes. I showed her how if you add a dollop of butter to the recipe on the box, the pancakes become fluffier.

We sat on the couch together. Jasmine tried the pancakes and agreed. "So much better."

That was the thing about Jasmine. I could teach her what I knew about life, and she always was impressed.

"Days like today make me realize what's important," Jasmine said after the pancakes. "I know you said you don't believe in love." She nestled close to me.

"I don't."

"And neither do I." She paused. "But I love you. If that's okay."

It wasn't.

Why did she have to say she loved me? Right then and there with the tears and the crazy mother with a knife and Sharon still on my mind? I wanted to say, "Listen, little girl, you might want to reevaluate whatever the hell you just said."

But I said the only thing I could say. "I love you, too."

Because that was what I did. That was who I was. And part of me did love Jasmine. I didn't want to make her more miserable than she already was. And if that's not love, I don't know what is. So, yes, when she said she loved me, I said "I love you" back. I didn't have much of a choice. I didn't want her to get all homicidal on me. Especially now that I know that sort of thing runs in her family.

So we cuddled longer than I would have liked until Jasmine rested her head in my lap and extended her legs out on the couch. I was the attentive boyfriend. I owed her that much. I rubbed her neck and shoulders.

I tried not to think, to just be present in the moment. I even attempted one of those bullshit Dialectical Behavior Therapy modules. I am a tree. I am grounded. I planted my feet firmly into the ground. My roots were in that moment with Jasmine.

But my mind kept floating back to Sharon.

How much I wished Sharon was in my arms or lying next to me, even after everything she did the first time we were together—or maybe because of it. Every time I saw her. Every time I thought of her. The pain. Sometimes a deep stabbing regret—the closest thing I knew to anything real.

So lying next to Jasmine, I grounded myself in grief and let myself hurt. Not healthy according to any book or article I've ever read, but when pain feels like love and anguish is all you have, you hold on to it even if it is dragging the rest of you kicking and screaming to hell.

CHAPTER EIGHT

If it wasn't for the sun casting a blinding wakeup call through my living room window, I would have slept right through Dean Dyer's Student Success meeting the next morning. I wrestled my arm out from under Jasmine and glanced at my watch. Just forty-five minutes until the meeting. Given Greenwood traffic, I'd be lucky if I got there on time. Add in potential Jasmine-related drama and I'd be lucky if I got there tomorrow.

I jostled a rumpled Jasmine good morning and told her I had to go.

"Can I come with you?"

"If you want."

Jasmine no doubt would take a year and a day to get ready.

"But you have to hurry up," I said.

And like that, Jasmine started to cry. Well, good morning to you, too.

"My par-ents," she sobbed. "They used to call me and I'd go talk to them, help them. Now they've given up. They're just going to get divorced. Di-vor-ce-d."

She was crying. Crying again over not being consulted before her parents decided to end their marriage. You're a grown woman, almost a quarter of a century old. Act like it.

I know I shouldn't have been so put out, but I didn't have time to comfort Jasmine again and get to work on time. I believed in an unspoken rule for relationships: just because you're upset, it doesn't mean I need to be upset, too.

Still, I guided Jasmine back to the couch and pushed a pillow under her head. I ran to the bathroom and grabbed an old bottle of sleeping pills.

"Go back to sleep," I said, with the practiced sincerity of a middle-aged, male Mary Poppins. "You've had a rough twenty-four hours. Take two of these and just relax. Your car is here. You can meet me on campus when you're ready."

It worked.

By the time I got dressed and pulled my stuff together, Jasmine was curled up on the couch. Eyes shut, breathing deeply.

I noticed a peanut butter and jelly sandwich laid out on the counter for me. Jasmine must have made it while I was getting ready.

I scooped up the sandwich and tiptoed past Jasmine. Asleep she didn't look so bad. And she loved me.

Although for the life of me I couldn't figure out why.

On the way to school, I considered if Jasmine and I could have a future together. There was nothing wrong with her. Except that she might be genetically predisposed to insanity. Oh, and she was using me for that stupid book of hers.

Maybe there was a lot wrong with her, but Sharon wasn't much better.

Sharon.

I checked my phone.

Five text messages. All Sharon.

Breakfast—now or never, the last one demanded. Sent just a minute before.

Heading to a meeting, I replied.

Skip it, she texted back.

Can't.

You can.

And longing.

Maybe I could. A rapid rendezvous with Sharon.

I glanced at the clock. Evergreen meetings habitually began late. Who knows why. A desire to please everyone, even latecomers? Or maybe the administrators themselves knew the truth: nothing we did in those meetings was essential. Dean Saunders, the dean before Dyer, told me that he would have scrapped our meetings altogether if they didn't give the faculty something to do. "Makes them feel significant, like they have a voice," he said. Probably why the poor bastard got fired—well, asked to reflect on if he was a team player. He reflected and determined he wasn't. Or maybe he reflected and determined he was. Or maybe he took too long reflecting. Before any of us knew it, he was gone.

Dean Saunders wouldn't mind if I was late, if I missed meetings, if I didn't even pretend to care. Dyer loved her meetings and took them seriously. She already had me on some sort of Improvement Plan. No point giving her more ammunition in her war against me.

Then a text from Sharon: Fine, Daniel. Don't reply. Your loss.

Loss.

I continued to tap out a quick reply. I'd see her, we could do this. I'd be late to the meeting—who cares—but Greenwood morphed into an endless school zone. No texting or cellphone use. Oh, the joys of living in a pocket of safety.

I tried to text Sharon down low in my lap so no one could see. Start. Stop. Start. Stop.

Let's, I managed. A little girl with a backpack too big for her body crossed the street with a female crossing guard. Traffic resumed just enough for me to slam on my breaks. Female crossing guard back at her post. This time a little boy wheeling a backpack behind him. Really, kid? That girl was carrying hers. And just when another of Greenwood's numerous Audi Allroad wagons eked through the intersection, another little boy stopped traffic with his bowl cut. It was too much.

Start. Stop. Start. Stop.

I've often thought it would make more sense if they'd group the tykes together and then cross the street. Not in Greenwood. Every pipsqueak is a delicate flower worthy of individual attention. Much like the actual flowers planted everywhere. Not a single one dead or dying. The association dues must pay round the clock flower girls to trim and replant before anyone notices a single peculiar petal.

Maybe it was the kids crossing the street or the stress of Greenwood living, but I remembered that summer before my father had his last heart attack. The freedom of going with him to Yellowstone. The endless possibility of heading anywhere and the danger of that, too. I never saw my father as happy as when he was forging a path in the woods, his hiking boots grinding into the dirt.

Well, I did see him almost as happy once. That time he flirted with his best friend's wife, but that was a different happiness. The exhilaration of control. Out West, he couldn't control anyone or anything. Out West, he was free.

Christ, he must have been forty-nine on that trip. I know he didn't make it to fifty.

Stop. Female crossing guard back at her duty station. I jerked to a halt for a tubby girl with huge glasses. The school bus behind me was dangerously close to my bumper.

Ding. A text from Sharon: Meet me at Auntie Dora's Donuts.

Which actually could work. The place was in one of Greenwood's many village shopping centers, right across from Evergreen, in fact. I'd never been there, but I'd seen its sign. As good a plan as any. I could see Sharon, feel her warm skin against mine, not that she'd let me touch her in public. But be near her. Even for a few minutes.

And the Mercedes station wagon ahead of me jerked to a halt, which made me slam on my breaks and hope that the school bus driver behind me was awake enough not to plow into the back of my "Puppy Porsche," as Frank called it.

Two kids wearing matching outfits crossed the street. At least the Greenwood I.S.D. crossing guard had the good sense to take twins across traffic at the same time. Tweedle Dee and Tweedle Dum, with Tweedle Dumber leading them across the street gesturing at her stop sign like none of us were well acquainted with our brake pedals.

Still, a good reminder.

The bus driver behind me slammed on his brakes just in time. A screeching success.

And like that, new respect for the crossing guard. Probably because I was just two cars away from the front of the line. Almost free. I'd get out of here unscathed. No worse for wear. Except for the time I'd never get back.

Another text from Sharon: Can't wait all day. I can meet someone else for breakfast.

Ridiculous. Some of us are risking our lives out here, battling the suburban start-and-stop and Sharon's immediately onto someone else, probably Alan or someone equally below her.

A quick right and I was at Auntie Dora's Donuts, or in the shopping center, anyway. Enough typing and driving. Might as well talk like normal human beings. I hit the call button instead of tapping out a misspelled reply.

"Can't talk long," she said. "Gotta get off the phone any second."

School zone, probably.

"Make it quick, Daniel. Told you, can't talk."

Why women have to waste time explaining that they can't talk is beyond me. If there's limited conversation time, no point using up precious resources talking about how we can't talk. I told her I was there, in the parking lot, that I was on a timetable, too, but that I wanted to see her, touch her, hold her.

Which was the truth. She groaned and said she'd be there soon.

With all of ten minutes before Dean Dyer's meeting officially began, all I wanted to do was see Sharon, maybe sneak a quick grope, and go. Something to feel alive.

Ahead of me, Auntie Dora's Donuts stood, the only mom and pop shop with the chutzpah to thrive in the sea of chain restaurants that comprised Greenwood's village shopping centers.

Made me glad to see she chose a place with character. Took a lot of effort in Greenwood too.

Might as well head inside, support this Auntie Dora woman, and pick up a Bavarian cream filled chocolate donut for Sharon. Bavarian cream filled chocolate donuts were her favorite. Maybe I'd have one, too. Walking into Auntie Dora's Donuts, I couldn't help but be overwhelmed with the mediocrity of Greenwood. It was as if everything average from everywhere found itself transported and plopped down in one place. Thank God for this Dora woman and her donuts. A sliver of something extraordinary.

I spotted a table in the corner. Perfect for Sharon and me to talk, if only for a second. I draped my jacket over a chair, while the ladies at the next table eyed me like I was trying to pull one over on them. Yeah, that's right. Better hide your purses. The guy leaving his jacket at a table might use it for a magic cape and, presto chango, you're pickpocketed. Given how little crime there was in Greenwood, the default mode should be trust.

Then again, maybe they could smell the lying and the cheating on me. That's right, ladies, don't trust the deviant in your midst.

Ding. A text from Sharon: Almost there!

A bit too giddy, I decided to order, but first, I made a big show about trusting the lady at the next table with my jacket. This is what trust looks like, lady. She wasn't impressed.

The disinterested girl behind the counter—not Auntie Dora—plopped two donuts, one for me and one for Sharon, into a bag.

"Do you want to up the ante?" she asked.

"Up the what?"

"Up the *Auntie,*" she pointed a slick menu behind her. "Up the Auntie."

"What does that mean?"

She rolled her eyes. "Buy one dozen, get a dozen free."

Like I was stupid or something.

"No," I said.

"Everyone ups the Auntie," she said.

"You'd think Auntie Dora wouldn't let just anyone up her auntie," I said, trying to make a joke.

The girl stared at me.

"I mean, the woman must have standards," I said. "You must know her. She's got to be a nice person, living the dream, baking donuts, selling them."

"I know Daryl at Corporate," she said. "If you've got a question about the menu, you can call him. He's in Dallas."

"Wait. Are there other Auntie Dora's Donuts?"

The girl nodded like I asked her if this planet right here was called Earth.

"In Greenwood?"

Another slow nod.

Great. I should have known not to trust Auntie Dora.

Sharon was probably sitting and munching on a donut at some other fake Mom and Pop donut shop, exactly like this one, but miles away.

I fished my phone out of my pocket and called Sharon.

"Where are you?" she asked before I could get out the same question.

"Auntie Dora's on Evergreen Avenue. Where are you?"

"I'm at the one on Greenwood Boulevard. Come to me."

"I can't," I said, looking at the retro clock ticking away above the counter. "I really need to get to this meeting."

"Auntie up! Auntie up!" the girl behind the counter bellowed with more gusto than I thought capable of a human being given over to apathy.

"This place is terrible," I said. "But I want to see you. Spend time with you."

Not my proudest moment followed.

"Brian still out of town?"

"I thought you were heading to a meeting then class."

"I am," I said.

"I thought you didn't have time to meet."

"I don't."

Sharon paused.

I tried to fill in the gap. I could feel Sharon slipping away.

"I can meet you after class," I said. "At noon. And I'm free all day. We can spend as much time together as you want. Noon until you're tired of me."

"I have to pick the girls up from Model UN at three."

"I get out of class at noon."

"But is that enough time? For you to—"

Thanks, Sharon. What did she think I was? A Thanksgiving turkey or some kind of rump roast?

"More than enough time," I replied.

Sharon didn't respond.

"Hello? Hello?"

"Yes," was all she said. "Still here."

Probably hurt that I didn't want to spend all day together. Even though I did, sadly.

Despite myself, despite my better judgment and everything I knew about the past, I needed Sharon. I wanted us to have a real go at a life together, but I would settle for another moment inside her. I wanted her to—oh, never mind. The point is I didn't even mind her insults, even though I wanted her respect. If that's not love, I don't know what is.

I wanted to get all that out to her somehow, but the stupid donut shop and the ally-oop of the girl behind the counter bellowing another "Auntie up! Auntie up!" made me sullen. I looked at the clock. 8:32. The meeting must have started.

"I really have to go," I said.

"Auntie up! Auntie up!"

Another genius, another two dozen. Buy one dozen, get a heart attack free.

Sharon sighed, rattling the phone.

"I bought you a donut," I said. "Chocolate. Bavarian cream filled.

Your favorite."

I imagined Sharon smiling at that.

But her voice was cold. "Come over at noon," she said. "Don't be late."

And Sharon was gone.

I might have hustled through a couple of almost-red—and really red—lights heading to Evergreen, but I got to my office and grabbed my lecture materials since I wouldn't have time to get to class if the meeting ran a minute over.

I could lecture on memory in my sleep, but I needed my flash drive with my slideshow presentations in order to perform the technologically enhanced rigmarole kids these days need to learn two plus two. Don't get me wrong. The flash drive just had some insipid slides I got from the textbook company. Nothing fancy, but who really cared. Anything to keep my success rates—or is it completion rates?—up for my favorite person in the world, Dean Dyer.

So I was feeling pretty good, not perfect given that I had to walk in front of the Don't Sleep with Daniel Conrad poster, but pretty good for a Wednesday morning. It was a day of possibility. I was going to see Sharon. And I had two donuts and a sandwich.

When I got to my office, taped to my office door was a brown envelope with Dr. Daniel Conrad scrawled across the front with a thick black marker.

Probably a student asking for a recommendation. Or maybe some stupid initiative the administration wanted to throw its weight behind. I looked at the office doors around me. Nothing.

Could be a test from Dean Dyer to see if I strolled into my office before noon. Wasn't I on an Improvement Plan? I wouldn't put it past her to have Tim monitor how long it took me to take the envelope down.

So I tore the envelope off my door and threw it down on my desk. I didn't have time for it—whatever it was—but it was down and off my office door if some administrator was looking for a reason to put something in my file. Look at me, I'm putting in my required hours on campus, ladies and gents. What more do you want from me?

Even though I was late. Fifteen minutes late.

Then I saw it. Another pink note on my floor. Die Motherfucker was all it said. Concise. I could give the note-writer that.

No time.

I grabbed the note and rushed to Dean Dyer's meeting. I didn't feel like dying, but as I crossed campus, the thought occurred to me that if the note-writer's knack for brevity translated into swift follow through and I was to be murdered, shot in chest, stabbed multiple times in the back, or beheaded sometime that day, he or she might as well get it over with right then and there. At least I wouldn't have to spend my last hour on earth in one of Dean Dyer's Student Success meetings.

It might seem that confronting my mortality like that would have been enough to say screw the meeting and go do something important: make love to a beautiful woman, write an opus, build a skyscraper, save a village from a despot, leave my mark on the world, but that wasn't who I was. If it was my last hour on earth, I wouldn't even know where to start.

Probably just a prank, a joke, nothing real.

Better not worry. Better keep moving forward.

So, with my head still on my shoulders and my body not maimed and my face not disfigured, I continued on to the meeting. Not happy, but who knew anyone who was? Satisfying myself with the pipe dream of finding a seat in the back of the auditorium, I told myself I had more time.

Because that was what people did.

CHAPTER NINE

When I arrived, the back of the auditorium was packed. Everyone was as far away from the front as possible, leaving the first two rows full of toadies and empty seats.

The meeting hadn't started yet, still the administrators and their hordes of secretaries—oh, excuse me, executive assistants—stared like I showed up to a state funeral dressed like a clown. How dare he? Who does he think he is?

Then, a voice. "Hey, buddy! Over here!"

Great. Frank.

I sure as hell didn't want to sit by Frank, but seats were limited, and I couldn't ignore the one guy in the room who appeared happy to see me.

I walked over to him. Frank gestured to the seat next to him.

I peered up at the downtrodden faces of my colleagues.

Did any of them have the get-up-and-go to threaten me?

Highly unlikely.

Most couldn't muster the energy to raise their eyeballs. Those who did returned my gaze with a glassy indifference. It was difficult to believe that those half-dead broke-dicks used to be the robust Evergreen faculty. Sure, we never were the Harvard professoriate, but there was a time when we possessed more vigor than Siberian refugees in a Dostoyevsky novel. No, these people looked too droopy to concern themselves with combing their hair, let alone harassing a colleague or planning his demise. Had Dean Dyer drained their drive that much since she'd been at Evergreen? Or had ennui replaced passion over the years? Maybe I just hadn't noticed the slow leak.

I stuffed the note into my shirt pocket. No one behind me was a threat.

"Dean Dyer's meetings might be the only place on earth where the nosebleed seats are the best ones in the house." Frank elbowed me.

"What time do you think they got here to get the good seats?" I asked, glad to strike up a conversation with someone, anyone, even Frank.

"You see Jimmy over there from Kinesiology? Probably camped out overnight to get that seat by the exit and on the back row."

"What about Judy Maggadino over there?"

"Oh, Judy knows a guy," Frank whispered. "She's connected, if you know what I mean."

"The mob?"

"Nanotechnology."

I could see us becoming friends, Frank and me. Then he asked a dumb question.

"How's that book of yours coming, the *User's Manual*?"

"It's not a user's manual."

"Some women would disagree with you on that one," he sniggered.

The man deserved a punch in the gut. First of all, I wasn't a user or a victimizer or a misogynistic monster or anything horrible. I was a guy who'd written a fairly successful book about dating women under twenty-five. If anything, I was underqualified to write the thing. I wrote it on a lark to see if I could, sure, but the idea was to get my mind off Sharon. It didn't hurt that the whole book attacked Sharon and every woman her age. Still, not a reflection on my character or what I "did" with young women. And even if, let's say, I believed what I wrote—which I didn't and still don't—did I deserve nonstop persecution? I wasn't a child pornographer. I wrote a book. Did writing a book merit abuse, scorn, hate, and—Dean Dyer was at the podium, beginning her presentation.

She babbled for ten minutes and flipped through slides. Too many numbers with green pluses and red minuses. Some categories appeared to be up, others down. This was bad apparently. But now a giant picture of a comet filled the screen.

"Many of you were here in 1997 for Comet Hayley-Bopp. Remember Hayley-Bopp?"

Dean Dyer's toadies nodded from the front row. Ph.Double D was among them. Really, Ph.Double D, weren't you in high school in 1997? Don't nod like you were here.

"Haley-Bopp was a dazzler," Dean Dyer continued. "One of our brightest comets. And she shot across the sky during this university's best year on record regarding outcome assessment."

She hit a button on her remote control. Numbers shot across the picture, coming to rest next to the comet.

"Nestled among the stars, you see the numbers from 1997. Ninety-eight percent. Ninety-nine percent. Miraculous. The comet was a good omen."

Really? A good omen? Wasn't that the Heaven's Gate suicide comet?

"Is she going to strap us into white sneakers and force us to drink her Kool-Aid?" Frank whispered to me.

And Ph.Double D whipped around in her seat up Dean Dyer's butt and glared at us. Her commitment to Dean Dyer made me respect her enough to make a show of giving Frank a look that said, "Stop being insensitive." Besides it was fun to reprimand Frank, even though it might be more entertaining to beat him with a witty response. Still, a victory.

"And then 2005," Dean Dyer said with a flourish as she hit her remote. An image of Hurricane Katrina. Where was 9/11? The Iraq War? The Japanese Tsunami?

"Hasn't she only been here a year?" Frank whispered.

I nodded. The man had a point. Strange that one year entitles Dean Dyer to a historical sweep.

"2005. Hurricane Katrina ushered in dark days on our campus."

The audience—mostly the front row brownnosers—collectively aww-ed.

An image of a young boy, who had to be no older than seven, filled the screen. He was stranded on a roof surrounded by a rising tide of muddy water. He grasped a scrawny kitten.

I wondered if the boy lived or died. Either way, he was lucky not to be at Evergreen. Sure, he'd been stranded once the levees broke, but I was stranded right there in a meeting that was making me want to claw my eyes out.

Numbers flew across the screen, once again coming to rest, this time near the boy.

57%. 61%. 63%.

"Deplorable," Dean Dyer said, shaking her head, making her minions nod. "Since 2005, our numbers have been hovering around this point." She used a laser pointer to focus our attention on the 61%. The red dot skimmed dangerously close to the boy's forehead. For a moment, it looked like she was attempting to take the boy out with a sniper rifle.

"But there's hope," she said.

And the boy was gone. Another comet.

"Comet ISON. Raise your hand if you've heard of Comet ISON."

Murmurs from the brownnosers. They hadn't heard of it. A few overweight profs from Astronomy and Astrophysics raised their hands from the back of the auditorium. Lucky bastards. Those were good seats.

"Comet ISON will be here soon, and she will be just as bright and powerful as Hayley-Bopp. And, like Hayley-Bopp, Comet ISON will usher in better numbers for this campus."

"Hale-Bopp," a male voice from the back of the auditorium said. "It's Hale-Bopp."

Gasps from the toadies.

Dean Dyer surveyed the crowd. "Doctor Moore," she said, "I'm sure you're not doing what I think you're doing."

Dr. Moore didn't respond.

"I understand that we have a longstanding culture of disrespect on this campus," she said, getting red in the face. "But I am a woman and I am your boss. I will not tolerate rampant disrespect and devaluation of women. Do I make myself clear?"

Everyone was silent but twisting in their seats to see Dr. Moore's reaction. I knew he had a Ph.D. in Astrophysics and had discovered something exciting early in his career, but I couldn't for the life of me remember what it was. At any rate, he was well known in his field. The guy most likely knew the name of a famous comet. He probably just wanted everyone else to know it, too. I doubt he was being sexist.

"No offense intended," Dr. Moore said.

"Intentions are not important. Actions are important," Dean Dyer continued with a glare.

She returned to her PowerPoint.

"Back to what we were talking about before we were rudely interrupted: Comet ISON will be good for us. Just like Hale-Bopp. Now, go and be successful. We need students passing. And not just passing. We need As, Bs, and Cs. Our numbers have been too low. We need them higher. Much higher. This comet will be a good omen for us."

The meeting ended. People began shuffling out of their seats. Frank sidled up to me.

"Hey, buddy."

I wanted to tell him, "Listen, Franky-boy, we are not buddies," but before I could say anything, he launched into another question.

"What's going on with you and Jasmine?"

"We're dating."

"No, I mean are you going to use her until your *User's Manual* comes out or are you going to stop seeing her before that?"

I really wanted to flatten him right there in the auditorium in front of everyone. What was this guy's problem? Was he interested in being with her? Didn't he have a wife and kids?

But "We're dating, Frank" was all I said.

"I know it's none of my business. It's just that ... a girl like Jasmine deserves someone who cares about her, someone who—"

"Doctor Conrad," Dean Dyer's voice pierced the crowd. "Doctor Grant." She motioned to Frank and me. "I understand you're both on the search committee."

What search committee? I looked at Frank, hoping he could fill in the gaps, but he was just as clueless as I was.

"Oh, we're searching for a committee, sure," I said, hoping the joke might diffuse the situation.

Nope.

"Quite a few faculty members have complained to me that the search committee you're on is quite contentious."

Contentious?

"I hear that you two are the ringleaders, inciting negativity and controversy. You know how I feel about instigators."

What was she talking about? There's a search committee and Frank and I are ganging up on other faculty members? Wouldn't I have to go to a meeting or exchange an email or two in order to be an instigator?

I wanted to tell her I didn't know about any search committees, and I certainly wouldn't be teaming up with Frank. But like Johnny-on-the-spot, Frank was already talking.

"I'm sorry, Dean Dyer," Frank said. "You're absolutely right. We need to be less contentious and more focused on the issues at hand."

Somehow Dean Dyer succeeded at smiling at Frank while shooting me a dirty look. "I'm glad someone around here understands."

Frank was eating it up. All smiles back. Bowing down like he was apologizing to a Saudi prince.

"I'm truly sorry if I've caused you any trouble, Dean Dyer," Frank said.

"I appreciate that, but you are only part of the problem and not really *the* problem," she said, like the word the was a bullet and I was an enemy of the state.

Clearly, I was *the* problem.

"You men just think you can railroad female committee members and get them to change their minds by dominating them into submission. Let this be a lesson. Women don't take coercion lightly."

Tim was at her side with a pile of papers. She turned away from us to address the poor guy, which gave us just enough time to slip away.

"What was that?" Frank asked when we were out of earshot.

"No idea. Are you on the search committee?"

Frank shook his head. "You have to admit what she just said about domination and submission was riddled with psychological implications."

I nodded in his general direction as I checked my phone. It was almost time to teach my class and I needed to get out of there before Dean Dyer called me over again or I found myself on a search committee. Search committees were the worst.

Frank kept going. "Did you read the study out of Maryland—"

"I've got to take this," I said, gesturing to my phone even though it wasn't ringing. I had been doing that a lot lately, using my phone to get out of situations.

"Say hi to our girl from me." Frank winked.

"Don't you have a wife?"

"Say hi to her from me anyway."

Fucking Frank.

As I walked out of the auditorium, I began to wonder. If I was being accused of doing what I knew I didn't do and I was receiving threatening notes for things I might have done, could I get away with doing something I wanted to do? I could kill Frank, for instance, and maybe pin it on the feminist protesters. Not that I actually wanted to kill Frank, but it was a thought. Women had to be mad at him. Countless women, maybe. Frank was a married man who flirted incessantly. Hell, I was fairly certain he had just been flirting with me, if that was even possible. He had to be sleeping with some—if not all—of the women he spent time with. Maybe I could frame him for a moral turpitude firing. With the heat on him, no one would look twice at me.

But I didn't have time to think it through and I didn't want to, either. I needed to simplify my life. Doing anything to Frank would only muddy the waters. Then again, keeping him around might not be a bad idea. If shots were fired, I could duck behind him.

CHAPTER TEN

Everything appeared normal in class. No stalkers, no unusual behavior. Most of my students were stress-free enough to snooze, which normally would leave me livid, but given the alternative of Stalker Boy showing up with an Uzi, it relaxed me to see others undisturbed, even if they should be listening to me. I wasn't just up there lecturing on memory for my enjoyment. They were supposed to learn something.

Maybe Die Motherfucker wasn't an actual threat. Maybe I wouldn't end up belly-up in a ditch before the end of the week. Die Motherfucker could be like Fuck the Police, an expression of anger and disenfranchisement. Maybe someone was angry at me—most people are. But it's possible the note-writer didn't actually want me to die. Maybe I could take a deep breath and just keep on living.

After class, I popped by my office to drop off my lecture notes and I must have been calm enough to feel hungry because I grabbed the sandwich Jasmine made me. It was quite good, which, yes, should have made me feel guilty since I was going to see Sharon, but no point wasting a good sandwich because I was unfaithful. Besides, Sharon and I needed to meet. We needed to talk things through. Even though, if I'm honest, I knew Sharon and I were going to have sex. Just like we used to. The kind of sex that makes you think this is why I'm here, why I'm on this planet.

Of course, I had to spot the envelope on my desk from that morning. Chowing down on the sandwich, I flipped it over. And then—red ink. Not again.

Consider yourself warned! in the same curly handwriting.

My blood pounded through my veins.

I tore open the envelope and pulled out a series of photographs. Three, four, five in total.

Who develops photographs anymore?

People who enjoy scaring the shit out of other people, apparently.

Each photo featured a separate moment from last night's dinner with Sharon at Mama Carlita's, all with that historically inconsistent mural in the background. The final picture featured Sharon's bare foot on my inner thigh. Near her foot—was that a circle, no, a backwards letter?

I flipped the photo over and more red handwriting jumped out at me: Dr. Daniel Conrad, 53, with Mrs. Sharon Vogel, 49, pre-coital dinner, Mama Carlita's last night.

On the back of each photo, the same message.

Who uses the term pre-coital? No one I knew referred to sex as coitus. People fucked. People had sex. They might even make love, if they were stodgy. But people didn't *have coitus.* And no one I knew referred to anything as pre- or post-coital. That was just bizarre.

Whoever it was knew Sharon was married. The Mrs. in Mrs. Sharon Vogel was underlined five times on the back of each photograph. They knew her age, too, which probably meant they knew other details they could find out about her online. It couldn't be hard to sleuth out her address and anything else people can dig up off blogs and social media.

When we were there, Mama Carlita's was deserted. Our waiter wasn't the culprit. He was in a few of the pictures. The angle wasn't from above, like it would be if the photos were stills from a security camera. Whoever took the pictures took them from slightly below us. But who? A Mama Carlita's busboy? Someone shimmying on the floor?

I hated Mama Carlita's for their revisionist history and how they pandered to suburban appetites. Now I had another reason to hate them. They had let Mr. Pre-coital take these pictures of me and Sharon.

I scoured the photographs for clues, but all I could focus on was how miserable I looked sitting there with Sharon. My face looked wrinkled and twisted. Not that Sharon looked better. If it was possible, she looked even worse. Like someone who might have been attractive twenty or twenty-five years ago—not head-turning-must-stop-and-stare gorgeous, just somewhat stunning—maybe. But that somewhat stunning person had baked in the sun too long and dyed her hair one too many times in the last twenty-five years to be considered anything but wrinkled and past her peak. Her skin looked discolored and thin in spots. I didn't remember her looking that splotchy in person.

I didn't look much better. My hair was matted. I was slouching. What was I wearing? Denim on denim?

We looked like two old people out to dinner. Two old, unhappy people.

Even in the picture with her bare foot on my thigh, she looked put out to be turning me on. I didn't look too thrilled, either. No wonder the waiter thought we were married.

The pictures made me wonder why I was attracted to Sharon, but the camera couldn't capture her eyes, the way they locked onto mine and pulled me in. Vulnerable, yet commanding. Daniel, it's just you and me.

Even though it wasn't.

Sharon's eyes. Those eyes made me want her, want to give her everything I had, knowing it would never be enough. And those eyes made me angry. A deep, shaking anger that made me think it was possible to tear out another human being's heart and wear it around like a trophy. If I was lucky, I could leave it at that. Beat it back. Distract myself with something else—my book, maybe. But sometimes it engulfed me, and I was drowning, flailing my arms about, losing who I was, and there was only Sharon. Sharon and anger. Sharon and me.

Maybe it was how content she was with her life. She broke my heart, destroyed my life, made me lose my wife and my home, yet somehow she was still happily married to Brian with her three kids and her Woodslake Grove house with her hand-carved furniture. She still took family trips to Hawaii every summer, now with added extravagance. Waterfront rooms with private balconies, endless manicures, facials, massages all while sipping Mai Tais. One picture she posted online showed her and Brian getting a couples' massage with roses and candles and chocolate. Sickening.

Sharon didn't deserve to be on Cloud Nine with her perfect family, lying on the beach after she surfed the morning away. She screwed around on me—not to mention Brian—and her life only got better. Brian and Sharon were doing fine, apparently. She opened a sinkhole under my marriage, she delighted in watching my existence crumble, and now she could rub her happy life in my face. Where was the justice? Didn't she deserve to be fucked up a little bit after she wreaked havoc on my life?

But it wasn't just that. It was her disdain for me. How she looked down on me. I wanted her to get off her high horse. I wanted her to beg to be with me. Maybe then she'd see that she wasn't better than me.

What was I doing?

Even if she wanted to be with me, then what? I'd roll right into bed with her and find myself back where I started, maybe more broken, but no less alone. Unless I could be with Jasmine.

Jasmine.

Thank God whoever was sending these pictures was contacting me and not Jasmine.

Unless, of course, they were sending them to both of us.

I called Jasmine. Voicemail. I tried again. One more time. Maybe she was relaxing at my home, still sleeping off yesterday's mother-father divorce drama. Maybe. That would be ideal.

Still, she could wake up any minute and head to the front door. On her windshield, there could be a brown envelope with red handwriting waiting to inform her about the *pre-coital* dinner and who knows what else. Sure, it was irrational to assume that Stalker Boy would come by my house since so far I'd only received threats at my office. Still, some click-happy, camera-wielding asshole was following me and knew about Sharon. He—or she—must be aware of Jasmine, too.

My mind raced. Maybe Jasmine woke up. Maybe she received the pictures and broke down. Insanity did run in her family. She could come up to campus and murder me.

I needed to put my mind to rest. I had to go to my place, intercept the envelope if it happened to be on Jasmine's VW Beetle, and then I could go over to Sharon's.

I sent Sharon a quick text: Running a little late.

Then I got to my car and battled housewife lunch, glass of wine, and a quick trip to the mall traffic. Almost home, just turning off Greenwood Boulevard, my phone rang. Jasmine.

"Sorry I missed your calls," she said, breathless on the other end.

"You feeling okay?"

"Not perfect, but I needed a distraction, so I came up to campus."

Well, there went the idea of getting the envelope off her car—if it even existed in the first place. Maybe someone could still try to reach her. I made a mental note to swing by the parking garage when I was done with Sharon. Might as well turn around, but NO U-TURN after NO U-TURN prevented me.

No point getting a traffic ticket. I kept ploughing forward, looking for a place to turn.

Jasmine continued, "Weird question."

Oh, no.

"Yes?"

"Have you ever cheated on anyone?"

My heart raced. What did she know?

"Well, hello to you, too," I managed.

"No, I'm serious."

"Do you think I could cheat on someone?"

"No. It's just that Mom called. She said Dad cheated on her and that's why she lost it and went at him with the knife. My dad's a cheater. A liar and a cheater. Can you believe it?"

"Let's not jump to conclusions," I said.

"No one's jumping to conclusions. He confessed everything."

"We don't know what he did, the situation, why he did it, if he did it."

"Because he's a douche," Jasmine said.

"Sounds like," I replied.

It was best to respond to Jasmine's "He's a douche" comments with noncommittal acquiescences. "Sounds like," usually worked. To tell the truth, half the time I didn't know what she meant when she said the word douche. I asked her once and she fumed.

As far as I can tell, sometimes she used it to mean entitled asshole, other times, jerk.

No matter what the word meant, when there's talk of douches, it's best not to be one.

"But you haven't answered the question. Have you ever cheated on anyone?" she pressed.

"No."

"You wouldn't cheat on me or be sneaky?"

Moment of truth.

Instead, "No, definitely not."

Jasmine sighed.

"I don't want to be with anyone else," I said. "Do you? Is that why you're bringing this up?"

"No. I've just been thinking."

"About?"

"Love and why we even try it if it makes us all crazy and desperate."

Jasmine was getting philosophical. She definitely hadn't received any pictures.

"Well, I love you," I said. "And I'm not doing anything sneaky."

"I know." She laughed. "How could you possibly find a woman hotter than me?"

"Exactly."

Another ha-ha from Jasmine.

"I've got to go. Meeting," I said, not really lying even though I was deceiving her. I was meeting Sharon after all.

An "okay" from Jasmine.

Then silence.

Jasmine was waiting for something.

"I love you," I quickly added.

"You don't have to say it every time. Unless you want to."

"I know. I love you."

"I love you, too."

And that was that. Conversation over. Unnerving that she brought up cheating, but if it really was about her father and not about the pictures or anything that she found at my house, it could be a coincidence.

Finally, a left turn signal that permitted U-turns. Might as well turn around and go to Sharon's. Jasmine wasn't at my house. No point continuing there. I pulled over to the left lane and proceeded to wait for a U-turn when I saw Jasmine's bright blue VW Beetle zip down the street. No. It couldn't be. But it was. Jasmine. Clearly her. She was talking on the phone and driving. I honked and waved, but she didn't see me.

Little liar. She just told me she pulled into Evergreen. Clearly not the case. What was she doing driving around? And who was she talking to on the phone? Not me.

Maybe she received the pictures. Of course. All the talk of cheating fathers and questions about my fidelity. It made sense. Maybe for the sake of her memoir, it was better if she pretended she didn't know. She could follow me, wait for me to bungle a lie, catch me with my pants down—perhaps literally. That would make that book she claimed she was writing all the more of a page-turner.

But that didn't make sense. Not really. Even though I slept with Sharon and I wanted to be with her again that day, Jasmine and I were doing well. Really well.

She told me she loved me, which made me wonder if she was trying to convince me to keep her around past her "expiration date," as Frank liked to joke. But if she was lying about loving me, could I trust anything she said? Maybe the story about her mother brandishing a knife like a Shakespearean actor wasn't even true. Maybe all that talk of her parents was carefully crafted to make me feel needed. Maybe the Jacobsons were happily married.

But who would make up a maniac mother and a philandering father just so she could cuddle next to me and tell me she loved me?

To be above board, our relationship had been running on the fumes of Jasmine's desperation for quite some time. All those annoying texts and emails. Jasmine must have known I was drifting away from her.

It made sense. Too much sense.

On that first day, Jasmine did say she was persuasive.

Maybe this was how she intended to persuade me.

Whatever she was doing was working. While the idea of a fake family crisis terrified me, the level of intrigue did make Jasmine more interesting.

Suddenly she wasn't the girl who sent me messages detailing the strawberry cream cheese she smeared on her bagel. Did she even eat bagels? Who knew? She wasn't the girl who texted me a dead turtle she happened to see by the side of the road. Oh, no! Maybe she killed it. Jasmine could be a social mastermind, spewing garbage that made her seem like she was saying everything on her mind when, in reality, she was hiding what she really thought.

Still, everything I knew about Jasmine told me she wasn't concealing anything too significant.

Then again, there it was: material proof of her lying ways. Or, to be fair, lying way. Singular. She was driving down the road when she claimed she was at school. I know, not a lot of material there.

But add in that she asked about cheating on the very same day I planned to cheat on her or the day after I cheated on her, it didn't look good.

Green left turn arrow. Decision time: follow after Jasmine, head home to check on what Jasmine might have left behind, or continue on to Sharon's?

I looked back. Jasmine was long gone. Then down at the clock. 12:01. I was late. Factor in Greenwood traffic and Sharon would be angry.

But I needed to rest my mind about Jasmine. The girl spent who knows how long at my house. Who knows what she discovered—or worse, what she left behind. Cameras, surveillance equipment, a landmine. Well, no, not a landmine. But something big.

From my house, I could go to Sharon's. I couldn't see myself relaxing any other way. And didn't great sex—or conversation, for that matter—require relaxation?

So I continued to drive home, not sure why except that I needed to do something. When I pulled up to my house and went inside, nothing appeared out of the ordinary. Everything as usual except someone, presumably Jasmine, had washed the dishes I piled in the sink from last night. First time I'd seen that in a while.

Enough looking around. No point wasting more time.

If I got to Sharon's in the next fifteen minutes or so, I could explain why I was late. About forty-five minutes late if Greenwood traffic was on my side.

I'd put off telling Sharon about the pictures. Maybe we could spend some time together first, and after the romance part was over, I could show her just what pressure I was under. Maybe she'd look at me and say, "Oh, Daniel, I'm so sorry I ever doubted you."

I texted Sharon along the way. Apologies, entreaties, promises: I'll be there soon.

By the time I arrived at Sharon's house, it was 12:42. I rang the doorbell and waited. Nothing.

I tried again. Then I knocked.

Sharon's SUV wasn't in the driveway.

I looked at my phone. No messages.

I texted Sharon: Where are you?

Then: At your place. Sorry late. Got stuck at work.

No response.

I waited another half hour before I called Sharon's cell again.

No answer.

Screw Sharon for not waiting. And screw Jasmine for lying to me. But most of all, screw whoever was stalking me.

If I found him, I would punch him in his sorry face.

Or maybe I'd just stick Jasmine or Sharon or—oh, this is good—Dean Dyer on him. They all were scary individually, but together, oh, God, together. The poor bastard wouldn't stand a chance.

CHAPTER ELEVEN

Back at my office, I immediately signed in to my email to see if there was something, anything, from Sharon. Hell, it didn't have to be an emergency. Maybe her son got into a fight at the high school. She'd mentioned a few times that he had anger management issues. Maybe she needed to meet with the principal immediately. Or maybe her cat was sick. Sharon was unusually attached to that pesky old furball.

No new email or text messages from Sharon.

Sharon was normal—well, not normal, but she wouldn't screw with my head. Jasmine's fake-maybe-real family crises wouldn't happen with Sharon, who valued honesty, even though in practice she was quite dishonest. "Honesty and authenticity," she'd say. She'd also say I was the only real thing in her life. That was before. Was I still? Together, we were the closest thing I knew to genuine. Maybe if I appreciated that about her, we'd be living together, married, in my house by now. Her kids would come visit us on the weekends. Even Brian would learn to like me. We could share a beer when he dropped off the kids. If the Yankees cap on his nightstand was any indication, Brian and I could talk baseball. I could give him that. It was the least I could do for stealing his wife and making him shuttle the kids back and forth.

I gave Sharon another call. Straight to voicemail. No point going overboard, but I needed to do something, so I wrote her a text: Sorry about this afternoon. My dean called me in and I couldn't just leave. I wanted to, but I couldn't. You know how it is. Emergency at Evergreen! I'm sorry I missed you and I really do miss you. I miss who we were to each other. And I'd like a second chance at being with you because what we had was authentic and real.

I knew she'd like the authentic and real part.

I re-read the message. I wanted to send it.

Then I thought how long text messages always arrive out of order. And I deleted it.

No point telling her the truth now, especially when I knew it would only cause me pain. Not that what I wrote was the truth. No, I'd be screwed if I told Sharon: Sorry, S, but I was late because I got these horribly unflattering pictures of us from this anonymous stalker. You looked really ugly, so ugly that I wondered why I was with you in the first place. Not that I looked much better. Anyway, I went home because I was more worried about what my girlfriend did or didn't know than

I was about spending time with you. And goddammit, my girlfriend—who I do want to break up with even though she just told me she loves me—has been on my mind because I'm fairly certain she's manipulating me in that way only women can. But don't worry. You're important to me.

The sad part was that I wasn't even sure if anyone was important to me. I knew Sharon used to be—and still was. Those eyes. Her touch. Although whenever she talked about her artistic free child, I wanted to shoot myself in the face. Not only did she consider herself an artist, so I had to put up with her artistic free child in person, but sometime in the last few months she had started a blog. She updated that thing at least twice a day with pictures from her walks combined with her subpar poetry. Without Alan the poetry teacher—or because of Alan—everything had gotten more melodramatic. Her favorite image happened to be a condom in a cemetery. That one showed up in more than a handful of her over-the-top poems. A condom in a cemetery. Yes, really.

Even though I hated reading her posts, I always found myself checking Sharon's blog. A picture of a downed tree across a dirt path, a close-up of the tree's roots and a poem entitled "Exposed for the World to See." A shot of various feathers she collected with a poem "Seven-Year-Old Wild Child" about her relationship with her Maw-Maw and an old quill pen passed down to her grandmother from her great-grandmother only to be broken in little Sharon's sweaty palms when she was seven.

Needing to act, I clicked on Sharon's horrible blog, hoping to see anything so I knew she was alive, but also hoping to see nothing because I despised her asinine insights.

Great. Uploaded at 12:16: photos of dead birds and a poem about death, death, and more death. Death and aging. But mostly just death.

Was she hormonal? Going through menopause maybe? PMS-ing? Depressed? Embracing her artistic free child too much?

The pictures were startling. One dead sparrow looked like it had been brained by a rock. Did she bludgeon the poor bird? Or did she happen across it while she was waiting for me? Either way, unnerving given that she and I were supposed to be together while she was off documenting and uploading death.

I wanted to call her again. Maybe text her a quick You okay? but at that moment, Jasmine strolled into my office.

She sat down like she owned the place, lifting my coat off a chair without asking me a thing. By all means, Jasmine, have a seat. Feel free to lie to me while you're at it.

"You okay?" she asked. "You look like you're going to throw up."

Maybe I wasn't doing so well. There was the stalker, not to mention Dean Dyer and her posters. I felt insane for having sex with Sharon yesterday when I didn't think I was going to, and then getting nothing that afternoon when I thought I was going to at the very least get the opportunity to spend three hours with her. Instead, wanting. Wanting to see her, wanting to touch her, wanting to know was Sharon okay. Then there were Jasmine's lies. Yes, little Jasmine might have a hidden dark side. Maybe even darker than Sharon's brained bird blog post. Hard to believe, but the signs were all there.

I remembered Sharon's comment. "Daddy issues." Did Jasmine have daddy issues? Was that why she was with me? A screwed-up childhood and a desire to please an older man?

"You never talk about your father," I started.

"Are you serious? You're asking me about my dad now?"

She slumped forward and groaned.

"It's just that, you may not realize it, but you could be—well, there might be a psychological reason you're with me," I continued.

She pushed herself up.

"You've got to be kidding me."

"It's a real issue. Daddy issues."

"You can't tell me that psychologists really call it daddy issues.'"

"No, but the family of origin ... the family of origin shapes how you interact with the world. The role you have in that family becomes the role you play as an adult unless you break free of the unhealthy patterns and unproductive cycles."

"Listen," she said, "if you don't want me to visit, just say so. Don't be a douche and psychoanalyze me because you can't—or don't want to—spend time with me."

There was that word again: douche. No point asking her what she meant. The bite in her voice told me enough. Asshole. She was calling me an asshole. That was if I was lucky. A motherfucking asshole or some compound curse word was probably closer to what she meant.

"I'm not psychoanalyzing. Just needing to know. Is your relationship with your father ... healthy? Is he normal?"

"Oh, it's very unhealthy," she said with an exaggerated smile that didn't mask the fact that she wanted to slap me. "My dad and I fight and then kiss and make up. Really kiss and make up. Sometimes we make up so much that we make out."

"Really?"

"No," she scoffed. "My dad's a regular guy. Our relationship is quite normal. Except now that you mention it, I've always wanted to sleep with him."

She looked at me and crinkled her nose.

"What's wrong with you? I'm kidding, of course."

"It's just that this father of yours, does he look like me? Act like me? Resemble me in any way?"

She whimpered, flattening her torso against her knees. Then she sat back up and tilted her head to the side. Deep in thought, she appraised me. Still silent, she got up and walked to my side of the desk and looked me up and down.

"Come to think of it." She paused and grabbed my shoulders. She didn't shake me, but she had a firm grip on me. "Listen, Conrad, I love you. I'm not with you because of my father. Although that would be funny, but, no. I'm with you because—"

"You're writing a book."

"Yes, that was the reason at first," she said. "But now I'm with you for other reasons."

"Such as?"

"Why are you looking at pictures of dead birds?"

Oh, no. Sharon's blog.

"Research. Nothing important."

I closed the browser and pressed. "I need to know all reasons or motivations. Why are you with me?"

"Because I love you."

She leaned in and kissed me. Too much passion? Overcompensating?

"I know I'm being difficult, but things are getting to me at home and at work and—"

"Hey, buddy!"

Not Frank again. Did he have a tracking device on Jasmine or something? Or was he her lapdog, woof-woofing at the sight of his master?

"Going to the department meeting?"

"What department meeting?"

He gave Jasmine a look that said, "Your old man's crazy."

"You know," he said. "The one we have the second Wednesday of every month since 1999."

Jasmine straightened up. "You better go," she said.

"I'll see you there, Frank," I said, turning to Jasmine. "We need to talk."

Hoping the cliché would jolt her into listening.

I just wanted to break up with her, get it done and off the list of things to do, but there was Frank loitering in my doorway like he was my department meeting prom date.

"It's fine. You're fine." She paused. "Go to your meeting. We'll talk about families of origin later."

"Oh, families," Frank interjected. "You telling him about your dad?"

Jasmine shushed him.

"These questions are really nagging me," I said, purposefully ignoring Frank as much as possible. What did he know about her father?

"I promise I'll answer your questions later. I really don't want to think about my dad or my family or—oh, God, my parents' divorce—right now, if that's okay."

"Give her a break," Frank said. "She's got a lot on her mind."

I didn't want to listen to Frank, but he was right, the bastard. Jasmine looked stressed. A tiny scar I never noticed on her face, right under her left eyebrow, stood out in that moment. Something about the florescent light or maybe Jasmine was pale or not wearing any makeup. The scar was oddly beautiful. An imperfection that made her face all the more alluring. She couldn't be as crazy as I made her out to be in my head.

I could ask her about it, how she got the scar. She probably would tell me the truth. Unless she didn't, in which case I wouldn't know since she could be an expert liar. She had lied to me about being on campus when she was driving down Greenwood Boulevard.

Maybe she was lying about loving me, too. If not, loving me was probably a sign of lunacy, given that she was who she was and I was—if those pictures were any indication—a slumpy old man.

I needed to get to the truth.

Instead, I did what I was told. I went to my meeting. What a colossal mistake.

CHAPTER TWELVE

Right before the meeting began, Frank whispered to me, "You got your second birthday surprise yet?"

I nodded. Sure, sure. That second visit must have been my second birthday surprise or maybe it was hidden in all the newly required I love yous Jasmine and I now shared.

"I drove her all around. All up and down this residential part of this nice neighborhood to get it. You know, off Greenwood Boulevard. Woodslake Grove."

Woodslake Grove. Sharon's neighborhood. Could she—could *they*—know about Sharon?

I wanted to grab Frank by the collar and shake him for clarification, but Ph.Double D was at the front of the classroom with an official frown and a glare that could jumpstart a dead battery.

Jasmine was my stalker. It made sense. She must have dropped the pink note at my door right when she gave me that sophomoric framed article on my birthday. The same with the second note and the brown envelope. It wouldn't have been hard for her to have developed those pictures while Sharon and I were together.

But the handwriting on the threats looked nothing like Jasmine's. Then again, she had a seemingly endless supply of female friends. Every day she mentioned more. Allie, Nessa, Michelle, Kara; one of them could have written the note for her. Maybe she and another girl were in on it together. Maybe they enjoyed destroying men. Maybe I was their perfect victim. I had fame and money—although the money had been spent and the little fame I ever possessed was fading fast.

I didn't have time for Jasmine's games.

I needed to get her out of my life. Before she did anything worse.

I had to protect my job, my reputation, my future success—hell, I even had to protect Sharon and her family. Poor Brian didn't need Jasmine taking pictures of his wife rubbing my inner thigh with her foot at a Mexican restaurant. The one time I saw the guy he was relaxed, too laid back to be married to a woman like Sharon, I remember thinking. I expected him to be more wound up, tense. That was before. Who knows who he is now. He could be all wiry, itching for a reason to crack. Anyone can go postal. Brian could stab Sharon. Or shoot her. They had guns. He could shoot Sharon and then shoot the kids and put the gun in his mouth and pull the trigger. People did that. Maybe not in

Greenwood and not in Woodslake Grove. But there's a first time for everything.

Yes, I hated Sharon's idyllic life with Brian, but I didn't want her dead. And I certainly didn't want to hurt Brian. Poor guy never did anything to me. Her daughters were beautiful and seemingly well-adjusted. One was into science. The other played the cello. Her son liked basketball. Seemed like a good kid. Sharon said he had some issues, but he seemed functional. No point having them discover that their mother has men all over town.

I couldn't concentrate on the meeting no matter how hard I tried. Ph.Double D was yapping about something she clearly thought was significant, and all I wanted to do was get more details from Frank on what the hell Jasmine and he were doing near Sharon's house.

There were six people in our department in total. Someone thought it was a good idea to line us all up in the front row of a classroom, which meant Frank was just an arm's length away from me. I thought I could get his attention and his attention alone. My mistake, obviously.

"Hey," I whispered to him.

Frank furrowed his brow at me.

"When were you in Woodslake Grove?"

He flipped to a page in his legal pad and wrote "last night" in big block letters.

"What time?" I whispered back.

Frank didn't hear or pretended not to hear. He was too busy nodding his head along with Ph.Double D like whatever she was saying was profoundly important.

"What time?" I poked, tapped, hit Frank, maybe a little forcefully. It looked worse than it was.

"Stop," Ph.Double D shrieked. "Just stop!"

I froze. Was she talking to us? Frank and me?

No. Just me.

"I just don't think I can do this anymore," she said. "I don't—" And then she burst into tears right in front of the department. Full on sniveling into her navy-blue dress shirt sleeve.

Susie, the grandmother in our department, jumped to her aid. She held Ph.Double D against her chest and rubbed her back. I turned to Frank, the only other man in the room, for support. Frank shook his head. "Don't look at me, buddy."

Thanks, chum.

"He's just so rude," Ph.Double D bawled into Susie's shoulder as Susie said, "There, there."

Who there, theres an adult? A toddler, sure, but a thirty-five-year-old woman? Wonders never cease at Evergreen.

"There, there," Susie said again to Ph.Double D. "Don't let him bother you."

Part of me hoped she was crying because of Frank, but, no, everyone—including Frank—glared at me like I was a pervert. *Et tu*, Frank? *Et tu*?

"I didn't do anything," I said.

"It's best if you leave," Susie said.

"There must be a mistake," I said.

But they all looked at me like *I* was the mistake. I was depraved and they knew it. A few of them, the middle-aged women in particular, had a glimmer of pity in their eyes like they felt sorry for me for not knowing how repulsive I really was. Their disgust still overpowered any sympathy I could perceive. Still, a vestige of compassion. A brief condolence for just how vile I was.

I looked to Frank. No hey, buddy conspiratorial grin. Concern, sure, but withdrawn concern like for a circus freak or a leper. Don't let him get too close; it might be catching.

"You should go," he said. I wasn't used to seeing detached, disquieted Frank.

"I didn't do anything wrong," I stammered, feeling myself getting shaky. "Maybe you should go. Maybe all of you should go."

And then Ph.Double D sobbed harder and bolted to the door. Susie scuttled behind her. "Only you have power over you," I heard her say, which must have been one of those affirmations women say to themselves in the mirror before going to work. "Only I have the power over myself. I am beautiful, smart, and successful. My friendship is a gift, not a right. No wonder no man will touch me with a ten-foot pole. I'm a crazy bitch who talks to herself every morning." Well, the last part I added, but, you know, no man has to give himself a pep talk to go to work every morning. Just women. Why? Because they're mad as March hares.

I turned to my other three colleagues. Clara and Elizabeth had always been rational women and there was Frank. But before I could say anything, Clara and Elizabeth were up out of their seats with Frank at their heels. All of them rushing out, like the room was filling up with mustard gas.

"Let me get the door," Frank said to them on the way out. He shot me a look that said, "Sorry, buddy. You're in this alone."

And that's how I found myself sitting in the department meeting without the rest of my department, wondering if Ph.Double D was crazy, if my whole department was crazy, or if there was something fundamentally wrong with me. Something that couldn't be fixed.

CHAPTER THIRTEEN

I felt silly sitting there, so I took a few deep breaths and walked back to our office suite. Time to figure out what the hell just happened. I needed to know what Ph.Double D thought I did. Sure, I disrespected her in my head regularly, but not out loud.

The office suite was deserted. Not a soul. Just that poster reminding me that everyone around me was nuts.

My colleagues probably all went to Dean Dyer's office to give statements against me. Ph.Double D was always kissing her ass. Maybe Ph.Double D would tell Dean Dyer "Daniel Conrad was mean, mean, mean" and made her cry.

Although I wasn't sure if I had been mean. As far as I knew, all I did was try to get answers from Frank. Not that I got any. The bastard.

At my office door, I thought about going home, but I decided to stick around. Might as well get ready for a call down to Dean Dyer's office, which was becoming my home away from home.

I opened my door fearing more pictures and another threat, but nothing. Thank God, Jasmine—I was fairly certain my stalker was Jasmine at that point—hadn't left anything else. Just as I was about to take a temporary sigh of relief, this work-study kid, Benny, who always looked homeless with his stained T-shirts, fraying pants, and pubic hair beard, lurched into my office doorway. He was a stumbler. I once saw him topple down a large stack of textbooks. Maybe he had bad balance—a perpetual inner ear infection?—or maybe his flip-flops were too big or his jeans were too long or some catastrophic combination of two or three of those issues.

I didn't know him, but my female colleagues sure did.

"I saw Benny looking for hot water for his Ramen this morning. It's just so sad. Ramen for breakfast," I'd overheard Elizabeth say in the faculty lounge to a small group of female colleagues after the kid stumbled by. "We have to do something for him."

He'd told them he was too poor to eat a decent meal. With the enthusiasm of small-town church ladies, my female colleagues took it upon themselves to adopt the boy.

A few of them made him food during the week. Others gave him snacks they picked up at committee meetings. Ph.Double D, who refused to eat anything with sugar or fat in it, made a point to always grab a slice of cake or a brownie at every meeting just to bring it back for Benny. I even heard talk of giving him gift cards to fast food restaurants for the weekends, something I would never do because, let's be honest, students are like raccoons. There are always more of them than you can possibly take care of and they're wily scavengers.

So this kid, this charity case, Benny, came stumbling into my office wearing a hoodie illustrating the zombie apocalypse and not looking much better himself.

"Doctor C," he said, pushing his stringy, dirty blond hair out of his eyes. "I found this on the floor outside your office. I think it's for you."

My heart began to race. Oh, no. Not a pink piece of paper or a brown envelope, but a wrinkled newspaper clipping. It looked like nothing. Maybe it wasn't even for me.

I thanked him and took the crumpled clipping from his hand. And there it was: more red ink. This time no handwriting. Just the latest column from Lacey Griffin-Smith with: Fire Daniel Conrad. He is a misogynistic monster who has taken advantage of countless women on this campus. Underlined. Twice. And a tiny arrow pointing off the page. I flipped it over in case whatever I was supposed to see was on the back. No. Just part of another op-ed on how undergrads should stop peeing in the communal showers even though doing so helps save water.

No, the arrow couldn't be referring to that.

But what was the arrow pointing to? Something missing?

"Where did you find this?" I asked Benny who was still standing there like a bellhop expecting a tip.

"On the ground," he said.

"Where? Show me."

"I don't know. The floor." He backed out to the hallway, spread his legs like he was going to do a jumping jack and flailed his arms about. "Somewhere here."

I stepped out into the hallway and looked at the floor and the walls. Nothing.

"Was it attached to anything?"

"I don't think so."

"When did you find it?"

"I think this morning."

"You think?"

"Or maybe yesterday evening. The days are blending together."

"Think. Yesterday or today?"

I resisted the urge to smack some sense into him.

"I don't know," he whined. "I haven't slept since Monday."

"So you just found this note on the floor somewhere in the hallway and you kept it until you saw me?"

"Yes. It seemed important. Like maybe you dropped it."

"Where did you keep it?"

"In this pocket." He jammed his hand in his front hoodie pocket.

"You sure nothing's in there?" I craned my neck until I felt a sharp twinge.

"Just air," he said, turning his pocket inside out.

"You wore this hoodie yesterday and today? You didn't take it off last night?"

"I haven't slept. I've been here all night working on my Civil Engineering project. A bridge. Wanna see it?"

No, I didn't, but Benny kept going.

"It's made of tongue depressors and it can hold the weight of a full-grown cat. Not an obese housecat, but a regular sized alley cat. I tried two different ones. It holds up."

What was he talking about? Did he bring alley cats into the office suite after hours?

"Have you seen anyone hanging around my office? Anyone suspicious? Anyone asking for me or not asking for me?" I continued on topic.

"Sorry, I've mostly been zoning out at the computer now that my bridge is done. Zoning out at the computer like a zombie all day long, just waiting to go home."

A zombie. That sounded right. He was supposed to be our office assistant, but most of the time, even when he was supposed to be unjamming the copier, on his good days, he was on the computer browsing websites designed for doofuses. Sometimes he would laugh out loud at what he saw. This little tee-hee that didn't match the size of his belly.

"I'd tell you if I knew," he said. "But I don't remember much except finding it and keeping it for you."

I believed him. And then I had an idea. Benny was always at the office. Why not ask him to spy for me, let me know who was coming and going and who might be threatening me?

"What are your hours?"

"I'm just about to get off," he said. "Going over to sell some plasma if they'll let me. Then sleep."

"Sell some what?"

"Blood plasma."

"You sell your blood plasma?"

"It's amazing. They really pay you. They used to give me fifty bucks, but that was the introductory rate. Now I get thirty-five. If I keep up the iron in my blood, I can donate twice a week. They wouldn't let me give last week because I wasn't eating enough." He paused. "Don't tell anyone how much they pay. I don't want any more competition."

Man. He sounded hard up for cash. Maybe my female colleagues were right.

Then I had an idea.

"How about if I pay you not to give plasma today?"

"I'm listening."

"Just stick around here and watch my office. Find out who's been dropping off messages like this one." I waved the newspaper clipping at him.

"Like a P.I.?"

"Sure," I said.

"Can I hire a team?"

What was this kid thinking?

"No, it's really important that this stays between you and me."

"Sure, sure," he said. "Discretion. I am the definition of discretion."

Was he really? He unzipped his It's the Zombie Apocalypse and We're all Going to Die hoodie revealing a sweat-stained T-shirt emblazoned with the phrase Talk Nerdy to Me.

Great.

"So I just watch?" he asked. "Watch and report?"

"Yes."

"And you'll pay me?"

"Yes. Maybe not cash, since that might look strange, but in gift cards."

"Oh, goodie," he said. "How much a week?"

"I'll give you two hundred for a whole week."

"Two hundred dollars?"

"No, two hundred pesos. Yes, dollars."

He scuttled forward and threw his arms around me, pressing me into his damp T-shirt and hoodie so I could smell his hair. When was the last time he showered? Maybe I could give him a stick of deodorant and a bar of soap as payment.

"Thank you." He winked with his whole body. "You won't be sorry. No one regrets hiring me. No one. Except my old manager, but he was a stickler. Retail's a tough racket."

And like that, regret.

Still, with Benny "on the case" as it were, I was at liberty to go back to my office and sit down to work on my idiotic *Practical Guide*. Get something, anything, done. At least if Jasmine tried to interrupt me, Benny could hold her at bay.

I had more pressing concerns. Between Jasmine the potential stalker and Sharon the missing-in-action blogger, weaker men would cave. Add in Frank who might be in cahoots with Jasmine and Ph.Double D who might be telling Dean Dyer that I hurt her fragile feelings, not to mention Dean Dyer, who was no doubt slipping notes in my file and most likely putting me on some sort of secondary vague Improvement Plan for something I didn't do. I was lugging around more than my fair share of challenges compared to the rest of good old Evergreen's faculty who did diddly squat with all of their free time.

Pushing thoughts of Improvement Plans and sniveling girls out of my mind, I double clicked on the computer file for that damn *Practical Guide,* the very thing I had been avoiding all those months. I read it. All five—well, four and a half pages of it. And here's the thing: it wasn't half bad.

Kind of frothy and funny. It rang true even though I knew it wasn't based on anything accurate. The pages had been written pre-Jasmine, but I doubted anyone could tell. I had a great section on cultural references your young woman won't understand, which included quotes from *Get Smart.* Would you believe twenty-somethings just don't know these somethings? was the title for the subsection.

Not bad. Not bad.

Except that the whole thing amounted to four and a half pages. Double spaced. I required more from my Psych 101 term papers.

I thought about where I could expand my ideas. Maybe consider pubic hair do's and don'ts. I remembered Jasmine saying something about young men manscaping. I could include that. And the manbun—an older man's do's and don'ts. Maybe it would be funny if I included a subsection on hair in general. What to expect from the bald "down there" women and what they expect from the bald "up there" in return. Maybe that would be a great place for a pie chart—or a pube chart, as it were.

In that moment, it felt like I could finish my *Practical Guide.* Finish it and do a damn good job, too.

Feeling proud of myself, I popped back out in the hall and looked around. No one. I checked my watch. 4:05 p.m. Made sense. These people had the work ethic of Social Security administrators during a government shutdown. And that was on a good day. They probably all went home.

Still, quiet. Calm. I could stay and work on my *Practical Guide.* Maybe churn out a few more pages. Something to be proud of. But as I was about to turn back to my office to work, I heard Benny flip-flopping near the kitchen. I tried to move away from the doorway as deftly as possible without alerting him, but I banged my elbow on the doorjamb. I instinctively froze in pain and, before I knew it, it was too late.

"Doctor C," Benny waved at me, rocking his whole body from side to side as I cradled my elbow. "Doctor C!"

He galloped to me, letting his sandal slip off his left foot along the way. "Just to clarify something, does the two hundred bucks include my retainer?"

"Your retainer?"

What did this kid think he was? A lawyer? And didn't he hear my elbow crack into that doorjamb? Considerate much, Benny, kicking a guy when he's down?

"I've been looking online and private detectives have retainers."

"You're not a private detective."

"I'm acting as your private detective."

"No, not really. Less Sherlock Holmes, more mall cop."

"So if, say, I see someone, poking around your office, and let's say that person sneaks by, but I catch a glimpse of him, should I follow him or not?"

"Follow him. Find out who he is."

"What if my personal safety is at risk?"

What was this kid talking about?

"Benny, it's very unlikely your personal safety will be at risk."

"What if he has a gun? Or a weapon? Maybe I need a gun or a weapon."

"No, definitely not. No gun or weapons."

I was fairly certain it was a felony to carry a gun on a college campus. That was all I needed. Daniel Conrad, seducer of "countless" twenty-something women and enabler of school shooting suspects. I might as well consider myself hanged in the court of public opinion.

I wasn't going to be able to work on my book anywhere near Benny. Besides, I had things to do. I had to get home, figure out what happened to Sharon, maybe see her or, at the least, break up with Jasmine who was most likely a psycho stalker.

"So, what I'm gathering is that I am to risk my personal safety to protect and to serve without a weapon?"

This kid.

"You aren't protecting or serving. You're just watching my door to see if someone comes by."

"And the expenses I might incur?"

I needed to go. I stepped back in my office and popped my flash drive into the computer. While Benny speculated on his future expenses, I downloaded my *Practical Guide* in case I had time to work on it that night. When he mentioned per diem for the second time, I had to cut him off.

"You won't have any expenses. You'll be sitting. Sitting for two hundred dollars a week isn't bad."

"What if I have expenses? What should I do?"

"Keep your receipts," I said, getting up from my chair and stuffing my flash drive into my coat pocket.

"You'll reimburse me?"

"I'll reimburse any real expenses you'll have while sitting here watching my door, which should be none, by the way. No sodas or meals or anything like that."

"Thank you," Benny said, extending his right hand.

Really? I shook his hand. Warm and wet. Maybe that meant we would be done with the conversation.

"You want me to walk you out?"

No, I didn't want him to walk me out. I wanted him to watch my door. Was he that dense?

"I'll be fine," I said. "I doubt anyone will shiv me in the parking lot."

Not that I was entirely certain.

"I'd be a great bodyguard if I had a weapon," Benny said. "I bet I could beat a black belt if I had a sawed-off shotgun."

Highly doubtful. If someone came up to us in the hallway right then and there, I wouldn't rely on Benny to save me. He'd probably run screaming down the hall. Weapon or no weapon. Or he might pee his pants. Benny wasn't the type who would throw his life on the line for someone else no matter how much he fantasized about the zombie apocalypse.

"No weapons," I said, closing my door behind me. "No weapons, please."

I continued down the hall, leaving Benny at my door.

"I'll keep my receipts," he shouted after me.

"There won't be any," I said, waving at him over my shoulder. "You're just sitting there."

Of course, Benny didn't just sit. But he sat still long enough for me to get out of there, which in of itself was worth the two hundred. Because that's what a man has to do these days, beg, fight, pay for a quiet moment with his thoughts. Alone time, the new American dream.

CHAPTER FOURTEEN

On my way home, I got a call from Jasmine wondering if I wanted to join her for an early dinner.

"I heard about the department meeting," she said.

Partially curious as to what she knew, but mostly knowing she was a woman I needed to get rid of in the kindest way possible so as to not activate any psychotic tendencies she might not yet be exhibiting, I agreed to meet her.

"After all you and I have been through lately, we need some quality fun time together; it'll lower our stress."

Speak for yourself, Jasmine.

I met her at the Jared's Deli across from campus for some of that quality fun time. Despite being across from a college campus with seventeen thousand students, according to Evergreen's public relations gurus, the place overflowed with senior citizens. Bald men in wheelchairs reading newspapers and white-haired women wearing socks under their sandals sat at every table, downing the deli's free coffee for seniors. Funny how a national offer for what had to be twenty cents' worth of coffee made the elderly come out of the woodwork. The coffee wasn't even good. You'd think doctor's orders alone would block a few of them from drinking the swill. But no. They chugged the stuff like they were corporate lawyers or Wall Street execs. Maybe that's how they stayed alive, running on coffee fumes, teetering back to the car and heading down the interstate to the next Jared's Deli.

Jasmine spotted me and waved me to come join her in line. In the swarm of gray and wrinkles, Jasmine's brown hair and smooth skin looked out of place.

"Two senior coffees, please," the old man ahead of her said to the clerk. His eyes were bloodshot and he darted his hands in and out of his pockets. In and out. In and out.

"Only one cup per person per day," she said.

"It's for my wife."

"I can only give your wife a cup if she's here."

"She's disabled, waiting in the car. Are you telling me she doesn't get free coffee?"

Was this man really going to stand there and argue over a dollar twenty-nine plus tax?

"Just bring in her ID."

"So you want me to go to the car and get an ID from my disabled wife? She's attached to an oxygen machine."

The woman behind the counter sighed and lifted a Jared's Deli cup off the stack by her register. "You didn't see that," she said to another girl frothing a cappuccino on the espresso machine behind her.

The old man thanked the clerk and shambled with his two empty cups to the condiments station. He slopped some cream into both cups and squeezed the honey bear's stomach until it spewed out what had to be a quarter cup of honey. Then he sat down at a table. Sat down with his two coffee cups full of anything but coffee. And he started drinking them. A sip here, a gulp there. Either he had decided to leave his wife in the car, or he'd made her up.

"You looking forward to the day you get free coffee here? Two more years!"

Thanks, Jasmine.

"That and the senior menu at Denny's. Can't wait," I said.

Jasmine laughed. Good old Jasmine. Always laughing.

I knew she wouldn't be laughing long. Not with the breakup on the horizon. We found a table and settled in.

"You know I've got a lot on my mind," I started.

"Your *Practical Guide*?"

"I'm stretched. Tired. Deep into my legs, back behind my eyes. There's no way I can get everything I need to get done in the hours I have in a day."

Which was the truth.

"Oh, I almost forgot. I had a really wackadoodle dream!"

That's all I needed. Reality with Jasmine was already confusing enough. I didn't need talk of wackadoodle dreams, too.

Attempting to get back on subject, I asked "What were you up to this afternoon? Last night?"

Ignoring me, Jasmine plowed forward with recounting her dream. I was going to hear about it whether I liked it or not.

"I was getting it on with Michael Douglas except Michael Douglas was my dad, but I wasn't worried that I was his daughter; I was more worried what Catherine Zeta-Jones would think."

"None of this is reality, right?"

Jasmine laughed and touched my arm. I took that for a yes. She kept going.

"I asked Nessa what she thought it meant, and she said I needed to think about what Michael Douglas represents to me. Is that good advice?"

"Why are you asking me?"

"You teach psychology and you used to be a therapist."

Not a wackadoodle dream analyst, Jasmine.

But I gave her what she wanted to hear. "Fine. Seems legitimate."

"Okay, cool. Well, I thought about it. Michael Douglas and Catherine Zeta-Jones have that kind of relationship I want us to have, except Nessa says she heard they might be separated? Anyway, I didn't know that when I had the dream. He's twenty-five years older than her, but it doesn't matter. Age doesn't matter when you're in love."

"He's twenty-five years older than Nessa?"

"No." She grabbed my hand. "Than his wife, Catherine."

"But in the dream, he was with you. He couldn't be that much in love with his wife."

"Well, it's not a perfect explanation."

"And he was your father."

"Don't you think that part came from seeing my parents yesterday?"

Probably, but I wasn't willing to let Jasmine off that easy.

"No," I said. "I'm no dream expert, but I think you're more worried about my age than you pretend to be."

"Doubtful," she said.

"You're dreaming about sleeping with your father. Age matters to you."

"It doesn't now," she said. "But I *have* thought about it. If we get married and I don't get in some freak accident, there will be a time when you die and leave me alone. Aren't you worried about that?"

"No," I said. "I'll be dead."

"You don't worry about me and what I'll do after you're dead?"

"I haven't really thought about it."

Probably because I wanted to break up with her. Not marry her. And definitely not wait around for a freak accident to put either of us out of our misery. I wanted out now.

"When I'm your age, how old will you be?"

Was she really this bad at math? Add thirty years, Jasmine, then subtract one. Jesus Christ.

"Eighty-two," I said. "I'll be eighty-two. When you're my age, I'll be dead. Or in adult diapers."

"You'll still be sexy."

No, Jasmine, I won't.

I shook my head. "That's what I've been trying to tell you. I'm feeling old. Not quite as young as I used to be. I just don't think I can do everything anymore."

"I'll help."

"No," I said. "It's a nice offer, but I need to do some things myself."

"What things?"

"The book, my research, dealing with Dean Dyer—have you seen the poster?"

"You mean, you don't *have* to trade sex for grades, but you *can* if you *want*?"

"Funny how you didn't mention it."

"I thought it might be a sore spot, given that it's right across from your office."

She reached across the table for my hand. I let her weave her fingers into mine.

"It's all these things," I said. "And the fact that I'm in therapy."

"Therapy?"

I wasn't in therapy. Did all that talk of Jasmine's dream make me say it? Maybe. Or maybe I needed therapy.

"I'm just really stressed, so I started seeing someone. And this therapist, he said I need to concentrate on my work. Concentrate on my work and get everything done and then I'll feel better. He said it was the only way for me to recover. Doing work. Lots of work. And cutting out my social life until I'm less behind."

Therapists rarely gave that advice. They mostly advocate for work-life balance, but Jasmine didn't have to know.

"So you're saying you're going to be spending more time at work?" she asked.

"Well, yes."

Damn this was hard.

"Number forty-one."

Our order was ready.

We both got up.

"Wait here," I said. Not that I thought she'd run away, but I didn't want her getting up and changing the conversation to something new. We needed to finish. We needed to break up.

I brought us our sandwiches and settled back in. Jasmine began fiddling with a mustard packet.

"So what I'm saying," I said, watching her pinch and pull on the mustard packet and then bite it with her teeth, "is that you and I might need a break."

"A break?"

"How is this difficult to understand?"

"Oh, I get it," she said.

Did she?

"You need time to work and I'm cool with that. Like I said, quality fun time over quantity not-so-fun time."

No. She didn't get it.

"It's more than that. I need to feel free to work. Not distracted."

"I'm distracting?"

Yes. Exactly. Not the good type of distracting, either. What with the maybe pretend family crisis and the lying and the stalking.

"No," I said. I wanted to spare her feelings—and get out of there without a fork rammed through my arm. Stabbing ran in Jasmine's family, after all. "Everything else is distracting me from you. I need to be able to give you my full attention, and I just can't right now."

"Haven't I been supportive? When you need to work, I let you. What did I do wrong?"

"It isn't about you."

But it *was* about her. I could tell by her face that she thought so, too. She started crying right there in the middle of Jared's Deli. Second woman blubbering in my general direction that day and it wasn't even dark yet.

Even with tears blotching her face, Jasmine stood out. Then again, the place was overrun with senior citizens. It would be hard for her to look ugly in that crowd.

"You know, I've been really understanding, right? I mean, ridiculously understanding." She sobbed.

"You have been … understanding."

"So what are you saying? You want to break up with me because you like me so much that you want to be able to give me your full attention, but you can't, so you want to break up with me?"

The old people around us started to stare. They no doubt thought I was a cad. Or a really shitty father.

"No," I said. A mistake, but I was trying to calm her down so the old people around us could refocus their cataracts on someone else.

"Then what?"

"I just need time to focus," I said. "Work without feeling distracted. All this—" I waved my hand in front of her weepy face "—is distracting."

"My parents are getting a divorce and now you're breaking up with me. Aren't I allowed to cry?"

"I've been sympathetic to your parents' situation. Now I have to put myself first because I'm going insane."

Which was the truth.

"You really can be a douche sometimes."

That was fair. Still it stung.

"I don't want to break up," I said.

Even though I did.

"What do you want then?" she asked.

"Time to think. Time to do work. Time to get stuff done and put my life together without worrying about hurting your feelings or not spending enough time with you."

"So we need a break, not a breakup?"

"Something like that. Maybe a pause? A hold on all this?"

"How long?"

"A few weeks. Just enough time for me to get into my therapy more. Figure out what's important. What I need in my life."

Not that I would be in therapy.

"What will we be in the meantime?"

Why did women always need a term for whatever we were doing?

"Friends?"

"No," she said. "Friends don't push friends away when their parents are getting a divorce."

"I can't do this," I said, pushing my chair back from the table. The metal chair legs scraped across the deli's tile floor. Everyone who wasn't staring before directed their full attention on me.

I was done. Done with Jasmine. Done with that comatose deli full of the dead and dying.

Jasmine reached out and seized my arm. "Wait," she said. "There's got to be something I can do. Something. Let me know and I'll do it."

She looked desperate. Everyone was staring. An elderly woman in a red hat shook her head at me. Disdain.

"Please," she said. "Let's figure this out."

I sat back down.

"I need to put all this," I said, "on hold."

"Okay," she said.

"Good." I nodded.

Silence then Jasmine blurted, "You can put me on hold. I'll be your On Hold Person."

"My on hold person?"

"Yes, we can be each other's On Hold People." She laughed. "Not that I know what that means. What do you think On Hold People do?"

"They give each other space."

"But they still support each other, right?"

"I guess."

"And they still say they love each other?"

"I don't know."

She smiled.

"I can do this. This will be good. We'll be fine."

Good one of us thought so. Jasmine looked hopeful like a kid whose parents just told her that the Easter Bunny was a fake, but "Oh, no, Santa Claus, that guy, he's the real deal."

"I'll be the best On Hold Person you've ever seen," she said.

Her adoption of the phrase "on hold person" disturbed me. Wasn't I trying to get away from calling her my girlfriend and treating her like she was special? How was on hold person any less of a label? And she'd be "the best?"

I could try, I supposed. Whatever the hell being on hold meant, it sounded less confining and less likely to end in one of us stabbing the other. I could always break up with her later if having her on hold began to be more of a burden than an advantage. Who knew, maybe keeping her on my side would be good for me. Someone in my corner. Someone who loved me. Even if that someone was unbalanced. Wasn't it always worse when deranged people's love turned into hate?

Besides, this on hold arrangement would give me time to pull my life together. Not that I thought even in that moment that I made my life any easier. In fact, putting Jasmine on hold made everything more complicated, and I knew it sitting there in that deli. It felt right at the time, though. A bit of a hindrance maybe. A bump in the road to breaking up, but at least we were on the asphalt.

Truth be told, it was hard eliminating my chance at sex with anyone, even Jasmine the lying stalker, especially when Sharon was MIA. Not that sex should have been a priority.

That's the thing about being a man. Sex and the desire for sex never goes away. You might think, "Hey, I'm done with this. I'm past my sexual peak and I'm a mess." I know I thought just as much during my divorce. Then you see a waitress with a gorgeous smile or a coed jogging on the treadmill in front of you at the gym, moving up and down—not that I go to the gym—then you think, "I want her. This could work."

So sitting there, I wanted Jasmine. She was intriguing and sexier than she had been in weeks, even if it was because I thought she could be damaged and deranged. Maybe she knew the truth about me. Knew I could never be her Michael Douglas. Or maybe she didn't. Whatever the hell she knew, she was smiling at me, her new On Hold Person, thinking somehow our relationship was fine when it would be anything but. And for a moment, I was okay. I didn't need Sharon. I didn't need anyone. But that's the thing about moments. They don't last.

My phone rang. A number I didn't recognize. Still, maybe I could use it as an excuse to dodge the meal with Jasmine. "I'm sorry, babe," I could say, "but I've got to go."

I motioned to the door, indicating to Jasmine that I had to step out and take the call. She nodded a go ahead. Out of earshot from Jasmine, I answered the phone. Sharon?

"Doctor C," whispered a male voice, "I need to speak with you."

"Who *is* this?"

"Benny."

"How did you get this number?"

"There's been a break-in," Benny said.

"A break-in?"

"At your office."

"How do you know?"

"The door's askew. I went to the bathroom and I came back and the door was askew."

"Askew?"

"Open. Askew."

"Ajar."

"Yes, the door is ajar. Your door is ajar. I think someone's watching me watch your door. This might be a Code Red situation."

Code Red? What was he talking about?

"Is anything missing?"

"I don't know. The suspect might be inside. I repeat, the suspect might be inside. Code Red. I repeat, Code Red."

"Stop saying Code Red and go in my office and look around."

"I don't think I can, Doctor C, not unless I have a weapon."

"Grab a stapler, something, and go check it out."

Not that I wanted Benny to assault anyone with a stapler. However, it was unlikely that anyone was in my office, so the stapler made sense. Benny could protect himself from the Code Red, and I could find out if someone had broken into my office—or, more likely, that the cleaning crew left my door open. Benny probably drifted off, didn't notice the cleaning crew, and woke up to his Code Red situation. Whatever the hell that was.

"I have a three-hole punch."

"That'll work."

"I'm at your door now. I just don't know, Doctor C."

"Go ahead."

He breathed into the phone. Two short breaths. "Okay. I'm going in, Boss. I repeat. I'm going in."

And then, Benny let out a long, raspy gasp. Followed by silence.

"All clear. I repeat all clear. No suspect in sight," Benny chirped. Then silence. "Unless he's hiding behind your bookcases. Or under your desk. Or behind me—holy mother!"

And then a screech.

"What happened? Benny, are you okay?"

He started to tee-hee and wheeze at the same time.

"That poster … that poster across from your office. Out of the corner of my eye I thought a man was standing there."

Oh, that. Don't remind me.

"I know, but anyone in my office? Anything out of place?"

"I don't know what I'm looking for."

"Anything roughed up or missing?"

Probably just the cleaning crew.

"Don't know for sure. Looks like a regular old office. A computer, a desk, a chair, two chairs, a lamp, two bookcases, some books. Oh, cool, I didn't know you drink green tea."

What was he doing? Looking through my drawers?

"I really love green tea," he continued. "Gives me mental acuity. Keeps me sharp. That and ginseng. Now, ginseng green tea. That would be a killer combo."

Uh-uh. I didn't have time to hear about Benny or his mental acuity or lack thereof.

"So everything's fine?" I asked.

"Yes. Everything appears to be in shipshape, right-o working order, sir."

"Thank you for calling," I said, hoping that would end the conversation even though I worried any acknowledgement or appreciation might only embolden him to keep calling, which I certainly didn't want. With Jasmine on hold, all I needed was another high-maintenance time sink on my hands, this one a man-child, scared of his own shadow. At least Jasmine's breakdowns came with the potential for physical connection. What did Benny possess? The potential for a sweaty handshake?

"I'm on it, Doctor C," Benny said. "Rest assured. Your office is safe when Benny's on the case."

Was he referring to himself in the third person?

"Would it be okay if I hit the vending machine? All this has made me hungry," he went on.

"Go ahead," I said even though I wondered how the very act of walking into an office with a three-hole punch could famish the kid.

"Because if it's easier, I could order in," Benny said. "Order in and pee in a bucket, but I'll need to get a bucket. I guess I could use your trashcan or the office recycling bin."

"No, Benny, you can pee in a urinal, like a real person, in the bathroom. Hell, you can even go to the vending machine. You don't have to be glued to the office door."

"It's just that the breach occurred when I was in the restroom. The whole thing makes me uneasy. I doubt I can go ever again."

"Go," I said. "There wasn't a breach. We're fine."

"If you say so, Doctor C."

"I say so."

"Okay, I'm going to grab a Honeybun, and then I'll sweep the perimeter."

"Sweep away."

Done with Benny, I hung up the phone and returned to Jasmine.

Damn. She didn't eat a bite of her sandwich in my absence. I wanted her to be done by the time I got back. But, no, there she sat like an obedient little puppy waiting for her master to return to feed her. It took everything I had not to yell at her.

Instead, I said, "I've got to go. Meeting."

"Frank didn't say anything about a meeting."

Did she and Frank communicate about every detail of their lives?

"Sometimes my meetings don't include Frank," I said, which was true, even though I didn't have a meeting. I really just wanted to go home. Alone.

"Oh," she said. "If you're feeling overwhelmed, you should reevaluate your commitments."

You can imagine my frustration. Still, I probably shouldn't have snapped, "What do you think I'm trying to do?"

Which might have been a little harsh. But, really, I already was being as selfless as one man could be since I didn't break up with her even though I wanted to. Redefining our relationship to be whatever the hell it was now should have given me enough good guy points. But no.

"I really need to go," I said, ignoring the tears welling up in Jasmine's eyes. If I could get out of there before she started to cry again, then I wouldn't be the guy leaving a woman sniveling on top of her sandwich.

So, for once, I did something for myself. Something I wanted to do. I got up, grabbed my coat, and got out of there.

No taking care of people. No taking care of Jasmine. If she wanted to cry, she needed to do so on her own.

Free at last.

But I was far from free.

CHAPTER FIFTEEN

For exactly two hours, I was comfortable. Well, not comfortable by Greenwood Planned Community's standards, but I could take a breath, kick my shoes off, turn on the news. See that the world hadn't changed much in the last few days. Coldest day of the year turning into coldest week of the year and some weight loss show contestant might have lost too much weight while another might not have lost enough. "How much weight should you lose? Doctor Alex will tell us when we return." Whoever Dr. Alex was, he looked like an idiot. But watching him blab about heart muscle and hormones, I felt normal. There was something comforting seeing that the world was still as insipid as it had been a few days before.

Not that I really relaxed. A couple of minutes into the news broadcast, which included an update on two brothers who trained a—and I'm not kidding—rabbit to ride a miniature bicycle, my phone rang.

"Doctor C," Benny said, panting into the phone. "The goose has eaten the biscuit. I repeat, the goose has eaten the biscuit."

"I have no idea what you're talking about. Unless there is a goose eating a biscuit."

"I texted you the phrases and what they mean. I repeat, the goose has eaten the biscuit, if you know what I mean."

"Stop speaking in code, Benny."

"Your stalker," Benny whispered. "I've apprehended her."

I jumped to my feet. Did Benny find Jasmine poking around my office? Maybe *we* were on hold, but her stalking wasn't?

I grabbed my jacket and I was out the door.

"Is it Jasmine?"

"What's a Jasmine?"

"The goose, what does she look like?" I asked as I started my car.

"About yay tall."

"Benny, if you're gesturing, I can't see you."

"This right here is why we should video chat, Doctor C."

That's what I needed, video chat with Benny. As if I didn't see or hear from him enough.

"Focus. What does the stalker look like?"

"I don't know. It all happened so quickly."

"Think. Remember her hair, her eyes."

"Her eyes were brown and white."

"Brown and white?"

"You know, brown in the middle, white on the outside. White eyeballs."

Dear Lord. If Benny were a girl, I'd think he was playing dumb. But no. He *was* dumb.

All I could hope is that if he had my stalker there, he didn't let her go.

"And her hair?"

"Short and weird."

That didn't sound like Jasmine. Maybe my stalker was someone else. Or maybe Benny captured an innocent woman walking down the hall, hoping to turn in a late paper. Great.

"Did you happen to get her name?"

"No." he paused. "Want me to make the canary sing, if you know what I mean?"

No, I didn't.

"Benny, listen to me. Don't make the canary sing. Whatever that is, don't do it. Just stay where you are. I'm coming. Don't do anything."

"Doctor C," Benny whined, "why can't I make the canary sing?"

"Because I'm on my way."

When I got there, Benny was sitting with his back against my office door, his right pant leg ripped up to his knee.

I gestured to his leg. "What happened to you?"

He pointed at the door. Did he get it caught in the door or did the woman rip his pants in the scuffle? A fracas, a fight, a disturbance in or outside my office. Just imagine the paperwork if Dean Dyer got wind of this.

"Benny, please tell me you didn't assault anyone."

"Shh," he whispered. "She's in there."

Wait—what? Benny'd locked up some woman in my office? That's all I needed: Benny kidnaps a woman and I get charged with aiding and abetting. I thought about getting the hell out of there, but I was in too deep. Besides, I wanted to know who the woman with short, weird hair and the brown and white eyes was. Maybe Jasmine in a wig? Serves her right to have Benny assault her for poking her nose where it doesn't belong.

I moved to the door. Benny, still on the floor, raised his hand up to me.

"Doctor C, we should come up with a plan in case she rushes at us. She's been eerily quiet in there, probably making a weapon. Do you have any pencils she could file down?"

"The door opens in, not out. All she'd have to do is pull the door open on her end, and you'd fall to the floor. Then she could overpower you."

"*Au contraire,*" Benny said. "I know a thing or two about power relations, Doctor C. All one needs to gain the upper hand is intellectual knowhow."

Knowing a thing or two about power relations myself and possessing intellectual knowhow about my own office, I reached over Benny's head and rapped on the door. Three short knocks. The door opened. And like that, Benny was flat on his back like a turtle.

"Not cool, Doctor C," Benny said, rolling to his side so he could boost himself up. "I have chronic pain."

I wanted to tell him he was a chronic pain in my ass, but by that point I was staring right at an insubstantial teenage girl with dark hair that sat squarely on her round, slightly squat face. She stood in my office, silent, her deep brown eyes widening at Benny flailing about on the floor. She had to be fifteen if that.

"Listen, girlie," I started, "I don't know who you are or what you think I did to you, but you need to stop."

"Okay." She shrugged. "I'll stop."

Could it really be that easy?

"Thank you," I said. "Because your threats ... your little game isn't funny."

"What threats? What little game?"

"So now you're denying it?" What was this little girl's problem? "Tell me, what did I do to you? Did I sleep with your sister, your best friend, your mother? What?"

"Actually you did." She smiled.

"Aha!" Benny said, suddenly on his feet and in an exaggerated defensive stance that he no doubt learned from a video game or an action movie. "I knew this was personal."

No shit, Sherlock.

"You're angry because I slept with someone?" I continued, ignoring Benny as much as possible.

"Not angry," she said.

"Why are you stalking me? Taking pictures of me?"

She shook her head. "You must have me confused with someone else."

I stared at her.

"I'm your daughter," she said.

My stomach dropped. This had to be a joke.

"You have a daughter?" Benny interjected. "You should have told me you have a daughter. That's need-to-know info, Doctor C."

"She's not my daughter," I said, looking at the girl, hoping she would laugh and agree.

"No, I'm definitely yours," she said. "I know what you're thinking. I wish I wasn't, but here I am."

"You want me to make the canary sing?" Benny said to me like the *canary* wasn't standing there right in front of him listening to every word he said.

"Nah," I said, digging in my wallet and pulling out a five. "Benny, why don't you buy yourself something from the vending machine?"

"Excellent," he said. "Can I keep the change?"

I nodded and he scampered off mumbling to himself that Honeybuns were eighty-five cents and he could buy five Honeybuns or buy one and keep four dollars and fifteen cents.

"Please tell me that's not my brother," the girl said, which made me laugh a little too much.

Discomfort followed until I said, "No, definitely not mine."

"That's a relief."

"You're telling me."

She smiled. "So, you're really Daniel Conrad?"

"Yes," I said, feeling a bit like a celebrity, half embarrassed to be recognized, but mostly flattered. "And you're?"

"Zoe," she said.

"Well, Zoe, don't take this the wrong way," I said, although there was only one way to take it. "What makes you think you're my daughter?"

I wasn't trying to be rude, but I needed answers. At least it was more polite than "What the fuck were you doing poking around my office after hours?"

"My mother told me."

"Your mother?"

"Donna Davis, but I think you knew her as Donna Winston."

The name was formless in my mind. Maybe there'd been a Donna in the late nineties, or early in 2000. No way a fling with Donna then could bring me a semi-full-grown girl claiming to be my daughter, although the timing was right. The girl looked to be fourteen, maybe fifteen. She could be a young seventeen tops. A young seventeen. When were Donna and I together? Everything was distant and dim.

"I remember Donna," I said, even though I didn't.

I shut the door behind us just in case Benny lumbered back to my end of the hallway. I gestured to the seat across from my desk and she sat down.

"So, this stalker," Zoe began.

"Probably just a prank," I said. "Nothing serious."

"Your bodyguard made it sound serious. He told me he was going to do me like a grizzly bear. It was quite disturbing. Is he altogether normal?"

"That's just Benny," I said. "He was most likely using code, not threatening you. Or maybe he was threatening you, in code. That's possible."

We sat in a prickly silence.

"I really am your daughter," she said. "We can do the DNA tests to be sure."

"I don't doubt that you're telling the truth or what you think is the truth, but if you *are* my daughter, you know how easy it is to lie about these things, to twist the truth."

"I'm sure I don't know what you're talking about." She smirked. "You're probably wondering why here, why now, why did this girl just pop into existence?"

"Those thoughts did cross my mind."

"I found out myself when the man I thought was my dad kicked me out a few months ago."

I must have looked confused.

"I'm not a child. I'm eighteen. It's in his rights."

She didn't look eighteen. Not even close.

"Are you in high school? College?"

"In between. This was supposed to be my first semester. But when my mom told my dad—I mean Ron—he refused to pay for school, stopped paying for everything. Then he told me 'Not my daughter, not my problem.' And that was that."

So she was looking for money. That made sense. Penniless and with a newfound father who no doubt had cash from his book, what did she have to lose? Worst case scenario, I could give her a job with Benny and they could split a Honeybun for eighty-five cents.

"What about your mom? Didn't she stop him, offer to help you?"

"You really don't remember my mom, do you?"

"Is it that obvious?"

"Just a bit. My mom's a wreck, but an ineffectual wreck. She's just clinging onto Ron's knees, hoping he won't divorce her for lying to him my whole life."

I was trying to keep these people straight. Ron must be her father, or her stepfather. I guess I'm her father.

"You said your mother's name is Donna?"

"I have a baby picture somewhere." She dug around in her purse. "Not of her but of me when I was a baby and her."

That sounded helpful.

She rifled around in her purse, clanging things together. Finally, she exhaled and dumped the contents of her purse in her lap. "Here we go," she said, fishing out a faded picture under a bright pink tampon and a wadded-up dollar bill. She peeled a gum wrapper off the front of the picture. Women and their purses. Could be useful for my *Practical Guide.* Not that older women didn't come with traveling freak shows slung across their shoulders.

She handed me the picture. She had small hands with slender fingers. Not that Jasmine had hulking hands, but Jasmine's hands weren't slight. They belonged to a full-grown woman. Zoe's wafer-thin fingers looked like they belonged to a child. Fragile.

I took the picture from her and, sure enough, there was one of my exes staring me in the face. And some of it came back to me. Dear Lord. Donna the dental hygienist. I remembered how persistent she was to "psychologically diagnose" me, which annoyed me to no end since I was the psychologist. She'd grab my DSM from the shelf, look at me, and say, "lack of intimacy" or "intimacy issues" or "problems with authority" or "dissatisfied" or "depressed," hoping to find a reason for my behavior, when in reality, I just couldn't stand her.

So this was Donna the dental hygienist's daughter. If I squinted, I could see her nose. Maybe her mouth. But damn me if I saw any of me in Zoe. I wouldn't put it past Donna the dental hygienist to lie to her daughter.

"I remember your mother," I said.

"Doesn't sound like a ringing endorsement. Don't worry. She doesn't like you, either."

"Well, that explains why she'd hide my daughter from me for eighteen years."

"She says you're a psychopath."

"Is that what she says?"

Zoe nodded. "*Are* you a psychopath?"

"No," I said. "But that's what all good psychopaths say."

"She says you like killing animals."

"Liked, not like. And who doesn't?" I joked.

Zoe looked at me like I was deranged. "Most people."

"It's not as if I reveled in killing them. I just enjoyed running over squirrels."

"Who enjoys running over squirrels?"

"Enjoyed isn't the right word. I liked letting bad things happen. So when normal people would slow down or swerve out of the way, I just kept going. I didn't speed up, but I didn't slow down, either. You'd be happy to know those bastards have good reflexes. I rarely hit one."

She shook her head. "That's beyond warped."

"Probably."

I didn't mention to Zoe that part of the fun was that her mother Donna the dental hygienist was the type of woman who always picked up wounded animals and took them in. Really, I was just offsetting Donna's good, which, come to think of it, probably made my actions worse.

"Besides a good psychologist would tell you there aren't psychopaths," I said instead.

"And a good psychologist would tell you letting bad things happen means you're sick in the head."

"Probably."

She laughed. "Don't worry, I'm sick in the head, too."

A knock on my door. Must be Benny. I ignored it. Then another knock. This time louder.

"Doctor C, Doctor C!"

I rolled my eyes.

"Doctor C! The queen bee is in the honeypot. I repeat the queen bee, she's—"

Then a series of swift thumps down the hall. Benny was running, clonk-clonk-clonking down the hall at top Benny speed.

And then another knock.

But this time Dean Dyer's voice resonated through my door.

"Doctor Conrad, I know you're in there. Open up."

I looked at Zoe, who didn't look eighteen, let alone sixteen.

This couldn't be good.

Open the door, I motioned to Zoe.

Might as well get it over with.

CHAPTER SIXTEEN

Dean Dyer took one look at Zoe and turned to me.

"What is the meaning of this?" she asked.

"The meaning of what? The meaning of life?" I said, trying to be funny.

Zoe laughed. At least someone was with me.

"The meaning of *this*." She gestured at Zoe.

"Oh, that. That's Zoey."

"Zoe." The girl glared. "My name's Zoe."

Then she extended her hand toward Dean Dyer. "It's nice to meet you. You must be my father's girlfriend."

Dean Dyer just stared at her, not taking her hand.

"I ... I ...am not," Dean Dyer managed to say.

It was fun seeing Dean Dyer squirm. Poor woman. She was turning yellow.

"Not my girlfriend," I finally said to prevent the dean from vomiting all over my floor. "That's my dean."

"Oh," Zoe said. "Sorry. I thought you were someone else."

Dean Dyer, still not taking her hand, scrutinized Zoe.

Zoe shifted her weight like an middle school boy at a dance. "You know who I am, right? Viola-playing Zoe? First in state? My dad must have raved about me over the years."

"Are you a student here?"

"No," Zoe said. "Just visiting my Pops. You work him hard. He's never home."

"You shouldn't be on campus," Dean Dyer said. "Wandering the halls late at night, after hours, going into men's offices."

"My dad's here," she said. "I'm fine."

Dean Dyer looked at Zoe and then glared at me.

"Doctor Conrad, can I speak with you in the hall?"

Zoe winked at me on my way out. "I'll wait right here, Daddy-o," she said. "Who knows what might happen if I leave this office. I might get attacked by a bear."

"Inside joke," I said to Dean Dyer, who shot me a look that said, "I don't want to know."

We stood a moment in silence. Dean Dyer rubbed her face, pressing her fingertips over her eyes.

"Doc-tor Con-rad," she said, drawing out my name as long as she could, "I don't know what you're doing with that little girl, but it needs to stop."

"I'm not doing anything. She's my daughter."

"I know you two think it's funny to lie to me, but this is serious."

"No, really," I said. "Zoe's my kid."

"And you haven't mentioned her because?"

"I was trying to cultivate an image," I said. "You know, of being a man's man, for my book, but I'm really a family man, not some user or abuser of women."

"Then be a family man," Dean Dyer said. "Be a family man and stop doing whatever it is you do with young—" She looked at the poster.

"I don't sleep with my students," I said. "And I don't trade grades for sexual favors or whatever that poster's accusing me of doing."

"No one said you did." Dean Dyer exhaled. "No one's accusing you of doing more than it is that you do."

I shook my head. "But what do you think I'm doing?"

Dean Dyer closed her eyes. "Doctor Conrad," she said, "be a family man, go home, get some rest, take your daughter to dinner, stop—" The color drained from her face.

"Stop what?"

"Drawing attention to yourself," she said under her breath.

"Zoe's really my daughter," I said.

"No one said she wasn't. I should go," she said. "You should go. The girl should go."

Dean Dyer turned on her heel and walked away.

"She's not some student I'm sleeping with," I called after her. "Zoe's my kid. She plays the violin beautifully and she sings like an angel."

I added the singing part. It sounded like something a father would know.

"Go home," Dean Dyer's voice shrilled down the hall. "Do this somewhere else. Off campus."

Zoe's head popped out of my office.

"It's the viola, not the violin," she said. "And if she hears me sing, she'll know you're lying."

"Violin, viola, same difference."

"Big difference," Zoe said. "A real father would know that."

"I'm your real father. Most likely. Or probably. Unless, of course, your mother is lying."

She picked up her purse. "I shouldn't have tried to cover for you back there."

"No, that was good."

"It was wrong," she said. "I don't know why I did it. Why I pretended like we're a father-daughter duo when I just met you."

"Well, technically, if your mother's telling the truth, we've been a father-daughter duo for quite some time. We just didn't know it."

"I should go," she said. "We're not good for each other."

"What does that mean?"

She paused in the hallway and shrugged. "It was nice to meet you."

"What about a hug?" I said.

"I'm not a hugger," she replied quickly, not making eye contact.

"You have a place to stay, right?"

Zoe nodded.

I didn't want to bother her, so I said it was nice to meet her and told her if she ever needed anything, she could call me day or night and I'd be there. We both knew she'd never call. Still, I played my part well with just the right degree of humor that hinted at real concern.

"Do you have a phone number I can reach you at if I need something, like a kidney?" I tried.

Zoe knit her brow. "No," she said. "I don't believe in cellphones."

"You don't believe in cellphones?"

"I should go," she said.

"Feel free to stop by later," I said.

She grimaced and then caught herself. "Okay." Zoe nodded.

Then she extended her arm and I took her little hand in mine.

"I hope you find what you're looking for," she said. And before I could wrap my mind around the fact that I had a daughter, let alone a viola-playing, non-singing wisp of a daughter, Zoe was gone, down the hall and out of my life.

CHAPTER SEVENTEEN

And that's where the anger crept in. How dare that little girl pop into my life, make a mess of things—including with my dean—only to disappear again? She made me think perhaps I wasn't alone, that I was connected to someone, infinitesimally connected on the smallest level, in our DNA and then—bam—gone. She gave me no way to contact her all because "we aren't good for each other," whatever the hell that was supposed to mean. Add that to my own flesh and blood's parting jab, "I hope you find what you're looking for." I wasn't looking for anything. She was the one who came looking for me.

So I sat there, seething. I was mad at Zoe, mad at Donna the dental hygienist for hiding Zoe, and mad at Dean Dyer for thinking I was "doing" my students when I most certainly was not.

Of course, I couldn't be left alone. Benny hobbled into my doorway and stood there, cramming his mouth with a six pack of powdered sugar donuts. He didn't have the decency to take them out of the package and eat them. Oh, no, he was dangling the package above his face and letting them fall into his mouth one by one.

"Doctor C," he said, letting another donut plop into his mouth. He munched on it whole as I stared at him wondering if that moment right then and there would be how I would live the rest of my life, watching Benny eat miniature donuts like a trained sea lion.

"You want a donut?" He held out the ripped pack. Two donuts remained. I'm fairly sure he might have licked one.

I shook my head.

Benny kept going. "I figured out if you eat them right out of the package, you don't get the white stuff all over your fingers."

"But it's still all over your face and shirt," I said.

"Yet the fingers stay clean," he said. "That's key."

I didn't want to argue with him. I just wanted him to leave.

"I'll need new pants," Benny lifted up his leg, letting the rip reveal his hairy shin. "That daughter of yours ripped them."

"They're not too bad. You can still wear them."

Benny wore clothing with rips and tears bigger than that one every day.

"It's the coldest week of the year," Benny bellyached. "My shin will be exposed to the elements."

"Fine," I said, hoping he would just leave. "I'll buy you new pants."

"We should talk about my salary. I've been on the front line of this, walking the thin blue line here, putting my life on the line for you."

I wanted to make a comment. Instead, I fished out my wallet. All I had was a twenty and a ten. I handed the ten to Benny. Probably not the fairest given that he had been *working* for me without pay, but he could go to the Goodwill or the Salvation Army and pick up a pair of pants for less than ten bucks if he wanted. Besides, I knew he'd pocket the money and wear the ripped jeans with duct tape he found in the office.

I hoped the ten spot would encourage him to leave, but Benny had more to say. "I checked with my sources. I have sources, Doctor C," he said, waiting for me to be impressed.

"And?"

"She sleeps in the basement in the PRs."

"The PRs?"

"The Dewey Decimal System. Really, Doctor C, how could you not know—"

"She's living here? In our library? At Evergreen?"

"Yes. For the last week or so. I knew I recognized her beady little eyes. She's the girl who's taken over the PRs. The PRs are prime territory, Doctor C."

So she didn't have a place to go after all. Poor little Zoe, curled up on the cold linoleum floor of the library basement. I could say that the image of Zoe alone in the library drove me to intervene, but that wouldn't be the whole truth. I was thinking of myself. Thinking of Dean Dyer finding her there. What kind of family man lets his daughter live in the library?

I told Benny I had to go, grabbed my coat, and I was out of there.

I was a man on a mission. I didn't have time for Benny. I had to get to the library. To the basement and then to the PRs. I had to find the daughter I never knew I had, the daughter I didn't even want, but now that I knew she existed, the one person I needed to take care of.

Especially before Dean Dyer came across her.

I found Zoe, shoes off, legs crossed on top of a sleeping bag, reading a book of all things, like it was perfectly normal to camp out in the library. She was surprised to see me. I insisted that she spend the night at my house. She was reluctant, but eventually she acquiesced. I might have mentioned that Benny knew where she was sleeping. That upset her.

At any rate, I got the girl. Before I knew it, there she was, at my house, looking at me with big brown eyes that radiated pity and empathy. Eyes that were my mother's when I broke one of her favorite dishes. Eyes that said, "Oh, Daniel. I'm disappointed." But eyes that understood. "I know you," Zoe said in a look. "I know who you are."

Which made me uneasy. Because, let's face it, any woman who knows who I am doesn't like me. Or shouldn't.

CHAPTER EIGHTEEN

Zoe and I had been living together for less than twenty-four hours when she stopped me midsentence.

"Wait, what are you talking about?" she asked from the kitchen. She was cracking eggs into a skillet even though it was late afternoon. After I taught my Thursday morning class, Zoe and I spent the late morning and early afternoon talking and drinking black coffee—the creamer I had in the fridge expired two weeks ago—until we finally agreed we were famished. So Zoe decided to cook and I sat at the breakfast table with my *Practical Guide* open on my laptop, although I wasn't working on it, obviously.

"This woman, Sharon," I said from my place at the breakfast table. "She's just gone silent. I'm worried she might be in trouble."

Zoe stopped what she was doing and turned around with a broken eggshell still in her hand. She didn't say anything. She narrowed her eyes at me like she was trying to determine if I was insane or joking.

"You know, Sharon could be dead," I continued.

"Then she'll continue to be silent," Zoe said.

"That's heartless."

"It's the truth. If she's dead, she'll continue to be silent. If she's in trouble and there's anything you can do, you'll hear from her or someone else soon enough. Otherwise, just calm down."

"Calm down?"

"Yes."

"Aren't you a woman? Aren't you supposed to be good at listening?"

"Aren't you a man? Aren't you supposed to be less whiny?"

"I'm not whiny. You're the one who isn't a good listener."

"All I've been doing is listening. I've heard all about Princess Jasmine and Aladdin—"

"Frank," I said.

"Frank." She groaned. "Frank the bastard, and the Wicked Witch of the West—"

"Sharon or Dean Dyer?"

"Listen to yourself." She sighed. "That's your problem: too many women and an inability to tell them apart."

"I can tell them apart."

"Really—" She stopped herself, and instead of finishing her

sentence, she pushed the eggshell into the garbage disposal.

"It's not my fault there are too many witches and I can't tell which one is from the east and which one is from the west," I said, not sure if Zoe could hear me over the pulverizing din of the garbage disposal.

She shook her head. Then she said, indicating that, yes, she had heard me, "No, it is your fault. Take responsibility."

"I am responsible," I said. "I take responsibility all the time."

"Oh, really."

"Look at you right here, right now. This is me taking responsibility for you."

"Maybe," she said. "Or it's me taking responsibility for you."

She scooped fluffy scrambled eggs onto two plates and put one in front of me.

"Not to diminish what you're going through," she said, "but other people could be jobless and homeless, dying of cancer, they could be sold into slavery, and they'd have more hope than you do."

"Oh, are you talking about yourself? Jobless and homeless."

"No, I'm talking about people with real issues. I have a roof over my head."

"Thanks to me," I said.

"I had a roof over my head at the library."

"Some roof," I said. "Maybe you should try living like an adult in the real world, instead of some squatter."

"Whatever. We're not talking about me. We're talking about you and how you have less hope than a leper."

"That's not fair," I said. "I have hope. And maybe the guy with leprosy should try working at Evergreen before he becomes all holier than thou."

A Mona Lisa smile.

"Eat your eggs before they're cold," she said. "Everything important is out of your control."

"That sounds vaguely fatalistic."

"Not vaguely," she replied, sitting down next to me. "We're on a path. You're on a path. I'm on a path—"

My phone rang. Sharon.

"I've got to get this," I said, stepping off of whatever path Zoe thought we were on to answer my phone away from her week one Philosophy 101 twaddle.

I looked down at the phone in my hand. Not wanting to appear too eager, I let it ring. It felt good to make her wait for me. Good to feel wanted.

Third ring. Fourth ring. Sharon calling me. That's hope, little girl. Right there. Hope.

When I couldn't stand it any longer—somewhere in the middle of the fourth ring—I answered Sharon's call.

"There's a concert tonight," Sharon began.

Well, hello to you, too, Sharon.

"Laurie Packard at the House of Blues," she continued.

"And you're telling me this why?"

"I want to go … with you."

The way she said *you* was soft and sensual. Progress. Maybe Sharon was coming around.

I wanted to ask where she'd been, why she uploaded those disturbing images to her blog, but I was afraid I might lose her again. Her artistic free child was sensitive.

"What time?" was all I asked.

"We could meet around five, grab dinner downtown after the show."

Of course. Another dinner on me. Predictable.

"What's in it for me?" I asked.

There's your honesty and authenticity, Sharon. Deal with it.

"A second chance at a second chance with me if you grab tickets from Craigslist. The show's sold out."

"Are you serious?"

"Yes, it's sold out."

"About the second second chance."

"You don't deserve any chances after you left me waiting for you. I cleared my calendar just for you."

Sharon sounded hurt. Maybe she cared about me.

"But I might deserve a second chance if I buy the tickets?"

"If you get good seats. Although really more of a third chance." She laughed, forcing me to laugh, too. The whole thing was ridiculous. Maybe Zoe was onto something about just how stupid I was.

"I'll do it," I said. "But remember you're giving me a second second chance or third chance. Whichever is better."

"Done," she said. "But you and I are still in a fight, additional chances or not."

"Listen, I'm sorry," I said. "Sorry for being late. Got caught up at work. The dean."

"I'm getting another call," she said. "Could be the school. Meet me at five tonight."

And Sharon was gone.

So I went back to my laptop, found a guy selling tickets online who insisted his name was Johnny Bob, first name Johnny, last name Bob, even though I'm fairly certain no one has the last name of Bob. $300 a seat, Johnny Bob insisted. Take it or leave it. So I took it, even though my expenses were adding up. Zoe, dinners with Sharon, Benny's two hundred a week, and now six hundred for tickets to see some woman singing about her problems. At least Jasmine still paid for her half of the check when we went out for lunch or dinner, but that wasn't much of a comfort. The hope was that those lunches and dinners would be *on hold* indefinitely or for the time being, anyway. I added pick up tickets from Johnny Bob at the Burger Box downtown to my list of things to do. Luckily, the Burger Box was just five blocks north of the House of Blues.

I headed back to the kitchen to update Zoe on the whole Sharon situation—well, I wasn't going to tell her about the promised second second chance and what I hoped it might mean in the bedroom. I do have boundaries, but I thought it best to put her mind at ease just in case she was concerned. When I entered the room, Zoe was on the couch, reading a book.

"Sharon's alive," I said.

Zoe made a little noise, an acknowledgement, sure, but her eyes didn't leave the page.

"I thought you'd be relieved." I loomed over her. "But I guess you're too busy reading your book to care about another human being's life."

She let her book drop.

"Listen," she said, "you didn't really think she was dead, did you?"

"I didn't *not* think she was dead."

She cocked her head to the side and looked at me like a lion assessing if the underweight bunny hopping by was worth a pounce and a chop.

"The problem with you—"

"Is it that I'm too generous? Too open to taking in a homeless girl out of the library?"

"No."

"I see. Not a problem because it benefits you."

"No," she said slowly. "The problem with you is that you don't believe in anything or anyone but yourself."

"That's hurtful."

"It's the truth," she said. "Prove me wrong. Tell me: What do you believe in?"

"I believe in things."

"Such as?"

"You. I believed in you when I picked you up from the library."

"You can't prove everything with that one action. Even if it was a nice action."

"It was nice of me, wasn't it? Some might say generous." I extended out the last word. Gen-er-ous. "I believe in you. See?"

"But believing in me doesn't make you a believer, someone who sees the extraordinary in the world, the beauty, the sheer power of—"

"I see beauty," I interjected.

She shook her head. "Why do you lie all the time?"

Which frustrated me to no end.

"Listen," I said, "I don't know where you get off coming here and accusing me of being morally bankrupt when I'm the one helping you."

"I'm just returning the favor," she said. "I'm trying to help you."

"No one asked for your help."

"You did," she said. "You obsess non-stop about all the people you've lied to: Sharon, Jasmine, your agent, your dean, me probably."

"I don't just lie to those people," I said.

"You lie to more people?"

"No. I mean, yes. I mean, I tell those people the truth, too."

"Which is what exactly?"

"That I'm a slumpy old man."

"A slumpy old man who believes in nothing but himself?"

"Sure," I said. "That might be the truth. A slumpy old man who believes in nothing but himself—and love," I finished.

"You sound like a Beatles mashup: When I'm Sixty-four mixed with All You Need is Love."

"Make fun of me if you want," I said. "There's nothing else to life. You live, getting older, deteriorating every day, and then you die. That's it."

She looked like she wanted to punch me.

"I thought you and I could be good for each other," she said, "but I'm starting to see that you're bad for me, just like I thought."

"You need to pull your head out of your ass," I said, being severe, but between Zoe, Benny, Jasmine, and my students asking for extensions every time one of them sneezed, I was tired of all these young people acting like I owed them something.

"Finally, the truth," Zoe said.

"Well, Sharon's alive," I said. "And you might not understand this because you're just a kid, but adults have relationships that are complicated sometimes."

"Only because you make them complicated," she said. "By lying."

My phone rang. Unknown number. No doubt someone I didn't want to talk to.

I told Zoe I'd get it later.

She glared at me. "Answer your phone. The truth can wait."

"Danny!"

Great. My agent, Alexandra Morris.

"Danny!" she started again. "I found you *the* perfect woman. Perfect. You'll be impressed. Smart, funny."

"Uh, thanks, but I can find women on my own."

I moved away from Zoe, who was giving me the evil eye.

"See, he's funny," Alexandra's voice sagged into a grumble. "Didn't I say he was … funny?"

"I thought he would be," a buoyant female voice trilled. Oblivious, light, whimsical. A voice that exclaimed, "Let's kick off our shoes and run across wet grass!" A voice who read Sartre with a smirk, bemused by the ridiculousness of the world. A voice who could be with a guy like me. We could—

"Sophia's our newest collaborator," Alexandra said.

"Who's Sophia?"

"I am," the voice said. "I'm looking forward to working with you."

Every man has a place he'll draw a line in the sand and say "I'm willing to die here on this hill." Having a ghost writer or a collaborator, however adorable she sounded, was my hill.

To think Zoe complained that I didn't believe in anything.

"We're not working together," I snapped.

I was rude, sure, but it was better than the alternative. That book, for better or for worse, would be mine and mine alone.

"Danny, you've got to get this book done. Sophia will—"

"Sophia," I said, addressing her directly, "I'm sure you're a nice girl. But I'm not working with you or anyone else."

I hung up.

I looked at the clock. A little before four. Time to be on my way so I could meet up with Johnny Bob and get the tickets before Sharon and I met at five.

I changed my shirt, gargled some mouthwash, ran some water through my hair. Sharon. I was going to spend the evening with Sharon. We were going to do something normal people do. We'd listen to a concert, not my choice of music, but, still, a date. We'd go out for dinner and drinks after. Sharon once mentioned that there was a bar she wanted us to try downtown, but we never went there. "Numi's ah-mazing," she said. "Everyone who is anyone loves it." But that was back two years ago. Perhaps *everyone* no longer liked it, but I could try. Maybe I could get us reservations. Surprise her.

So I was in a good mood, excited, hopeful about Sharon when I skipped out into the living room to say goodbye to Zoe. The girl hadn't moved an inch as if she needed to stay perfectly still or we wouldn't finish our conversation.

"Wow, you're all dressed up," she said.

"Going out with Sharon."

"She's married, right?"

"Well, it all depends on how you look at it."

"Yes or no. On or off. Married or unmarried."

"Sometimes people can be separated."

"Is she separated?"

"No."

"Married." Zoe shook her head. "A married woman."

"She's my friend," I said.

"Some friend. It sounds like you two abuse each other."

"No, we're friends," I said.

"Oh, sure," Zoe said. "Tell me something that's true."

"Okay," I said. "You're annoying."

"Real mature," Zoe snorted.

"Here's something else that's true: I've got to go," I said, looking at my watch. I needed to meet up with Johnny Bob who was now texting me nonstop like we were coordinating a missile strike against the USSR. And then there was Sharon.

"Have a good night," Zoe said.

"I'll try not to get shot by any jealous husbands."

"Jealous husbands are the least of your problems."

CHAPTER NINETEEN

Driving down the highway, out of the suburbs, I was on my way. First, I needed to meet Johnny Bob at the Burger Box just five blocks north of the House of Blues. Then I'd meet Sharon, see the concert, go out to dinner—which reminded me, I still needed to call Numi to see if they took reservations. But Johnny Bob was texting me constantly and I spent most of the time I should have been paying attention to the road dodging accidents and quelling Johnny Bob's endless stream of panic. Another text. Maybe I wasn't coming. No, I'm on my way. Why wasn't I there yet? Just hit a bit of traffic. Maybe I was "the fuzz." No, I am a college professor. Back to maybe I wasn't coming and he should just sell the tickets to someone else because "they'll be worthless once the concert starts." He knew other people who wanted them and he'd do it, too, if I didn't show up in five minutes. He could even make more money. He was giving me a deal at three hundred a pop. Oh, Johnny Bob, thank you for the charity!

There's something about being on the open road all alone that normally lets me clear my head. I'm sure I'm not the only one who feels that way. In fact, I'm sure most people do. Give me time alone in the car with my music and my thoughts over colorless conversation with someone else in the passenger's seat, and I'll take the solitary drive.

I needed time. Time to think about my *Practical Guide*. Time to think about Sharon. Time to think about Zoe, even, and that nonsense she spouted about how bad I was for everyone including myself. But there was Johnny Bob and traffic and then Johnny Bob again. Ding. Stall. Ding. Ding. Stall.

Traffic. Patchy at first. Then long and drawn out. Not moving an inch. Sirens. I was stuck behind an eighteen-wheeler. I looked at my watch. 4:46.

My phone rang. Sharon.

"Where are you?"

"Traffic. Almost there. Just hitting downtown."

Even though downtown was another thirty minutes away at least. All I could be hitting was the back of this truck, especially if I didn't pay more attention to the start-stop in front of me.

"They're seating people."

"I'll be there."

"Can you give me the seat number so I can—"

The phone cut out.

Another call.

"I'll be there," I said, hanging up on Sharon and taking the other call.

"Where are you?" a female voice said on the other side.

"Downtown."

Might as well keep everything consistent even though I was still thirty minutes from downtown.

"You want me to meet you down there?"

"Down where?"

"Downtown."

"Who is this?"

"Jasmine."

Oh, Jasmine. I almost forgot about her.

"Nah. I'm going downtown to work on my *Practical Guide*, get away from it all, you know."

"Sounds relaxing," Jasmine said.

"It will be. If I ever get out of traffic."

"When you get back, let's talk," she said. "I need to tell you—"

Another call. This couldn't be Sharon again, could it?

I lurched forward.

"I can't hear you," I said to Jasmine, even though the reception was fine. "It's … cutting out … the phone … oh, no."

I clicked over to the next caller.

Sharon again.

"Why are you hanging up on me and not answering your phone?"

"Traffic. Bad cell reception." Which was somewhat true.

Then an idea hit me.

Sharon was at the House of Blues, just five blocks north of the Burger Box. She could pop over there, buy Johnny Bob a burger, keep him occupied, maybe even buy the tickets off him if she could grab cash from the ATM, and then I could meet her at the concert. Thirty minutes. I'd be there, no problem.

She hemmed and hawed at the idea.

"Isn't that neighborhood dangerous?" she asked. Suburban code for "Isn't that an"—insert racial minority here—"neighborhood?" In this case, she meant, "Isn't the House of Blues in the barrio?"

"Nothing you can't handle," I said, which was the truth. Sharon always carried a gun in her purse.

"And you just want me to meet this unknown man and *keep him occupied*?"

"I'm not asking you to sleep with him. Just buy him a burger."

I was only partially joking. With Sharon, you never know.

"Stop being a bastard, Daniel."

My phone whined. Another call.

She agreed to walk to the Burger Box, gun in tow. As soon as I ended the call with Sharon, I texted Johnny Bob about the change of plans. More panic. She could be an undercover cop or a murderer.

I asked him how many times he'd heard of a man getting murdered by a woman at a Burger Box.

To which Johnny Bob didn't reply, hopefully because he and Sharon were talking by then. She was buying him a burger, not shooting him in the face. Unless all that darkness on her blog and the brained bird was a sign of psychosis. Don't know what else it could be. Still, not a sign that she would just shoot a guy at a Burger Box, especially not a guy selling Laurie Packard tickets. Me, maybe. She might shoot me. Not some random guy. Propriety and whatnot.

Finally, the traffic eased up.

Still fifteen minutes away from downtown and another twenty-five from the House of Blues.

Sharon.

"It's almost time to sit down. Where are you?"

"I'll be there," I said, pulling my car on the shoulder and flooring the gas pedal.

"You better," she said. "You can't have me meet with some jittery miscreant in a criminal neighborhood and then leave me standing by the side of the road, waiting for you twice in two days."

"Five minutes," I said. Because that's who I was lately: too spread out, without enough time.

I drove on the shoulder, ran two red lights, and pissed off a homeless man who yelled at my car and hit my hood with his fists. Still I didn't make it on time. No surprise there. It was a fool's errand. Not that Sharon appreciated my efforts.

When I pulled up to the House of Blues, the doors were closed and Sharon was standing outside, arms crossed and dour. I pulled up to the curb and unrolled my passenger side window.

I leaned as close as I could to the window and the curb and planted a big smile on my face.

"Here's the money," I said, waving my wallet at her. "You can give it to Johnny Bob, get the tickets, go in and have a seat while I park the car. Where's Johnny Bob?"

She glared at me and rose up from the curb. Silent.

"It's not too late, is it?"

She leaned into the open passenger's side window and threw a pair of Laurie Packard tickets in my face.

"Did you buy these?" I asked, curious how Sharon got the tickets in the first place.

"No, I prostituted myself," she hissed. "Of course, I bought them. No thanks to you."

"I'll pay you back," I hoped it would make Sharon feel better to know I was taking responsibility for my actions. Look at me. I was a guy who cared.

"I don't want your money. Might be better if Brian saw the ATM withdrawal, asked questions, and kicked your ass."

Might be. Although Brian wasn't the ass-kicking sort. Obviously. The man knew about me the first time Sharon confessed everything two years ago. Instead of shooting me or challenging me to a duel, he'd probably sign up for another round of marriage counseling. He was a good suburban dad after all.

"I can take Brian. If he wants to fight, I'll kick *his* ass," I said, hoping it would make Sharon feel better. Here was a man who would fight for her. Every woman's dream. I half-expected her to swoon and say, "Oh, Daniel, you're wonderful." Although Sharon wasn't the swooning kind. That was more Jasmine.

But instead of swooning, Sharon clenched her jaw and said, "Screw you, Daniel." Vitriol dripping from each syllable. Scr-ew you, Dan-iel.

Before I could stop her, she whipped around on her heel and strode down the street, in the opposite direction of my car. I called after her, "Come back, please," but she didn't flinch. She kept walking.

CHAPTER TWENTY

Stop her. That was all I could think of. *Stop her. Don't let her walk away from you.*

I considered abandoning my car and following after her on foot, but a skinny police officer was already giving me the bum's rush. I knew if I left my car, he could chase me down. He was wiry and could catch up with me on foot if he wanted to. Not one of those rent-a-cops with a big gut.

I'd probably find myself in jail or at the very least without a car since the officer would no doubt tow my "abandoned" vehicle as soon as he got the chance. Already my expenses were adding up. I didn't need to add towing and bail to the growing tab. Besides, without a car, even if I could catch up with Sharon on foot, what could I do with her? Throw her over my back and carry her home like Tarzan?

So I made a quick U-turn despite the officer's whistles and tried to follow Sharon, who was surprisingly swift given that she was wearing skintight jeans tucked into her high-heeled boots. I guess resolution breeds expediency.

I floored the gas pedal and pulled up to her.

"Sharon, stop. I'm sorry."

Her brisk walk turned into a jog. I let her win a bit and pulled back, watching her go at it until her gait slowed. When I thought she had enough, I pulled back next to her.

"I'm not talking to you," she said, as we rounded the back of the House of Blues.

"That explains the sound coming out of your mouth."

"Fuck you, Daniel."

"Get in the car," I said. The back of the building looked more like a House of Crack than a House of Blues. A few feet from Sharon was a group of men huddled around a trashcan fire. "You can be mad at me, but you need to get in the car."

"No," Sharon said. "I'm walking to the Greyhound station and taking a bus home."

"Greyhound's not the metro bus," I said. "You'll find yourself in Los Angeles or New York or somewhere in Oklahoma."

"I don't care. I'll figure it out. Bum a ride or call a cab or something."

"Do you have any money?" I lurched in my seat so I could pull my wallet out from my back pocket, unfortunately attracting the notice of the men huddled around the trashcan.

"What do you care?"

"Here," I waved a wad of cash at her. "Take it."

"I don't want your money."

"I'll take your money, boss," one of the guys from the trashcan said, leering at Sharon. "And I'll show your lady a good time. You like younger men, Mommy?"

"Sharon, get in the car."

"No."

The men continued to laugh at their own jokes.

"Come over here, cowgirl," another goaded. "Nice boots. You lookin' for a stallion to ride?"

I pulled over to the curb and got out the car, leaving my engine running.

I sprinted to Sharon's side, not sure what I'd do, but when I got to her, I grabbed her elbow and yanked her toward the car.

"You're coming with me," I said.

"You can't make me."

"Hey, hey," one of the guys said. "Leave her alone."

Great, now stallion over here thinks he can defend my woman's honor.

"You're coming with me," I repeated, tightening my grip on her arm. "Now."

But she struggled, wiggling out of my grasp. She lunged toward me, shoving me toward my Porsche. I stumbled. While I was regaining my balance, Sharon must have pulled her gun out of her purse or shimmed it off her belt buckle or pulled it out of her boot like a prostitute in the Wild West. No matter where she got the gun from, there she stood, pointing a bright pink lady gun squarely at me.

Why Annie Oakley thought I needed to be threatened and not the men huddled around the trashcan was beyond me. They looked surprised. That's when you know you're loco, when your actions shock the homeless.

"Really? You're going to shoot me for missing a dumb concert?"

"Laurie Packard isn't dumb."

"Why not just shoot me in the back?" I said, turning around. "That's more your style."

I began to walk to my car. "If you're going to do it, do it now," I said, as I opened my car door. "I'm a perfect target."

She stood, gun drawn. Silent.

"Last chance," I said, as I sat down in the driver's seat. "You can shoot me directly between the eyes if that's more satisfying. I'll keep my head still. Do it."

She froze.

"Fine," I said. "Good luck with your new pals."

And I pulled away, leaving Sharon in the back of the House of Blues, a good half mile from the Greyhound station.

Then worry. Sure, Sharon had a gun, and she took kickboxing at the Y, but she was a woman, alone, and out of her element.

I gave her a call. Straight to voicemail. What if those men hurt her? Maybe they overpowered her and took her gun.

I had to go back for her. I couldn't just leave her there. Not Sharon.

I made an illegal U-turn, causing an old lady in a worn-down Buick to almost rear-end me. She honked her horn, but it didn't matter. I needed to save Sharon. Maybe when I swooped in to rescue her, Sharon would see the passion in my eyes, and she'd reward me with a third second chance—or at least not a stray bullet in my brain.

But when I pulled back up to the House of Blues, Sharon and the men were gone, the fire still burning in the trashcan, a woman's purse—I assumed it was Sharon's—on the ground, empty.

CHAPTER TWENTY-ONE

I picked up the purse and went back to my car. From there, I circled the building looking for Sharon. Or the men. Anyone. Anything. All I saw was a smoldering fire in the abandoned trashcan.

I pulled back up to the front of the building, hoping to run into the skinny police officer. He was on his cellphone, waving the few cars that passed by with his free hand. I parked and approached him on foot.

"Sir," I said, "there's been an abduction."

He craned his neck and looked at me.

"Hold on, honey," he said in his phone. "There's another crackpot here talking about aliens."

"Not aliens," I said. "An actual abduction by actual humans." I didn't want to confuse him by mentioning the fact that the abduction could have taken place by illegal aliens.

"I'll call you back," the officer said into his phone. Clicking it off, he put it in his pocket, all the while eyeing my hands.

"What makes you think someone's been abducted?"

I held up the purse. "I think this is my girlfriend's—well, not my girlfriend; I don't know what she is really—but I think this is her purse."

"You *think* it's someone's purse?"

"Well, it *is* someone's," I said. "I mean, it most likely belonged to someone at some point in time. But I think it's hers."

"You *think*."

"Listen," I said, feeling myself getting agitated, "she had a gun, one of those lady guns."

"A Ladysmith?"

"Yes."

"So this woman, your maybe girlfriend, was held up by a woman with a Ladysmith?"

"No, my girlfriend—well, she's not my girlfriend; she's married to someone else—well, she's the one with the gun."

"The woman your girlfriend's married to?"

"No, my girlfriend's not married to a woman. And she's not my girlfriend because she's married to a man, not because she's gay. And I have another girlfriend, so I guess this woman isn't my girlfriend."

"No judgment," he said, even though his grimace told me he was judging me for something, maybe not my morality but my sanity.

"So this woman of yours had a gun and you think she's been taken?"

"Well, I left her with a bunch of men at the back of the building. They were huddled around a trashcan."

"Okay, let me get this straight. You left her with a bunch of homeless men. Just left her?"

"Well, she was threatening to shoot me."

"Let me get your name," he said. "For the report."

"Conrad. Daniel Conrad. But there's no time for a report—"

"First things first. Are you on any medication, Conrad Daniel Conrad?"

"Not relevant," I said. "And my name's not Conrad Daniel Conrad."

"Okay, okay, no need to get agitated Mister Conrad. It *is* Mister Conrad, correct? I have to ask before we proceed. Have you taken anything? Maybe even something legal with one of those do not operate heavy machinery warning labels?"

"I'm quite sober. Listen—"

His eyes narrowed. "Don't get defensive."

I wasn't.

He continued, "Just slow down and tell me what happened."

"My girlfriend was mad, she walked away, I grabbed her, she drew a gun at me, I left, and now she's gone."

"You grabbed her? You mean, physically assaulted her?"

"I didn't do anything to her."

"But you grabbed her, you say."

"Time's running out," I said. "We need to move."

I must have grabbed his arm.

"Whoa, whoa, whoa," he said, pushing me off him. "You're not going anywhere. Give me that purse."

"No," I said, perhaps more forcefully than I would have liked. "It's mine."

"Oh, it's yours now."

"I told you. It's my wife's purse."

"Your wife?"

"Not my wife, my girlfriend—no—my woman's purse."

"Give it here," he said again.

I pulled the purse to my chest and crossed my arms over it. He tried to yank it away from me. I might have jerked the purse—and him—back into me. He might have wrenched it from my hands. I might have shoved him. Like I told the other officers, it's fuzzy. It wasn't my fault he was a slight guy. I didn't more than vaguely look at him and he was on the ground and then he was up and on me.

Before I knew it, I was face down on the pavement, my hands cuffed behind my back.

"You have the right to remain silent," he said.

And that's how I found myself in the back of a squad car, heading to jail for a crime I didn't do, but feeling oddly like I belonged there given the way I'd lived my life up to that moment.

CHAPTER TWENTY-TWO

The whole way to the substation, I tried to explain to the officer what had happened and that, no, I didn't assault him—or Sharon, for that matter—even though, yes, it's true, he did end up on the ground. The officer didn't listen even when I told him that I wasn't the type to go around punching people and to check my records: no arrests, thank you very much. Check my records and see that I have been nothing but good. Even I paused as I said that because, let's be honest, I've done what everyone else has done: I've lied, I've cheated, I've—well, anyway, he didn't seem to believe me.

When we got to the substation a tubby cop, who now was in charge of me, said, "We'll figure all this out," after I protested a little too much. "This is a process," he said, not really comforting me because the tone in his voice said, "Yeah, yeah, you're innocent and I'm the Queen of Sheba." At booking, the tubby cop took my fingerprints, my cellphone, my keys, my belt, my shoelaces, my cash—seven hundred twenty-three dollars and sixty-seven cents in total—all of which I was told I'd get back once I made bail or served my time. "Whichever is longer," the tubby cop deadpanned. A joke, I think, but not a funny one. I looked at the tag on his uniform and made note of his name—Officer Gatz—something I should have done earlier with the short cop who was accusing me of something I most certainly hadn't done.

At this point the officer next to Gatz was laughing at his joke, telling him, "That never gets old." Officer Williams was his name. Officer Williams walked around the barricade and approached me. "Come with me," he said. Williams led me to a long cell, had me strip, and assigned me a paper-thin jumpsuit and a pair of communal sandals that were too big in the toes and too small in the heel if that's possible. "This isn't the bowling alley," Williams said when I asked if there was a smaller size, which made me think that if one was going to pick a place to illustrate the height of footwear comfort, a bowling alley isn't the first place that should come to mind.

Officer Williams was chuckling to himself, so I tried to laugh, but before I could cough out a ha-ha, I felt someone jerk on the crook of my arm: a petite female officer. Well, hello to you, too, but, no, she wasn't hitting on me, obviously. "We're heading to the Tank," she said, wrenching me down a long hallway.

I tried to talk to her. Stephens was the name on her tag. I told

Stephens I was innocent, that I was looking for my friend Sharon, who might have been mugged or killed or worse. I told her I needed to get out of there, needed to find Sharon, needed to save her from those homeless guys. She listened, I think, but by the time I reached the part of my story where I explained that I was an upstanding member of society—a college professor for Christ's sake—all she said was, "Here we are," as she gestured to the bars in front of an elongated cell. "Home sweet home."

I peered inside. Everything in the Tank was concrete or metal. Long metal benches and a telephone welded to the wall. A metal toilet, exposed, but fused to the wall and the floor. No moving that sucker, which meant that someone somewhere had ripped the phone or the toilet out of the wall and used it as a weapon. Not a bad idea.

I looked around, hoping no one else had an unfair advantage. Not sure what I was looking for—a filed down toothbrush, a smuggled in razorblade, a scimitar? Eight men peered back at me like I was some kind of degenerate, looking at their hands and laps, scanning the room to see if any of them had who knows what, a shiv? Not that I could tell if there was a shiv in one of their jumpsuits or wedged in their state-issued sandals. So I glared back at them steely eyed.

"Almost full and the evening's young." Stephens smiled a toothy grin that should have made me feel at ease, except I had seen enough prison movies to be fairly certain that the guys in the cell were looking at me, sizing me up to see if I was bitch material, especially now that the female officer was acting chummy all of a sudden.

Of course, this was jail, not prison. Probably not too many bitches at the substation. Still, I tried not to smile back. No point looking like a narc or some kind of police sympathizer. I was a cop killer, after all. Okay, not a cop killer, but I did assault a police officer—not that I did, but that was what I was being charged with. Doing something—anything—to a cop should get me somewhere with the guys. Yeah, man, those pigs, man. Someone's got to stand up to them. Fuck the police. Yeah, fuck them.

As Stephens called to open the gate and the bars clanked and slid to let me in, a big tattooed guy lumbered over to the metal toilet and began to relieve himself. The other men didn't laugh. They didn't wince. They just averted their eyes.

Truly remarkable. No one was that polite at Evergreen. Not that we took craps in front of each other. Still, a little more civility couldn't hurt the place. Maybe confinement helps with some of that. Maybe it triggers courtesy. It's possible.

But even if I was locked up with the Psychology Department, we wouldn't get along well enough to take craps in front of each other. We might kill each other, sure. But be polite?

"Ladies," Stephens called out, "a new recruit."

The men, who were already eyeing me, continued to glare.

"Move along," she said.

I must not have moved fast enough because Stephens grabbed me by the collar like I was a feral cat and shoved me into the Tank. I stumbled as the door bolted behind me. Thanks a lot, lady. Was she trying to make me into the Rodney King of Green County? Not that I was beaten to a bloody pulp, but shoving like she did, that's unnecessary force right there. Excessive unnecessary force, some lawyers might say.

Which reminded me: I needed to call my lawyer, not that I had one. But first Sharon.

I walked across the sloping floor, across the drain at the center of the room, to the phone. Sure, it looked desperate, immediately rushing to the phone, but Sharon could be in trouble. I had to do something.

I reached over a hulking guy and tapped Sharon's cellphone number into the phone.

No luck. Voicemail plus "This is a collect call from Green County Jail. To accept charges, please hit pound in 5-4-3—" I hung up and tried her home number. Yes, I knew the number by heart. Okay, I admit it, there were times after we broke up when I called Sharon's home number. Those times when it's after midnight and your drunkenness outweighs your self-respect and you start to think how tragic it is that you no longer remember someone's voice. So you find yourself dialing the number you told yourself you forgot, hoping to a hear a soft, sultry "Hello" that probably never existed in the first place. Unfortunately, Brian answered more often than not.

But this time, no Brian, either. Straight to a canned answering machine, one of those that involved everyone in the family introducing themselves like chuckleheads. "This is Brian," he boomed, "And Sharon," she chimed in, "And Cam, Sarah, and Sasha" the kids said. And back to Brian. "We're not in right now. Leave us a message and we'll get right back with you as soon as we can" all the while my canned "This is a collect call from Green County Jail" message played.

Oh, the suburban dream. I hung up. Then called Sharon's cell again. Voicemail and the collect call warning, but Sharon's voicemail message was short enough and the "This is a collect call from Green County Jail" message wasn't over yet.

"Listen," I shouted over the collect call warning counting down. "I'm in prison—well, jail, because of you. You've got to come here and spring me. I'm in County Jail, Substation Seven."

3-2-1. Over.

Not sure if Sharon could even hear me.

I called back and waited for the right moment where her leave a message overlapped with "from Green County Jail," and then I started shouting again.

"I'm sorry about the concert. I'm worried about you. Tell me you're okay. Please—"

3-2-1.

I called her house again.

This time a female voice answered.

"It's me," I said. "Accept the charges."

She did.

"Thank God," I said. "Are you all right?"

"Daddy?"

Oh, no. One of Sharon's daughters?

"Hi," I said. "Hello. This is a routine call. A call from a concerned citizen. It's quite possible that your mother—do you know where your mother is?"

Then I paused. All I could hear was breathing on the other end.

"Don't hang up," I said, not sure what to say next. I didn't want to scare the girl if Sharon was fine, but I didn't want her daughter to think it was a prank call. Sharon might need help. Her daughter could—

I cleared my throat. "Just a routine call," I said, "from the county jail. There have been a series of kidnappings and murders in the area, so if your mother doesn't come home soon, please follow up with the proper authorities."

I hung up and the worry set in. Why would there be a routine collect call from the jail warning little girls about their mothers' possible murders? Sharon lived in one of the safest suburban neighborhoods in the country. A prank call, obviously. But maybe one of the other kids would put two and two together. There was an older boy in high school. Maybe he'd come home, ask his sister where his mom was, she'd say, "I don't know, but I got this weird call from the jail," and the boy would dial 911. But it would be too late. Sharon was gone, and no one seemed to notice or care.

I tried Sharon's cell again. Straight to voicemail.

And then it hit me. Jasmine. Jasmine could help. But for the life of me, I couldn't remember Jasmine's phone number. Beyond the Greenwood area code, nothing else came to me.

It's not my fault that I couldn't remember Jasmine's number. She always called me and I replied, hit the little call back button if I really wanted to talk to her before she called me again and I eventually answered. The calling and not answering was a dance Jasmine and I did. The only one we did, really. She'd call, I'd ignore, she'd call again, leave some message indicating some disaster, which would turn out to be something fully functional adults dealt with on their own every single day.

I tried to visualize Jasmine's number. Nothing. I closed my eyes and tapped numbers into the keypad. The phone rang. "Big Billy's BBQ," a woman's voice slurred on the other end and "This is a collect call from Green County Jail" triggered. Big Billy's BBQ hung up.

So much for calling Jasmine. Then I remembered Frank. I didn't know Frank's number, either, but all our phone numbers at Evergreen depended on our office location and Frank was just down the hall. His number had to be one or two digits different from mine. Frank was five, maybe six, doors down. I could find Frank, Frank could give me Jasmine's number, and Jasmine could help. Yes, it was late, but didn't he have a Thursday night class?

I began to dial Evergreen numbers, five or six digits higher or lower than mine. More random than a rational mind would have, probably, but I was in lockup and running low on time if Sharon was in trouble. So I kept hitting numbers until, after a few tries, I lucked into Frank's annoying yet familiar voice. He accepted the call with a laugh. "You got me, buddy. Good one. What can I do for you?"

"I need Jasmine's number."

"Why?"

"To call her."

"Don't you have her number, being her boyfriend or her paused person or whatever you two are these days?"

I wanted to punch him—and Jasmine, too, for blabbing to Frank about our on hold situation. But Frank was someone who could do something for me, so I played nice.

"Of course, I have the number," I said.

"Why are you calling me then?"

"I am away from my phone at the moment and I don't know her number."

"You don't know her number? Really? Come on, buddy."

"Just give it to me."

"Conrad, what's this call really about?"

"I'm in jail," I said. "Through no fault of my own."

"Naturally," Frank said.

"And they've taken my phone and I thought maybe Jasmine could help me, but first I need you to help me so she can help me, if that makes sense."

"Is this some kind of joke?"

"No, no joke. There's this woman, Sharon, I think she could be kidnapped or murdered or worse by a gang of ruffians."

"Ruffians?"

"Homeless guys, hoodlums," I said. "But that's beside the point. She's gone missing and I need someone to find her. Please. You've got to help. Call these numbers, go to her house, find her."

The idea of putting Frank in contact with Sharon made me want to vomit. I couldn't stand the image of another woman of mine tee-heeing with Frank. Still, I gave him Sharon's cellphone and home numbers and her address. Made sure he wrote them down, made him repeat everything back to me. Twice.

"Be discreet," I told him. "If you reach her husband, don't tell him who I am or anything about me."

"This keeps getting better and better," Frank said.

"And she's got kids—an older boy who might be able to help."

"Conrad," Frank said, "this is insane."

I shook my head even though I knew Frank couldn't see me.

"Give me Jasmine's number," I said. "She'll do it."

"You know I can't do that," Frank said.

I wanted to curse and scream at him, but he was my only hope.

Frank continued, "I'll call those numbers for you. I'll even figure out what's going on with—what's her name—Sharon. Whatever you need. And I'll call my friend who's a lawyer. Just relax."

"You're going to find Sharon?"

"I'll do everything I can."

"So you've got it handled?"

"Conrad," Frank said, "stop underestimating everyone around you. I've got this. Just promise me you won't call Jasmine."

"I don't see why—"

"Promise me."

I promised. Not that anything I said should mean much—wasn't I in jail?—but Frank was satisfied.

Before he hung up, he assured me that he had managed much worse.

"If you think I can't find some suburban housewife who's no doubt mad at you because you're Daniel Conrad—the challenge would be finding one woman who isn't mad at you. That's the challenge."

CHAPTER TWENTY-THREE

Off the phone, I slogged over to the only open spot on the metal bench, which unfortunately happened to be right across from the toilet, but luckily, near the phone, if I reached over the hulking man next to me. Probably not the best idea, reaching over men you don't know in prison. Not that I was in prison. County jail. But still. Same idea.

"That's Big Al's spot," the hulking guy next to me said.

"Who's Big Al?"

The guy on the toilet grunted. Big Al.

I looked down the bench. The men stretched out as wide as they could, knees spread apart, elbows out. No space.

I looked at the floor. Fairly clean. Cleaner than my bathroom at home anyway, which needed a woman's touch, but not just any woman's touch, preferably one with the muscle and dexterity of an Olympic gymnast to clean all the mildew and mold out of the crevices in the aging tile. At the jail, there were regulations. They had to power wash or slosh dirty mop water across the concrete more often than not.

But no point coming across as weak and acquiescing to the first guy who looked like he could take me down. This was prison—well, jail—after all.

So I sat down right then and there on Big Al's spot. Next to the phone and next to Hulking Guy who looked shocked that anyone would dare do such a thing.

"Really?" Big Al said from the toilet.

"I'm entitled to this seat. Any seat," I responded, pushing back on the bench and digging my heels in.

"Oh, he's entitled," Big Al said. "What else are you entitled to?"

The thought did occur to me that Big Al could easily get up from the toilet with his jumpsuit around his knees, puff out his chest, and deck me. My second altercation of the evening. Not that I punched that police officer. But this was prison—well, jail. Hostility should have been the norm.

But Big Al just laughed.

"If you want to sit between my irritable bowels and the toilet, be my guest."

"Hey," a high-pitched voice from the other side of the Tank called out. "There's space down here."

I nodded at Big Al, and walked down the other side of the cell where the high-pitched voice beckoned.

A little Latino guy with glitter on his face and long fake blue eyelashes patted the bench next to him. Fabulous. A gay guy coming to my aid. And a little one at that.

"Make love, not war." He winked. "Besides, it smells like butt down there."

A strange comment from a gay guy, but I let it go.

I thought about sitting on the floor again, not that I was homophobic, but my better angels told me to take a seat next to this little guy. Besides, I'd rather take my chances with Little Gay Guy than Big Al any day. Not that I would be taking either of them in a fight, especially not a gay guy. I wasn't some gay-hating, Bible thumping ignoramus. I was a college professor.

So I sat down, even though we were a little too close for comfort, our legs touching. Little Gay Guy shifted to give me more space, inching his thigh on top of mine. Great. Now he was sitting in my lap, although not quite, more on an angle. Angling on top of me, really. Nothing two regular guys wouldn't do if forced to sit on a bench together in close quarters.

"What did you do?" Little Gay Guy asked.

"I'm a college professor," I said. "And a famous author."

Okay, maybe not famous, but it couldn't hurt to let people know you have clout on the outside. Maybe it could even help give me a place in the prison hierarchy. I could be the convict who helps write appeals, letters to the press. I could be popular, if popularity was something one wanted to achieve in prison.

"Not what do you do. What did you do to end up here?" Little Gay Guy tittered.

"A little of this, a little of that," I tried. Better to maintain an air of mystery. "You first."

"It's all unfortunate." Little Gay Guy sighed like Scarlet O'Hara during the burning of Atlanta, his body wriggling on top of mine. "An unfortunate misunderstanding brought on by an initial case of mistaken identity and misjudgment, not on my part, you understand. A miscalculation, really. A difference of opinion, but the wrong impression of who I am and what I was doing."

"Oh, me, too," I said, not sure if I should give up my street cred, but by that point Little Gay Guy was beaming, looking up at me like I was his hero.

"I had a feeling," he said. "They pick you up for prostitution, too?"

If I had been drinking water at the time, I would have spit it all over the floor.

"Do I look like a prostitute?"

"Maybe," Little Gay Guy said. "I don't know what straight women want."

"Me neither," I said. "Not that I'm gay."

Little Gay Guy giggled.

I laughed ,too. This could be good. Me and Little Gay Guy. Sure we were in jail, but for once in a long time, I was spending time with someone who seemed genuinely interested in who I was. You'd think between Jasmine and Sharon and all the other women in my life someone would find me amazing. No, I had to rely on some random gay guy—most likely a soon-to-be convicted prostitute—for that bright eyed "you're wonderful and I enjoy your company" look.

"I'm writing a book," I said. "A practical guide."

"Oh, that's good," he said. "You mind if I use that excuse, too?"

"It's not an excuse. It's the truth. I'm writing a practical guide."

"Oh, me, too," Little Gay Guy chirped. "A practical guide to getting it on. Not prostitution; a guide for men looking to branch out of their comfort zone, within the confines of the law."

"Sounds marketable," I said.

Little Gay Guy sighed. "The world's not ready for it."

I wasn't sure if Little Gay Guy was serious or looking for an excuse to sell his body in some alley, but something about his small frame combined with his dark hair made me think of Zoe.

Zoe.

I could call Zoe. She could help me.

I excused myself from Little Gay Guy, shifted out from under him, and rushed to the phone.

I reached over Hulking Guy so I could dial home.

And stopped myself. Sure, Zoe needed to know sooner than later that her father was an idiot who got himself in jail, but maybe she didn't need to know now when all she could do was worry. Frank was on it. He was an adult who could do something if he set his mind to it—the man did write a dissertation after all, even though I had never read it. To put it bluntly, Frank was no Benny. He had a full-time job, although the fact that I had the same job didn't give me confidence in his competency or mental fitness.

Still, Frank should be able to succeed in getting me a lawyer—he'd mentioned having a friend—finding Sharon—although there was a part of me that hoped he wouldn't—and maybe, just maybe, keeping his mouth shut about me landing myself in jail because of another woman. Frank was a psychologist, a professional, and there was—or there should be—courtesy between professionals when one of them reveals a dollop of excrement that's sloshing around in the stained toilet bowl of life.

Frank was on it. Unless he wasn't.

Maybe I'd made a mistake calling Sharon's house, leaving a message with that daughter of hers who could react or not react but in all the wrong ways. So I did what I could. I tried calling back. No luck. Just that annoying voicemail and "This is a collect call" ready to go.

I called Sharon's cell. Still straight to voicemail. Then the house again. No luck.

Maybe Frank would visit the house or call and leave an indiscreet message that Brian or the kids would hear.

So I did what I could. I called Frank one more time, but he didn't answer.

Then I dialed 911.

CHAPTER TWENTY-FOUR

"Nine-one-one. What's your emergency?"

"I've got a tip," I said. "Sharon Vogel. She's disappeared near the House of Blues downtown. She's been kidnapped or worse."

"What's your name, sir?"

"Doesn't matter," I said. "An interested party. Someone who knows. Listen, Sharon Vogel's been—"

"Hey," female guard Stephens' voice boomed, "stop making prank calls."

Fastest police response time in Green County and of course I happen to be the perp.

I dropped the phone.

"Sit down."

I did. Nearly in Hulking Guy's lap.

"I don't want to see you near that phone."

I wanted to shift blame onto Big Al, but I thought better of it. Not that I was afraid of him. Being in jail hadn't softened me. I just couldn't figure out why Big Al would be the one calling 911 when I was caught with the phone in my hand. Maybe he forced me to call on his behalf? Maybe it had to do with Stephens and police brutality? Little Gay Guy and—? I was out of ideas and Stephens was glaring into the Tank like she could see right between the bars into my twisted soul. She shook her head, disgusted.

"But there's a woman—"

"You have the right to remain silent," she said. "Use it."

That made the guys in the Tank hoot and holler.

"Quiet down." Stephens hit the bars with her nightstick. Then she turned to me. "I don't want to hear a peep from you, Conrad Daniel Conrad."

She glared at me—at us—and walked on.

I sat in the Tank, quiet as can be, for hours.

Well, I tried to strike up a conversation with Hulking Guy and Big Al, who eventually got off the toilet.

That conversation didn't go so well.

I thought, why not? If I'm stuck in jail, waiting for Frank to do whatever it is he could do—which might not be much considering who Frank is: a professor at a mediocre institution who enjoys doing less than me most days—maybe I should work on that damned *Practical*

Guide. Maybe I could take a bad thing, this unjustified incarceration, and turn it into something good: time to work on my sure-to-be future best sell out. Although, really, I wasn't sure what was worse, being held for something I didn't do or writing something I didn't believe in. Maybe all this was the universe telling me to buckle down, unplug, make something of myself.

Of course, I didn't have paper or a pen and Stephens wasn't going to pass me a Bic. Okay, I could write in my head, plan, think. So, I thought. I remembered why I was having trouble writing the damned thing in the first place: I had little to say on the advantages of dating young women. I could think of the disadvantages, sure, which could and should be included in a real practical guide, but the advantages I no doubt needed for the type of book I was supposed to be writing? I didn't have a clue. I needed help from someone who knew.

So I made the mistake of asking Big Al a couple questions for my *Practical Guide*. Despite his irritable bowels, Big Al looked like a man who knew a thing or two about dating women. How did I know why he was behind bars? All I said was, "You look like you work out. Do you have a girlfriend?" He furrowed his brow like I was asking him to wrap his brawny biceps around my waist. No, no, I'm not hitting on you, Big Al. No need to pummel me. I quickly clarified by asking him if he's ever been with a younger woman, which was my mistake.

At the time, I couldn't quite figure out why he reacted the way he did, but Little Gay Guy tells me I committed a *faux pas* by asking an accused child molester if he had a young girlfriend.

Everything went downhill from there.

I wasn't trying to create enemies. I was just trying to work on my book.

Did Martin Luther King, Jr. endure as much in Birmingham Jail?

After that, I left Big Al alone and sat back near Little Gay Guy. To maintain the peace, I told Big Al no hard feelings, I wasn't accusing him of anything he didn't do, and even if he did it, I wasn't one to judge, which only made him look at me like there was something wrong with me, something he wanted to fix with his fists.

Down near Little Gay Guy, I tried to sit silently, even drifting off for snippets of time between Little Gay Guy's discussions of life, liberty, and the case against gay marriage, which was interesting coming from Little Gay Guy, who told me that it "only makes good gays who are married and bad gays who aren't, which only divides the community and makes us act like straight people who are fucked up."

I told him he had a point that straight people were fucked up and straight women in particular were the worst of them all.

He nodded sympathetically, but he disagreed. "Women, men, all of us just want to be loved."

"Sure, sure," I said, but I also added that women were particularly insane, and insane people sometimes don't want to be loved. Even when you try your hardest to do what they want and take them to concerts, they'll still wave a gun in your face and run away.

"Honey, that's not just women. That's men, too. I'm sure there's someone somewhere who thinks you're insane for the same reason."

I drifted off to sleep somewhere in the middle of our conversation.

Ten minutes here, five minutes there, who knows. But before I knew it, I was spending the night in jail with Little Gay Guy breathing deeply into my shoulder—and still no Frank.

Sunrise came and went and then a loud bang across the bars. Stephens.

"Conrad Daniel Conrad," she said, "come with me."

"Good luck." Little Gay Guy winked.

I walked to the gate and Stephens called to open it.

"You're one lucky bastard." She grabbed me by the shoulder and pushed me a little harder than necessary down the hall.

I must have chuckled or asked why she thought so. Hell, I might have asked if I was a lucky bastard because I was going to get lucky. Bad joke, I know, but I was running low on sleep and I hadn't eaten since the day before, which reminded me that there should be meals behind bars and maybe the lack of food and water was a further sign of just how out of hand the Green County police were.

Officer Stephens sighed. "You know what you did," she said. "Those charges shouldn't be dropped."

My charges were going to be dropped? I wanted to grab Stephens and kiss her like that sailor in that old photograph. Wrap my arms around her waist and pull her to me like she was a nurse and we were in Times Square and the war was over. Then it occurred to me that this could be some sort of a trick, a good cop, bad cop routine. I played it cool. I said, "They should be dropped. I didn't do anything." Which was the truth.

"I've seen people like you before," she said. "You might get away with it once, maybe even twice, but eventually it will catch up to you."

I wanted to ask her if that was a threat, but we were already at another gate. Stephens passed me over to someone else, a splotchy-skinned female officer who shuffled papers and groaned more than necessary.

Through the bars, I could see the outside world: a waiting room full of unfortunate souls, including some poor schmuck in a suit and tie who looked like Frank. No, it *was* Frank, except he was talking with a woman in a bright red dress, definitely not his wife. Jasmine? I squinted. No. It couldn't be.

Zoe.

My heart raced. Fuck Frank. Fuck him for bringing Zoe to this place.

If the splotchy-skinned female officer hadn't been groaning and shuffling those papers within Tasing distance, I would have reached through the bars and punched Frank right then and there. Would have been worth another stint in the Tank with Big Al and Little Gay Guy. No problem.

Of course, Frank and Zoe spotted me, and before I could wave Zoe away, they were up and on their feet.

I told myself that there'd be time to punch the asshole later. Maybe once I was out of the substation, down the road, I could sock Frank right smack dab in that fat face of his. I could wait. Just as long as he didn't say—

"Hey, buddy."

"Other side of the line," the female officer boomed.

Frank jumped, stumbling over Zoe, as he bent forward a little too much to see the yellow line that would have been obvious to a Kindergartener. Good boy Frank then overcompensated by careening back a good five feet or so. Entertaining to see Frank doing what he was told. I wanted the female officer to shout at him some more, maybe threaten to throw him in the slammer, but she just eyeballed him, saw he wasn't a threat, shook her head, and groaned.

I tried to exchange glances with her so she'd know that I, too, was familiar with Frank's stupidity, that I commiserated with her having to deal with Frank at all, but she didn't meet my gaze, which was fine. It would have been nice if she and I could have communicated, if she could have understood that there was someone who appreciated her and that someone was me. There she was, a woman doing her job, enforcing the law and the rules for the good of our nation. But all she did was grunt as she stamped and signed another paper.

Frank and Zoe, appropriately behind the yellow line, stared at me like they were the only mourners at my funeral.

Frank leaned into Zoe and whispered something. She smiled, but quickly returned to what had to be a practiced scowl given how much her eyes danced.

The female officer proceeded to muss papers about, stamping a few at random before she handed me a cardboard box with my clothes and shoes, a plastic bag with my wallet and phone inside, and a sheet to sign that said I got everything back and that the Green County Police didn't steal anything. I signed the form, wanting to get out of there even though I didn't trust them one bit and I thought about making a stink. Luckily for them, nothing was missing.

Besides, Zoe was watching me, and I thought it best not to embarrass her.

Something was off with that dress she was wearing. It drooped off her shoulders and made her look deflated, like she had shrunk in the wash. Strange that right in front of me on the other side of the bars was this human being, this person who was my genetic material walking and talking and wearing a dress too big for her small shoulders and slim hips.

I signed a discharge form. The overweight female officer called to another guard who walked me to a changing room, and, before I knew it, I was a free man, sprung on the other side, looking Frank and Zoe in the eye.

"Why did you bring her here?" I asked Frank before he could "Hey, buddy" me again.

"She insisted. She showed up at the office late last night looking for you, saying that you didn't come home and that I better tell her where you were or she'd—"

"Or she'd what?"

Zoe shrugged. "I didn't give him much of a choice."

"She was quite useful." Frank dug his own grave. Useful. That's what he said. "She knew where the prison was and how to get here."

"Jail," Zoe said. "Not prison."

I turned to Frank. "What's wrong with you? Taking an innocent girl on a tour of the seedy parts of town. You could have used GPS."

"It's no big deal," Zoe said. "I've been here before."

I should have stopped and asked her why she had been to the Green County substation, or why she knew the difference between jail and prison, for that matter, but Frank put his hands on my shoulders and ushered me out the door like he was a police officer. Jerk.

In the safety of Frank's beat-up Civic, Frank and Zoe traded barbs about giving cover, which annoyed me to no end, because if anyone should be talking like an outlaw, it should be me, the guy who spent the night in jail, not the two boobs who barely showed up the next morning.

I was about to interrupt them, tell them we needed to move like real outlaws, not self-congratulating morons, when Frank started the car.

Turning around, he asked Zoe, who was wrestling with one of Frank's seatbelts in the backseat, "You okay back there, Pardner?"

"Fine and dandy," she said before they launched into a jubilee of self-compliments fit for a Fascist regime.

Frank pulled out of the parking lot and onto the street.

The two "pardners" in crime continued to tip their hats to one another for a job well done until I pointed out that neither of them had spent the night behind bars despite their mutual over the top praise for "pulling off the job" and "picking up the package," which as far as I could tell was me.

"I'm pretty sure we might have committed a felony getting you out of your felony," Zoe said to my comment that they hadn't really done much of anything.

"And the Fashion Police are after that one," Frank gestured back at Zoe, sending her into hysterics.

"The Fashion Police," Zoe squealed, pulling at the shoulder of her dress, stretching the already too baggy fabric out a good foot from her shoulder. "The real police should have intervened. This dress is horrible."

"Stop stretching my dress!" Frank turned around, right as he merged onto the highway.

"Your dress." Zoe laughed harder. "You told me it was your wife's!"

"Same difference," Frank said, still not paying attention to the road. The man really was an idiot.

"Explains the broad shoulders," Zoe said. "Being a guy's dress and all."

"My wife is a gorgeous, if broad shouldered, woman."

Zoe hooted, which in turn set Frank off on a deep convulsive belly laugh that made me wonder if he was fit to drive given that we were on the highway by then and the man was spending a little too much time looking in the rearview mirror at his "pardner" in crime, who was beaming at him like he was Father of the Year or something.

Why Frank had to yuk it up with every woman who came along was beyond me.

Who knew why Zoe was wearing Frank's wife's dress. He could be wearing it himself for all I cared. I just needed them to stop whatever it was that they were doing, laughing, making fun of a very real situation with jokes about dresses and the Fashion Police.

Frank almost merged into a semi. I shouted and reached for the wheel until we were back in our lane.

"Thanks, buddy. That was scary," Frank said, as if he wasn't the one driving.

I wanted to curse him out for nearly killing us. Instead, I just said, "Pay attention."

Frank kept his eyes on the road and his hands at the ten and two of the wheel after that. Good. Of course, he couldn't keep quiet.

"Was it cold in there?" Frank asked out of nowhere.

"Where?"

"The jail. I read a study about how the correctional system is preventing fights by reducing the temperature by ten degrees. Really works, apparently."

What was he talking about?

"Focus," I said. "Or if you're going to talk, tell me what you two did to get me out."

"Us?" Frank teased. "We didn't do anything."

"We're innocent! We've been framed!" Zoe chortled.

"It's time to be serious," I said. "Tell me."

"Don't get mad," Frank said.

I refused to make any promises.

"Fine, but listen," Frank said. "When you called last night, there weren't any lawyers I could get on such short notice, so I asked around, but no one I knew was a criminal defense attorney, except, well, I know someone who is married to one. You know her, too, in fact—not that you're going to like it, but remember there was that woman of yours to deal with and to try to find—"

"Sharon," Zoe said.

"Sharon." Frank nodded a thank you to Zoe. "And then there was this little daughter of yours, looking at me, wanting me to tell her where you were—"

"Hey," Zoe said. "Don't blame this on me!"

Frank nodded. "So I had a lot going on, and so this sounds much worse than it is—"

"Don't sugarcoat it, kid," Zoe said in a strange voice that made me think she was quoting from a movie. "Tell her straight."

"What?" I asked.

"It's *Butch Cassidy and the Sundance Kid,*" Zoe said like I was developmentally delayed.

"Hey, is that what you call giving cover?" Frank attempted his best Robert Redford with a wink back at Zoe in the rearview mirror. The guy had the attention span of Benny.

"Stop," I said.

"Fine. Your dean," Zoe said. "Her husband's somebody and she got you out of this mess."

"Dean Dyer?"

"Yes," Frank said. "Her husband's a lawyer. He called in some favors. He knows a judge, went to school with him, fraternity brothers or something."

"Wait, you told Dean Dyer?"

"No choice," he said. Short and sweet like if he got it out quick enough it just would be a fact. The bastard.

"No," I said. "There's always a choice when it comes to telling employers about felonies."

"To be fair, I didn't say you did it, just that you were accused of doing it." Frank winked.

I wanted to clobber Frank, reach right over the stick shift and punch him even though he was driving us down the highway at seventy miles an hour and accelerating. If Zoe wasn't in the car, I would have done it, too, but Frank had brought her along and told Dean Dyer, betrayed me twice so that I was stuck there like an idiot in the passenger's seat unable to do anything apart from fantasize about kicking his ass when we got to campus.

Zoe intervened. "Listen," she said, "Frank tried his best. Your dean tried her best. Maybe it's time for you to say thank you and realize that there are people in your life trying to help you."

"Thanks for getting me fired," I said to Frank.

Zoe whacked me across the back of my head. Either I was weak after a night in jail or she'd really put her whole body into that smack.

I looked back at Zoe, who clearly wanted to hit me again, so to avoid what would no doubt be another blow to the head, I thanked Frank for trying his best. I asked him if he located Sharon. Frank hedged. Nope. So I thanked him for trying his best even though his best obviously wasn't good enough given that Sharon was still MIA, and I was on my way to being fired thanks to him. He edited the venom out of my comments and kept the appreciation.

"It wasn't easy." He nodded, glad to hear that I was thanking him. "It took a lot of guts to tell Dean Dyer and ask her for help."

"I'm sure," I said. "It's always hard to tell your boss when someone else commits a crime."

"When someone else is *accused* of a crime." Zoe thumped me across the back of the head with what felt like a shoe, but by the time I turned around, she was back to sitting in her seat with her hands in her lap and her shoes on her feet.

"Stop hitting your father," Frank said.

"Nothing else works with him."

"My car, my rules. You can beat him to a pulp when you're home."

"I'm right here," I said. "And I would like to know why you—" I chose my words carefully, keeping an eye out for Zoe's backseat attacks. "—how you got Dean Dyer involved in this mess."

"It really was no trouble. Dean Dyer was very nice about it," Frank went on. "She told me she'd handle it. She's basically a good person, despite her irrationality."

I thanked him for involving a known nutcase in one of the most important moments in my life.

"No biggie. That's what friends are for," Frank said.

I reminded myself to breathe, count to ten, remember that he—

"And did you even try to find Sharon?" I blurted.

"We both went over to her house," Zoe said. "Her nice house that she shares with her *family,* her *husband,* her *kids.*"

"While I'm thanking everyone, I'd like to thank my daughter for the guilt trip," I said before I dug in the government-issued plastic bag and pulled out my cellphone. Dead. Great. The officers could have turned it off and saved me the trouble of losing my battery life in addition to a night of my actual life.

Zoe was going on about Sharon's house, the beauty of married life, the commitment, the love that a man and a woman share and how it shouldn't be cast asunder.

"Give me your phone," I said to Frank, ignoring Zoe and her moral high ground.

Frank fished his cellphone out of his pocket and handed it to me. I dialed Sharon. Straight to voicemail.

"We should talk," Frank said. "About this Sharon woman and Jasmine."

"Yeah," Zoe said. "We should talk."

"Talk," I said, feeling confident enough that I could continue to dial Sharon's number from Frank's phone and listen to them with one ear. We were almost at Evergreen so maybe we could get this conversation done with and I could say "Thank you, gotta run, this has been fun" before rushing to class or a "meeting."

Voicemail again. I redialed.

"Jasmine's a good kid," Frank said. "You should leave her alone."

"I'm trying," I said.

"Try harder," Zoe said. Another whack.

"Sorry," Zoe said to Frank.

"It's okay," Frank said. "He deserved that one."

Voicemail. I hung up and redialed.

"I don't know why Jasmine and I are any of your business," I said to both of them, but mostly to Frank since I knew Zoe wanted to hit me no matter what I said. "Jasmine's a big girl. She knows who we are to each other."

"She loves you," Frank said. "And she might be a big girl, but she's not as adult as you think."

Zoe nodded. "Isn't that why you're with her? Because she's a puppy not a dog?"

I ignored Zoe. Might as well talk to the adult in the car.

"You trying to move in on Jasmine?" I asked Frank. I hoped to catch Zoe's eye. Frank was married after all.

"She's my friend," Frank said. "I know that's hard for you to believe, but I'm teaching at this level because I enjoy mentoring young people. Young people like Jasmine."

Sure, sure. Mentoring. I wanted to ask him if he planned on

mentoring her mouth right down on his dick, but Zoe was in the car. No point having her hear how men talk about women.

"You know Jasmine's using me. She's writing a book about me," I said.

"She's not writing a book," Frank said. "She loves you."

"Who knows why," said the pipsqueak in the backseat. "From what I can tell, you're horrible to her. You put her on hold and got yourself locked up for punching a police officer when you were out with your other girlfriend."

"Allegedly," I said.

"Not allegedly," Zoe said. "You were out with your other girlfriend. Your *married* girlfriend, who has a *family*."

I ignored the backseat moralizer.

We were almost at Evergreen. Just a few more moments and I'd be free.

I dialed Sharon again.

"Do you love her?" Frank asked.

"Who?"

"If you have to ask, let Jasmine go," Zoe said.

Frank nodded. "The little one's right."

I turned back to Zoe, hoping she would tell me something different, maybe crack a joke or two. She shook her head. With Frank, she had been all smiles, but I revolted her. She looked at me like she had stuffed her face on cotton candy and funnel cakes, gone on too many roller coasters, and then someone had asked her if she could do them a favor and down a half dozen hotdogs. No, I'm done, her eyes said. Done.

And in that moment, I knew if some cosmic prankster had said to Zoe, "I'll give you a choice: which one of these two men in this car do you want to be genetically linked to?" she would have picked Frank to be her father. No questions asked. Hands down Frank was the better guy. At least from Zoe's perspective. Not that Frank was actually the better guy. The bastard just had a way of making women feel comfortable. Still, I felt bad. It was hard enough to hear from Frank that I somehow ruined Jasmine's life by existing, but to see Zoe's face killed me.

I hung up on Sharon's voicemail and handed the phone back to Frank.

"I'll change my life," I said as we pulled into Evergreen's gates. "I'll stop being a loser. I promise."

I almost believed it myself. Or I wanted to anyway. But life had taught me—and everyone else who knew me—one thing: Daniel Conrad is a liar. The good part is that sometimes even liars tell the truth. Or they stumble face first into it.

CHAPTER TWENTY-FIVE

When we got to campus, Frank pulled up to the curb and motioned for me to get out.

"I better get her home," Frank gestured to Zoe, who had dozed off in the backseat. "She stayed up all night worrying about you."

Just when I thought I couldn't feel worse, a new depth to my self-reproach. Not only did my daughter hate me, but she put me first in her life, something I probably should have done for her, not the other way around.

I nodded to Frank.

"She's a good kid," Frank said. "She's been through a lot in that little life of hers. She could easily become you, a Conrad."

"Could be worse."

"Bitter, put upon, tired, alone; all classic Conrad. Even you can't deny it."

"What about smart and resourceful and—"

"No need to get defensive, buddy," he said.

Don't buddy me, Frank.

"Zoe's been through a lot. I worry about her. If she's under the wrong influences, she might lose some of that joyful spark makes her Zoe."

"Sure, sure," I said. "I know all about that."

Even though I didn't. No point letting Frank think he could psychoanalyze my daughter better than I could.

"Well, that's a relief," Frank said. "Because she's a good kid who needs to keep believing in—"

One of the many ever-present Evergreen campus police officers rapped on my window interrupting Frank's expert analysis. The campus has no crime, but its police presence rivals an Israeli airport. Our tax dollars at work.

"Move along." The officer waved. "No loitering."

"We're faculty," I mouthed because the window was up and I didn't want to wake Zoe.

"You better get out before you're in handcuffs again," Frank nudged.

"You'd enjoy that, wouldn't you?" I said, opening the car door.

"Let's just say I wouldn't dislike it," Frank leaned in so the officer could see his face. "Good morning, Officer Jim."

"Professor Grant," the officer said. "If I knew it was you, I wouldn't have harassed your friend here."

"You can never be too careful." Frank chuckled a little too much. "Better safe than sorry. Shoot first, ask questions later."

They both yukked it up.

I'd have thought Frank would know better than to make law enforcement-related jokes given how I'd spent the last night of my life with the threat of police brutality hanging over my head. The whole thing made me think that Frank wasn't a good psychologist at all, that he didn't understand trauma, let alone Zoe and what did or didn't happen to her. And he sure as hell didn't understand me.

"Keep your eye on this one, Officer Jim," Frank said. "He might be a professor, but that won't stop his deviance."

Officer Jim laughed. He waved Frank out of the parking lot.

When Frank's Civic disappeared, Officer Jim deflated like a poorly patched air mattress with one too many holes. He lumbered back to his golf cart without exchanging two words with me.

"You better get on it," I called after him. "Big crimes to solve. Serial killers and armed robberies and students parking in the faculty lot."

Officer Jim shook his head and jerked the golf cart into drive. Probably all for the best. I needed to get to my office. From there, I could call Sharon, see if I could catch the tail end of one of my classes, or at the very least begin damage control before everyone found out about my night behind bars.

Of course, I'd missed my morning classes. Not too much of a loss, really. My absence probably gave my TAs a moment to shine. Hell, the students probably enjoyed class more. I was always up in front of the class, droning on and boring everyone, including myself. Over the years, teaching my classes felt like watching the same rerun of *Gilligan's Island* on repeat. Gilligan does X, Mary Ann does Y, The Professor says—who cares. Over and over again.

Back when I tried, I knew just how to pace my Psych 101 lectures. What jokes to say to nail home theories of motivation, for instance. When to pause so I seemed, oh, so pensive regarding Emile Durkheim's Collective Consciousness. How to sigh just right to indicate that, yes, students could chuckle over psychosexual disorders. With every movement, I told them I was the type of guy who had hidden depths, the type of guy they should think about beyond the class. I was Daniel Conrad, a guy worth wondering about.

Somewhere during my umpteenth lecture, I stopped caring. I started skipping over the jokes and examples. I mumbled more and read my notes without memorizing them. Some days I figured out what to say on the spot while I was up there, which led to more hemming and hawing than anyone wanted to hear from a professional lecturer. And then I found myself getting more frustrated.

Looking back, I blamed Evergreen's students for not knowing what I should have taught them. Not that the little bastards deserved my sympathy. Even if I was Albert Einstein up there, they'd be on their phones, texting their girlfriends, elbowing each other over who would buy the beer kegs for the party on Thursday night. Then, one by one, they'd have the nerve to come by my office and ask me to cut them a break. "Do me a solid," this kid said just the other day, whatever that meant. "You've got to do me a solid." No, I don't *got* to do anything for you, kid.

Others who were dissatisfied with their grades threatened to speak to my dean because they weren't getting what they paid for, which might be true if they were complaining about my lectures or my engagement, which was far below that of a faceless government employee at the Department of Motor Vehicles, but given that they were upset with their own exam performance, it was ludicrous. A girl said to me, "Your dean will make this right," and I thought, really? Since when did it become socially acceptable to go all "I want to speak to your manager" on your professor's ass about a test you took? Her classroom performance wasn't some undercooked burger at a fast food restaurant. I didn't take the test for her. She took the test all on her own. Maybe I should ask to speak to *her* boss.

The good news: all the grade grubbing would be over soon.

Dean Dyer knew from her husband just how many strings he pulled to get me out of my felony charge. No doubt she would find a way to use the moral turpitude clause to fire me. Might as well start packing up my office—or updating my résumé. Sure, Evergreen might want me gone, but other universities would bite. Controversial hire with one book—really, two books; my *Practical Guide* could be published any day. A promising pop psychologist with the potential to do real psychological research. I always had potential. Just not motivation. True, I was no spring chicken. But I was tried and tested—or tired and testy. Other schmucks might not be worth the paper their diplomas were printed on. *Puppy Love* had made twelve thousand four hundred sixty-eight dollars. In today's nonfiction market, that's an asset to any institution, thank you very much. Someone worth hiring.

I alternated between patting myself on the back for a job well done and raging against Dean Dyer and Evergreen for letting me become a disappointment to myself. I could have accomplished greater, more important things if someone, anyone pushed me. Wasn't that the point of having colleagues? To inspire, to question, to set your ideas in motion? So I've got to admit that, walking down the hall, I was angrier than I needed to be at the Psychology Department. Every office door I passed aggravated me. Waste of space here, waste of space there. All clowns. Which even I knew wasn't quite fair. But no time for objectivity.

I was on the way out. The feminist protesters, my colleagues, Dean Dyer: the winners. Me: the loser. Probably could convince Dean Dyer to allow me to resign. A professor—even a disgraced professor—beating up a police officer? Horrible for Evergreen's reputation.

The idea of resigning, heading out, trying something new wasn't entirely unappealing. I glanced at that ridiculous poster across from my office. If I had the money, I'd leave Evergreen in an instant. I'd abandon this place along with its pettiness and accusations of things I most certainly didn't do. But I'd leave behind the things I did do, too.

Sharon. I wanted to arrive unnoticed, slip into my office, and call Sharon. Damn Frank hadn't made any progress. I needed to know if she was okay, but before I could even open my door, Benny was at my side like a panting bloodhound. Seriously, did I emit some sort of sound or smell that attracted him?

"Doctor C, why didn't you return my calls?" Benny whined.

"Hello to you, too." I fiddled with my keys, hoping the boy would get the hint or, alternatively, that I could get my door opened and shut before Benny could angle his body in my door frame.

"You really should've returned my calls."

"Benny, I've been a little busy." The tone in my voice screamed "Leave me alone. I'm not in the mood" to a normal person, but only encouraged Benny.

"Things have been going on here, big things, crazy big things, disasters, really, and you left me here to deal with them all alone," Benny griped like I'd left him to manage Mission Control during the Apollo 13 fiasco. Nothing at Evergreen should ever justify that much moaning and groaning. Disasters? Crazy big things? Unlikely.

"Listen," I said as I dug in my pocket for my wallet. Damn, it was still in that plastic bag. "I don't have time for this. I'll pay you whatever I owe you. Just leave me the hell alone."

I opened the bag and pulled out my wallet. "Here take it." I waved four hundred bucks at him. I just didn't care anymore.

Benny scrunched up his face like he was Jasmine about to unleash the waterworks.

"He said you were horrible, Doctor C. I didn't believe it."

"Believe what?"

"That you were who he said you were. That you were," his voice dropped to a whisper, "an asshole, but I guess you are."

"Who said?"

Benny scuttled down the hall without responding. Was talking with me like a decent human being just too much for his delicate sensibilities?

"Don't you want your money?" I called after him, knowing cash would lure Benny back to me like a mouse to a cheese-rigged trap.

The word money made him stop in his tracks. He turned around. Shook his head and then he did the unthinkable. He kept going. Not only that, but he picked up the pace, moving faster than I thought possible for a boy of his girth.

I thought about chasing after him, but what was the point? I'd sung the harmony to that ditty with Jasmine and countless women before her. "Daniel Conrad, you're an asshole," the woman would yell and rush off, no doubt prompting me to step up and do my part and chase after her. If I did what she wanted, if I followed her, then she'd scream at me some more, maybe throw things. I got hit in the head with a vase once. A lamp another time. All this made me see that it was quite dangerous doing what women wanted me to do. If I didn't follow after the woman, she might still throw things at me, launch insults in my direction, but she might calm down on her own, too. The chances were fifty-fifty. So I started letting crying dogs run, which meant that even when it came to Benny, it was better to let the boy rush off, cool off on his own. Although, because of his Y chromosome, even Benny on little sleep wouldn't hurl home goods. Men—even boy men—know that's just insane.

Feeling pretty good about my decision not to follow after Benny, I opened my office door. Someone was at my desk, fiddling with my computer: a teenage boy.

What? Who?

But before I had a chance to ask him any questions, he started shouting, "You motherfucker! Can't you just leave her alone? What's wrong with you?"

"What's wrong with me? What's wrong with *you*? Who *are* you?"

"You know who I am," he spat. "And you know what you've done."

"Really I don't. I have no idea."

"Oh. You have *no idea*," the kid taunted. He clenched and unclenched his fist as he looked me up and down, trying to determine his first point of attack. Maybe the nose. The gut. The jaw.

"You're angry," I said. I had no idea why.

He lunged toward me. I stepped back into the hall.

"I'm sure you have your reasons," I said.

Who didn't? Although I sure as hell didn't think this kid had reasons. What could I have done to him? Was he a student? He looked familiar. Maybe he didn't pass the last exam? That wasn't my fault; besides, isn't this why I had TAs? To deal with these disgruntled whack-jobs?

I backed further into the hall.

"Running away isn't going to help you. You're gonna get your ass kicked. My dad might not be man enough to do it, but someone's gotta make you pay. Someone's gotta stand up for what's right."

"Your dad?" I scanned my brain for men I could have possibly offended. Frank? Did Frank have a son? The police officer I sure as hell didn't hit? Even if I had, this kid was overreacting. His father was fine, no worse for wear. He didn't even have a scratch on him.

And where were the ever-ready Evergreen campus police?

I said what I could to delay. Come on, coworkers, call the police. *111 from a campus phone. "If your dad has a problem with me, he and I can figure it out."

"You have no fucking idea who I am, do you?"

He lunged toward me and ploughed me into the wall, forcing the plastic corner of that Don't Sleep with Daniel Conrad poster into my back.

While I attempted to edge away from the poster, the kid struck me hard in the gut. I doubled over to defend myself, but the kid knew how to fight. He pinned me back up to the wall, digging the hard plastic poster further into my skin. I resisted, I wriggled and thrashed. Then the kid opened his mouth.

"I'm Cam Vogel," he said.

Sharon's son. I knew I recognized him.

I stopped resisting.

"This is for my dad." He socked me in the jaw.

"This is for my mom." He whacked me square on the nose.

Blood gushed from my face. From my nose? From my mouth? Who knew?

"And this is for me, having to follow you two around, watching you make—" By that point, my eyes were closed, hoping Sharon's son would get his aggression out, and I could wake up in a pool of my own blood alive enough to ask if she was okay. I braced myself for the third punch, but nothing. Cam Vogel stopped attacking me.

I opened my eyes to see what had happened. And there he was, head in hand, squatting on the floor. Crying?

Dear Lord. You'd think I'd be the one crying. I was the one assaulted after all. Still, that was Sharon's kid over there.

I hobbled over to him and patted him on the back. "It's good you did that," I said.

"Fuck you, old man. You looking for more?"

Okay, so he wasn't crying. Just closing his eyes, regrouping, reassessing. Probably an anger management strategy, if anything.

"I admire what you did just now. Really," I said.

And Cam was up on his feet. "Shut the fuck up!" Punctuated with an uppercut that sent me to the floor.

I got up on my hands and knees. "I mean it," I said. "Your mother needs protecting."

"Seriously, shut the fuck up!"

A kick to my side. I fell on my back.

Shit. Maybe I should shut the fuck up.

Of course I didn't.

Cam eyed me as I pulled myself up.

"I get why you're doing this," I said, attempting to stand.

"What about 'shut the fuck up' don't you understand?"

Cam channeled his scorn: another punch.

I doubled over. When I could breathe again, an apology spilled from my lips. "I'm sorry ... sorry that me being with your mom has hurt you."

Cam looked like he wanted to slug me again.

But before he raised his fists, I asked, "Is there something I can do? To make it better, to make you feel better?"

Not because I wanted to save myself the pain of another punch. Surprising, I know.

"Stop doing it. Stop helping her hurt my dad."

"I love your mother."

Another blow to the stomach.

"Love." Cam slammed me against the wall with his body. "That's not love."

"I love your mother," I gasped. "I'll always love her."

Cam backed away enough for me to breathe. "I don't care. Leave her alone," he said. "You're not good for her. You're not good for us."

"But she's okay?" I asked.

Speaking was a mistake. Cam shoved me harder into the wall.

"Listen, asshole," he said, "her life doesn't revolve around you."

Sharon and I had talked about that the first time we were together. She called me nosy for trying to find out about her everyday life. I asked her if being with me was the best thing she had going. She laughed. I remembered wondering if her laughter was on account of the ridiculousness of the question or if, of course, the snippets of time we had together allowed her to patch up her problematic life and hold on. Now I wonder if the very idea that I could have been the best part of anything in her life was preposterous. It's like a symptom wondering if it's the cure. Although I guess sometimes fevers break and it's a new morning—

"You hear me? She doesn't need you."

I must not have responded fast enough.

He punched me.

And I was back on the floor.

Cam loomed over me. "Leave her alone and you won't get any more beatings. Understand?"

I nodded. I understood.

I wanted to tell him "You opened my eyes. I won't see your mother anymore," just to make him happy, get him off my back, but sometimes a man needs to own up and tell another man the truth. And there was a spark in this Cam kid's eyes that made me treat him like a decent human being, the same spark Zoe no doubt would say is in all human beings, but this time I felt it. That pesky need to tell the truth. Tug tugging like a toddler clinging on my pants leg, asking for a cookie. No, not now, honey. We're having dinner in a few minutes. Tug. Tug. Not that I ever had a toddler, but still—an irritating, harassing demand that yanks at something in you. That was the need to tell Cam the truth.

"I won't lie to you," I said.

Miraculously, dishonesty didn't follow.

Probably because Cam Vogel was long gone.

CHAPTER TWENTY-SIX

I limped into my office and lowered my body into my chair. A message flashed on my office phone. Maybe it was Sharon. I could tell her "Your boy just beat me up." Not that I'd rat on Cam. He was right about a lot of things, including the fact that sometimes I should shut the fuck up.

A message from Jasmine, acknowledging that yes, we're on hold, but maybe, just maybe we could grab lunch. "I know you're in therapy," Jasmine said, testing the water. "It's just that some Quality Fun Time"—there were those capital letters in her voice again—"would help us, both of us, because when you shut me out—"

I stopped the message. My head hurt enough from Cam's fists. I couldn't hear Jasmine try. I didn't know why I lied to her, why I told her I was in therapy when I wasn't, why I cheated on her, or why I kept her on hold, except that was what I did.

Zoe was right. Sure, her advice was holier than thou and grated on my nerves, but the girl knew the truth: I needed to do the responsible thing. I didn't want to make Zoe or Frank too self-satisfied, but they'd got me thinking.

Keeping Jasmine around really wasn't fair to her.

I had been myself—well, not completely myself, but I had been a good version of myself with Sharon's son—and that made me wonder if there might be something to the whole honest, authentic self movement I had previously written off as bullshit. Not that I'd tell Jasmine all the facts. No point hurting her.

The end result would be the same: she and I would go our separate ways.

Not that I knew how to do it. A man my age most likely should know how to break up with a woman. The sad truth is I just pussyfoot until women are done with me. If that doesn't work, I force their hands. I cheat, I ignore their needs, I wait until that steady drip—this isn't right, not right, not right—amounts to an ounce of self-respect. Inevitably, they say "I deserve better" or "You can't love me the way I deserve to be loved." And they go.

No grief. Just relief.

On my end, at least.

Of course, sometimes they left when I didn't want to lose them, but that was the rare woman. Sharon, the first time we were together, and my ex-wife Elle. Two women I loved. One more than the other, although that took me years to admit. That I loved them both equally was a lie I told myself.

Before Sharon self-destructed and told Elle everything, Elle and I had a good marriage. A struggling marriage, but what marriage isn't a bit of a grind? Life was going fine, too fine maybe, when I took up with Sharon. Elle and I had everything a couple could want for eight years: a house in the suburbs, cars that got us from Point A to Point B, financial stability, and career success. Elle's practice was thriving. I was planning my first book, not *Puppy Love,* but a research-based tome on anxiety's effects on the family. Elle was fifteen years younger than me. We were going to have children. My in-laws liked me. I was going to be the father to their grandchildren.

But I cheated on Elle with Sharon, Sharon told Elle, and I did what I always did: I lied.

Strange thing, I never wondered what might have happened if I had told Elle the truth. Maybe I could have explained Sharon's gravitational pull. Maybe I could have told her, "Elle, I love you. I'll always loved you. I'm just a stupid man. You know men and sex. What is it they say? A hard dick has no conscience?"

But I needed Sharon. More than she needed me, true. I woke up hoping to see her and I fell asleep fantasizing about the next day with her. Maybe I'd get the opportunity to touch her, maybe she'd write or call.

With Elle, I lived on the tip of an unlit candlewick, not knowing the darkness. Then Sharon appeared, igniting everything I knew. Around her, the air was different; oxygen was precious.

Sharon was everything I needed, and Elle was … Elle. I wanted to be with both of them. Sharon to live. Elle for who we had been, for the life we created together, for the comfort of tomorrow.

Elle was enough. Smart enough, beautiful enough, loving enough. Turns out Sharon was more, an adventure I couldn't abandon.

So I had it all for a few years: a wife and a lover—and longing. I lived in uncertainty, the ground always shifting under my feet. I wanted. I prayed to anyone or anything that might listen. Not that anyone replied.

I held onto shards of glass, sliding dirt, dissipating dreams, the scraps of hope Sharon tossed my way. She said she was angry with Brian. And possibility! They could get divorced. Sharon and I could be together. Where did Elle go? I hate to say this, but it wasn't about her. It was just me and Sharon. When there was hope, Elle faded away.

I lost both of them in one day, one normal October morning. Elle said she wanted to meet for breakfast at the bistro near her office.

Sharon and I were in the throes of a fight. I knew Sharon and I would get through it; we always did. But I screwed up. I called her a whore for sleeping with ah-mazing Alan the poetry teacher. Sharon said she was going to "fucking destroy" me before she stormed off, nothing unusual, except she had follow-through. She contacted Elle.

I arrived late to breakfast with Elle because I decided to swing by the coffeeshop Sharon frequented, just in case I could bump into her. I waited longer than I should have, hoping to see her. To grab her hand and tell her I was sorry. Sharon, we'll be okay. Other people don't matter as long as we, Daniel and Sharon, get to exist somewhere together. If the only world we can live in is a world populated with Brian and ah-mazing Alan and who-knows-who-else, then that's fine. We have to survive.

But Sharon didn't answer my emails, texts, or calls. She never picked up her morning latte.

I told Elle an excuse for why I was late, but she stared at me, her uneaten grapefruit and cup of coffee in front of her, untouched.

"The light on Third and Woodslake Grove was out again. So much traffic."

"Don't," Elle said. "You need to treat me like an adult and tell me the truth."

So I lied. I know. Bad idea. "I've been telling you the truth. Do you want me to make something up?"

She fixed her eyes on me.

"Are you sleeping with someone else?"

"No."

"Seeing someone else? Going to dinner with him or her?"

"Him or her? I'm not gay—"

"Answer the question. Are you seeing someone else? Going to lunch, dinner, coffee with him or her?"

"Of course not. This is ridiculous. And I take offense—"

"You're lying."

"I'm not."

"I see the way you looked off, up and to the side, when you said no. The internet says liars look up and to the side when they're lying."

"Oh, and the internet is always right."

"Daniel, you've been cheating on me, sleeping with another woman for years. Admit it. Please."

"No."

"Put your hands on the table," she said.

Elle's dad had been in the Army. Maybe this was some sort of field lie detector test. I read once that if you curl your toes or clench your butt cheeks during the baseline questions, you can throw off the whole test.

It was worth a shot. I clenched my butt cheeks and curled my toes.

"Say you haven't cheated on me."

"I haven't cheated on you."

"Liar."

"Because I looked off to the side? I can't control that. You know I have trouble making eye contact sometimes."

"No." She pulled a stack of papers out of her briefcase. "Because of this."

She plopped the packet on top of my hands. The binder clip rapped across my knuckles, scraping my skin.

On top was an email I had written Sharon two years before. I thumbed through the pages. Each another email. There had to be hundreds. The binder clip was big and at its breaking point.

Emails telling Sharon intimate details about my life, the particularly offensive chunks of text highlighted in yellow. The final one making fun of Elle's new haircut from last week. "Those bangs. God. What was she thinking? Don't cut your hair like that, okay? Promise me."

Another mocking Elle's love of pop music. "She has no taste," I had written Sharon the year before. "She wants me to go with her to a Teen Bop concert. Yes, that's right. My wife has the emotional intelligence of a thirteen-year-old. Lucky me."

And then there were the comments about her family and her weight. "Her mother's fat. Her sister's fat. Poor Elle does everything she can to avoid getting large, but it's inevitable. She's Polish. I see it in her thighs. She'll have a belly in no time."

Horrible.

Worse, there were the emails I sent Sharon detailing how much I wanted to make love to her, highlighted in pink. "I miss your taste." "I can't stop thinking of your amazing tits." and "I need you, S," flashed in front of my eyes. Our whole relationship—or the highlights of it—printed out and held together with one big binder clip.

I wanted to ask if Sharon had given her the emails pre-highlighted or if Elle had taken a highlighter to them herself. It seemed more Sharon than Elle to emphasize the hurtful bits. Instead, I did what I always do. I lied.

"You know Sharon made all this up," I said. "She knows you. She knows me. She just took what she knows and made it look like I sent these to her."

Elle was quiet.

"This is illegal." I kept going. "Sharon can't make this shit up and put my name on it. She really is insane. We need to get her out of our lives before she stabs one of us in the parking lot."

"Danny," she said, "they're from your email."

"My email?"

She nodded.

"You hacked into my email?"

"I don't want to hear it."

I stammered. I probably shouldn't have felt betrayed. I was the one cheating.

"Sharon told me … what you've done. I pulled up your email, not wanting to find … this … proof of just how much you hate me."

"I don't … hate you."

She crossed her arms and grunted. "Funny way of showing it."

"I didn't mean those things. I love you, Ellie."

"Not good enough," she said.

"I never wanted to hurt you."

Which was the truth.

"You shouldn't have done this then," she said.

"If it helps, I actually like your bangs. I don't know why I wrote that. I guess I was trying to make Sharon happy."

She looked tired.

"I want a divorce," she said.

That was the last time Elle and I sat down at a table alone together. We saw each other a couple of times in mediation. We didn't have any kids, so it was easy to avoid each other after the divorce. She got the house. I lived in an apartment complex near campus, overrun with college students. I wrote my book, *Puppy Love,* a fuck you to Sharon, not even thinking about how the book might affect Elle. I had to hurt Sharon. Show her that I found her undesirable.

And I became Daniel Conrad, the man who dated young women, women like Jasmine. Women I never should have been with in the first place, not when Sharon existed.

So I called Jasmine back and explained that I first needed to pick up my car from the impound lot.

Her only question: "You need a ride?"

That Jasmine. Always accommodating.

"Nah. I'll take the bus. I need some time alone."

"Wanna meet at Our Place in an hour and a half?"

I wanted to protest—there must be a better spot to meet than that god-awful Jared's Deli across from campus—but she sounded so damn happy that I took my lumps. Fine. As long as I forced myself to be honest.

I caught the bus and blended in with the men and women around me. Old men with canes, day laborers bundled up in layered coats, young professionals with headphones. They were on the move. I didn't know their stories; they didn't know mine. But it felt good to travel somewhere together.

A Latina woman with a toddler and a baby boarded the full bus. When I gave her my seat, she said something in Spanish, as she touched her hand to her face. Concern. Are you okay?

Shit. My face, no doubt bruised and bloody. Frankenstein's monster.

I'm fine, I smiled at her. No need to worry.

Her eyes said she would worry anyway.

I picked up my Porsche at the impound lot. Driving down the highway, back to Greenwood, it didn't feel like my car anymore. Maybe I was suffering from some light brain damage, but the steering wheel felt too high, the heated seats felt too low, and I could have sworn I used to be able to feel the road more. Everything was too effortless. Too comfortable.

But the gouges were still on the door and the bruises were still on my face. That was something. A clue. My car, my life. And maybe, just maybe, those marks meant my actions had consequences.

Consequences. My head throbbed. I needed to lie down. Pull over by the side of the highway, push back my seat, and rest. My eyelids felt heavy and sore.

I flipped on the radio. No closing my eyes just yet.

Keep moving. Keep your foot on the gas pedal, your eyes on the road. What is it they say? Sleep when you're dead.

CHAPTER TWENTY-SEVEN

Of course, the drive turned into an additional five minutes and then an additional fifteen minutes, no matter what I did. Good thing I didn't stop to rest.

I was late, hightailing it back to "our place," which was quite possibly the worst place I'd ever been to in my life, even counting jail.

I instinctively wanted to hold my breath and run out of there in case whatever was inside could spread like a virus, but Jasmine was waiting on me, wearing a diaphanous top that made me wonder if the octogenarian at the table next to her would have a heart attack looking at her. He appeared to be in that gray area between life and death. One nip-slip from Jasmine and he'd be gone. To keep the man on earth a little longer, maybe give him time to get his affairs in order, get right with his God, I went inside. Maybe I could block his view or ask Jasmine if she had a sweater in her car.

When Jasmine saw me, she got up from the table and smiled, ignorant of her surroundings like the inevitable girl in the horror movie who encourages her boyfriend to make out in a haunted house by saying, "Come on. Those things people say? That's an urban legend."

She grabbed my arm and cried, "Oh, God! What happened to your face?" like I was missing a nose or an eye.

"Someone beat me up." I shrugged.

"How horrible!"

"Not really. I deserved it."

"Who did this to you?"

"A kid, no one important."

I was off to a good start, lying to her, but I couldn't tell her it was Cam.

"Are you okay? Can I take you to the doctor?"

"I'm fine. Better than I've been in a while."

She sighed and shook her head, her chest heaving up and down. All the while, I fought the uphill battle not to look at her cleavage, despite knowing that she'd no doubt worn that top to make men, particularly me, gape. Jasmine shifted forward in her seat and leaned toward me, which only revealed her breasts more. Intentional? Perhaps. The nearly-departed octogenarian next to her noticed, too. Nah, no point asking her to cover up. Glad to see the old man's still looking. Even on death's door, a guy's going to look at a woman's breasts and think, "Maybe I could be with her. Maybe there's a possibility. Maybe, just maybe."

"Here! Coffee and cream, no sugar," she chimed. "I hope it's not cold, but I thought you'd be here sooner."

Great. Diluted room temperature coffee for the dead and dying. Could this get any better?

I wanted to say something snarky, but I was a half hour late, so instead I thanked her and got to the issue at hand.

"Jasmine," I started.

She looked at me with a huge grin on her face, like I was going to get down on one knee and propose marriage.

"Jasmine," I said, "this isn't working."

"We can go somewhere else."

"No. You and me."

Jasmine scrunched her brow. "But you love me … don't you?" Her voice cracked.

"I do—no, I should … but I don't. I could have. I just, I love someone else."

Jasmine sat, silent, until she said, "That woman from the pictures. It's her, isn't it?"

She fiddled with her phone and pulled up one of those god-awful pictures from Mama Carlita's with Sharon's foot on my thigh. That Cam. I almost admired his follow-through. Of course he'd contacted Jasmine.

"This woman?" Jasmine jiggled her phone in front of me.

"Yes."

I tried to reach across the table to grab Jasmine's hand, but she pulled away from me.

"I just don't get it." She thumbed at Sharon's face in the photo, zooming in and out. "Why this woman? She's not even prettier than me."

"Sometimes you can't help who you love," I said.

"Well, I love you," she whined. "And I'm beautiful and smart and talented and you're really lucky to be with a woman like me."

I didn't say anything.

"I really do love you." She started to cry.

Love and tears. I could have said "I love you" back to make her happy, but no point telling her something that wasn't true.

"Give me a few years and I'll be in a wheelchair."

Jasmine stopped crying. "Wait, is something wrong? Do you have a degenerative disease I don't know about?"

As if that could explain my irrational behavior of loving the wrong woman.

"No. Just hypothetically. Hypothetically, it's a real possibility."

Jasmine relaxed. "Hypothetically, I'd still love you."

"Then you know how love is," I said.

She nodded. "Which is why I'm willing to put all this behind us."

"Are you insane?" Probably a little too harsh. "I'm telling you I love another woman, that I don't appreciate your superior beauty, brains, whatever it is you said you had."

"Talent," she said, smearing her makeup with a paper napkin.

"Talent," I repeated. "The thing is I'm telling you I love someone else."

"I know, but you're my person."

And then she started to sob again like the possessive "my" set her off. I was no longer her person. I was some other woman's person. She plopped the paper napkin she was blubbering into on the table and picked up another napkin to snivel into. Luckily, Jared's Deli had napkin dispensers on the tables.

"Is this because of your book?" I asked. "Because if you want, you can say you got me to keep you past your birthday."

She shook her head. "There's no book. There never was a book," she said. "I just wanted to meet you."

Preposterous. Why would a woman like Jasmine go through such lengths to get to know a guy like me?

"I shouldn't have lied. I just didn't know how else to get to know you," she said.

"Well, now that you know me, it should be a relief to get rid of me," I said.

She shook her head. "No, you don't understand. I love you. Real love. The kind you can't turn off. What am I supposed to do? Just keep loving you into a void?"

Another napkin covered in tears balled up and abandoned on the table.

Maybe she did love me. Or maybe she thought she did. Who was I to judge what was real and what wasn't?

"You can't leave me. You just can't," Jasmine continued. "What am I supposed to do?"

I am sure every eyeball in Jared's Deli was focused on us, but I didn't notice.

"I don't know," I said. "I'm really not the person to ask. I hear it gets easier. Eventually you'll start to see yourself for who you are and the other person for who he or she was, and then the void shrinks or maybe you realize someone or something else was always there all along. And suddenly what's important will be bigger than just you and me."

I had no idea where any of that was coming from. Maybe my psychology training? Maybe Zoe? It felt like bullshit, and maybe some of it was. But as I said it, it rang true.

I believed it.

Jasmine stopped crying.

"Well, I hope that happens for both of us," she said.

Jasmine and I talked a little while longer. I'm not the monster everyone thinks I am. And besides, there was something to the real, raw Jasmine I enjoyed. The girl who loved me into a void, devoid of pretense and laughter. No point leaving her all tear-stained and sniveling.

I bought Jasmine a piece of chocolate cake and refilled our coffee cups while she popped into the bathroom to run water over her face. Settling back into her chair, she handed me a handful of wet, warm paper towels. "For your face," she said. The towels were exactly what I needed.

"You really are a mess," she said.

"If only you knew."

Jasmine and I talked. She told me about her parents and their impending divorce and what a gentleman Frank was and how when she was down, he listened. The whole thing made me want to kill Frank or point out to Jasmine just what a jerk he can be, but I let it slide. Maybe Frank was better at listening and caring.

Jasmine said she didn't want to write, that she didn't even start that book about dating me, but that she wanted to go into teaching. "Not like how you do it," she said. "But more like how Frank does it." Which made me angry at myself. Why did I waste all those years being a professor if I didn't inspire anyone? Fucking Frank. Maybe he was better at mentoring, connecting with his students. I could give him that. He was a hack who could get up and teach the same class over and over again for the rest of his miserable life. Or maybe teaching made him happy. Maybe I was the hack.

So I listened.

Jasmine asked me about my life, who I wanted to be, what I wanted to do.

"Before you're in adult diapers and a wheelchair." She grinned.

"Get out of Evergreen," I said to my own surprise. "But I'll probably be fired before I quit anyway."

I told her about the arrest, how I was innocent, but how I might have been to blame given how upset I was about Sharon's disappearance.

"That woman has a hold on you," Jasmine said. No tears. Almost like she admired it. Like she wished she could have a hold on someone. Or that someone—maybe any man except me—could have a hold on her.

"You mean she's my On Hold Person?" I asked, mimicking her knack of talking in capital letters.

"Oh, please, no! Too soon!" Jasmine choked back laughter.

And I got a taste of who we could have been to each other if I hadn't been me and Jasmine hadn't been who she was and—well, no point thinking about that now.

"Let's say you get fired tomorrow. What would you do if you could do anything? Keep writing books?"

"No." I surprised myself again. "Definitely no more writing."

"What then? Imagine you can do anything, be anyone."

"If I could do anything, I'd leave Evergreen and this stupid suburb. I'd never write another book. I'd leave everything behind. I'd go … west."

Who knows where that came from.

But it felt right. For the first time in my adult life, I wasn't treading water.

"West?" Jasmine said. "That doesn't sound like you."

"That's why I like it," I said.

CHAPTER TWENTY-EIGHT

West. Jasmine asked what I planned to do out west. I said I didn't know. "But definitely not academics. Real work. The type of work men used to do. I could build things with my hands, be a lumberjack, a ranch hand. I could work in construction, build a railroad."

"A railroad? Is anyone still building railroads?"

I shrugged. "Metaphorical railroads then," I said. "What my father did, what his father did before him. I could build skyscrapers, airplanes, cars."

"What about that woman? Would she go west with you?"

I shrugged. "Maybe I feel like falling in love with the first woman I meet, putting her in a wheelbarrow and wheeling her down the street."

Jasmine made a face. "Isn't that a Bob Dylan song?"

It was. Weird that Jasmine knew Bob Dylan. Embarrassing that she caught me quoting a song at her.

"Never mind, I'll find someone like you. I wish nothing but the best for you, too." Jasmine grinned a little much for the sentiment.

"Harsh."

"That's a song," Jasmine said. "From the CD I burned for you. It's the first one on there. It's by Adele. You know, Adele, my favorite singer?"

No, I didn't know Adele. And I had no idea where that CD was. If I still had it.

"You never listened to it, did you? You said you did, but I had my doubts."

I shook my head. Nope. Never listened to it. I felt bad. Maybe those songs were important to her.

She sighed. "Well, I really should go. You have women to meet and wheelbarrows to buy."

"Wheelbarrows are better than wheelchairs."

"Go west, Conrad," she said. "Just go west."

"Just like that?" I asked.

She smiled. "Just like that."

And she got up and walked away. Jasmine. My Jasmine. The woman who said she'd strap me in adult diapers when I was in my eighties and she was in her fifties if I just loved her a tenth of the amount she loved me. That woman, that idea of who we could be to each other, walked out the door. I felt a pang of regret. Not because I loved her, but because

I never should have been with her in the first place. It was as if I'd violated a law of nature, made a deal with the Devil, and when I got what I wanted, all I had left was "Maybe none of this was meant to be."

"Go west, Conrad," she said.

"Go west, old man," I heard.

But that was okay. Sure I was older. Sure my father, his father before him, all those American men had been younger when they had set off on their own, when they took dirt in their hands and built something, did something extraordinary. But I could do it. I had gone to school, earned a Ph.D., and landed an easy job a million other people would die for. I had written a meaningless book about something I never believed in and made something of myself. Hell, I even dated a beautiful woman when I was past my peak. I could do this, too.

I wanted to tell Zoe about my idea. It sounded just like the type of thing she'd love.

It wouldn't be hard to take her with me. Zoe and me on the open road. Father and daughter. Sure, it would be a responsibility taking care of her, but isn't that what fathers did? And she'd get to see a good example, me changing my life, making something of myself. Maybe I'd inspire her to become a musician or a painter, and we'd travel the country together sweeping into town as the railroad expanded north or south or whatever way railroads are being built these days. If anyone is building railroads anymore. We'd go where the work was. I'd work with my hands, provide for my family. That way, when my head hit my pillow at night, I'd feel the tired tranquility of a day well spent. I could almost feel it from when I was a boy, when my father forced me to work with him after school repairing roofs. The joy of stillness from striving and doing all day. The cool sheets a contrast to the harsh sun.

Sharon. Maybe Sharon could come with us. We could recapture whatever it was that we used to have, that fire. Cam would be mad, but even Cam would respect it with time—hopefully. Sharon and I wouldn't be cheating. We would be chasing a dream, together. Isn't that what people with integrity did?

I tried Sharon's number. Straight to voicemail.

I left a message: Let's run away together.

But even as I said it, my heart sank. I hung up. Sharon wasn't going anywhere.

Before I could feel too sorry for myself, my phone rang. Sharon.

I remembered the gun, her anger, the stupidity of it all. I dreaded Sharon mocking me, "Daniel, are you dumb? Me? Run away with you? Stop making me laugh."

But it was Sharon, so, of course, I answered before the second ring.

"And she's alive," I said with the acerbity of someone who no longer cared. Even though I did. And I always would. No matter what Sharon did or said. Damn love.

"Don't even start, Daniel."

"I got arrested because of you."

"You deserve what you got," she said. "If not more."

"Do you even like me?"

"Yes and no."

"Well, thanks and no thanks."

"It's the truth," she said. "What was that ridiculous message? Some kind of joke?"

"I've been thinking about us. Maybe you and I—"

Sharon let out a deep guttural sigh. "Can't talk now. Meet me in fifteen."

I agreed to meet Sharon at The Wood, Greenwood's newest whiskey bar. Not to be confused with The Green, Greenwood's whiskey bar on the other side of Woodslake Grove. But if I was going to change my life, I might as well start with Sharon. Talk to her like a man. A man who loves her. Even Cam did me that courtesy eventually after the stalking and punching got him nowhere.

So, in spite of my own sense of who we were and who we would be, I battled Greenwood mid-afternoon traffic, circled two parking garages before I finally found a spot—overpriced at almost four bucks an hour—and made my way up to The Wood, which from the look of the heavy wood paneling on the outside would cost me pretty penny. All to see Sharon. And get my heart broken.

If that's not love.

The bar was dark. When my eyes adjusted to The Wood's discreet candlelight, I could see Sharon waving me to her table. Already halfway through a bottle of Chardonnay.

Before I could make a comment about The Wood's lack of lighting—what were they afraid of, forest fires if they lit a couple of candles?—Sharon leaned into me and whispered, "It's time for that second second chance."

So much for her liking and disliking me.

I settled into the cushy chair across from her, thankful for the shadows cast by the flame between us. Maybe Sharon wouldn't notice my face. I didn't want to lie, but I wanted to protect Cam, keep Sharon from putting two and two together, grounding him. But more than that, I didn't want Sharon to know. Then Cam could safeguard her, keep her from—

Doing exactly what she was doing. Reaching under the table, caressing another man's knee. My knee in this case.

I'm glad you're here, she communicated with each stroke.

Good Cam's not here, I thought, fully believing he was just around the corner, maybe at the bar or lurking behind some wood paneling, probably in disguise as a whiskey-swilling gentleman—the bar was full of them—if he could find a way to slip past the well-groomed man at the door tastefully carding everyone under forty.

"I'm sorry if I was too passionate yesterday," Sharon whispered.

Passionate? She acted indifferent unless she was pointing a gun at my head.

I squirmed out from under her even though I was putty in her hands.

"There's passionate and there's homicidal," I said.

"You're the only man who's ever gotten my ire up like that."

"Well, that's something," I said. "Glad you're not going around town stuffing gun barrels down men's throats."

A waiter with a frothy beer for me.

"No thanks," I said.

His smile was too wide for the situation. "Perhaps I can interest the gentleman in some whiskey?"

Well, whiskey in a whiskey bar would make sense. What was with the wine and the beer? But, no, I didn't want to drink. Not then. I needed to be in control.

"Bring him a rum and Coke. Use the good stuff. More rum than Coke, if you *comprendez*."

A wink from Sharon.

The toothy waiter was off before I could express that I didn't want him to *comprendez*.

"I don't feel like drinking right now," I said.

Drinking after the day—or days—I've had would be a mistake.

"Stop punishing me, Daniel." She tilted her head to the side. Her eyes said "Let's have fun like old times. Just try it. You'll like it. We could—"

She whispered something I won't repeat. Sharon's breath on my skin made me want her. Right there. She knew exactly what I wanted to hear. What I craved.

"I can't," I managed.

"Can't or won't? I said I'm sorry. What more do you want? I won't draw down on you again, if that's what you're worried about."

Then softness. Yearning. "Come on, silly boy. I know what you want."

She weaved her fingers into mine. Not under the table, but across the table. Where everyone or anyone could see. I let myself be happy. Maybe there was hope for Sharon and me. Maybe we could—

"Sharon, do we have a future?"

"Of course we do," she said. "We have a past."

"A good future? One that doesn't involve sneaking around? One we can tell people about. One that involves just the two of us. No Brian."

"Brian got a new job, a promotion."

Was I supposed to congratulate him?

I squeezed her hand. "Is there a good future for you and me?"

"Are you asking if Brian is going to find out again? I sure as hell won't tell him."

"That's not what I'm asking."

"What then?"

"Let's say if I could have gotten the concert tickets and Laurie Packard was pitch-perfect, and we had a splendid evening with dinner and drinks and earth-shattering sex. Let's say all that happened last night. What then? Does our second second chance have hope? Can we be more?"

"Your rum and Coke, sir."

I thanked the toothy waiter and pushed the tumbler as far away as I could, placing my water glass in front of it. No point shooting back the liquor on reflex. I needed a clear head. I needed to know.

"Drink up." Sharon reached across the table and pushed the tumbler against my hand.

"Answer my question, please."

"Sure, we can do more. I always like when we do more, especially when you relax and let me … please you."

"No," I said despite myself.

"No?" Sharon staggered. "You're saying no to—"

"Yes," I said. "I need to know, do we have hope?"

"Hope?" Sharon took a swig of her Chardonnay. "Daniel, you're lucky I'm here at all after what you did yesterday. There's hope for more for us, sure. I miss the way we were. We used to have fun. Are we going to run away together? No. I don't want to. You don't want to. This works. My arrangement with Brian works."

"Arrangement? So he knows?"

"God, no. He's clueless, but that works for me. For us."

"Don't you want a man who will love you, pay attention to you, be enough for you?"

"I'm fine. I like what Brian and I have together."

"You deserve better," I said.

"Have you seen my house?" She pushed the drink to my hand. "Drink up."

I grabbed the glass of water instead. Sharon sloshed more wine into her glass.

"I've been thinking. I need to go, try something new, leave

Greenwood," I said. "I want you to come with me."

"What are you talking about?"

"I have this dream," I said. "This dream of going west."

"To San Francisco? Los Angeles? For a conference?"

"No, a move. To somewhere uncharted. The great unknown. The frontier."

"Okay, Grizzly Adams."

"No, I'm serious."

She eyed my untouched drink. "That rum and Coke must be strong."

"I love you," I said. "But sometimes you make me hate myself. I hate who I am here."

"No one is forcing you. You can leave."

"Sharon, I love you. You love me, right?"

Sharon said nothing. I kept going. "Maybe it's time for us … to grow up. Maybe it's time for us to strike out on our own, attempt to follow our dreams, succeed or fail miserably, as long as we're not miserable. What do you say?"

Sharon reached across the table. I thought she was going for my hand again—maybe I inspired her?—but instead, she grabbed the rum and Coke.

"No point letting this go to waste."

She took a gulp and pushed it across the table to me. "Drink."

I shook my head.

She drew the drink back. "Good liquor's wasted on you anyway."

Not that good liquor should be drowned in soda, but I kept my mouth shut.

Sharon guzzled the rum and Coke until she hit the ice cubes while I talked about heading out on the open road.

"I have to go. I have to be free. But I want you to come with me. We can be free together."

"We're not—you're not going anywhere," Sharon said, almost to herself.

"I am."

"Then why is this the first I'm hearing about this little move of yours?"

"Because I forgot."

Sharon scowled. "Forgot to tell me?"

"Forgot the dream existed."

"You applied to other colleges? Got a job? All without telling me?"

"No job," I said.

She looked confused. Then relieved. So not reality. Just a pipe dream. The ramblings of a mad man.

She relaxed. "Daniel," she whispered, "let's talk about something real."

"This is real," I said. "You can come with me. I want you to, but I'm leaving Evergreen with nothing on the other side."

"You can't do that."

"Yes, I can."

Even though I didn't know if I actually could.

"You must be joking."

I shook my head. "Like I said, I'm heading west to build something with my hands. And I want you to come with me."

Sharon flushed. Too much alcohol? The effects of mixing a rum and Coke with a bottle of Chardonnay?

No. Anger.

"What are you talking about? You barely have the stamina to get up and flap your gums in an air-conditioned lecture hall. What makes you think you can build something with your hands in the heat and the rain?"

"Because that's what men did up until recently," I said. "My father, his father before him, your father, his father, this whole stupid town, this whole stupid country. We used to be pioneers back before we flapped our gums."

"My father was a schoolteacher," Sharon said as if that one fact disproved my point. She replenished her wine glass and lifted it. Touché, Daniel. Touché.

"You know what I mean. Men used to work, toil, sweat. Now we just sit. We sit in traffic, behind desks, in nice bars like this one if we're lucky. When did we make the trade?"

She humored me, probably to keep me quiet. It was an upscale bar after all.

"Those men you're talking about, they were younger. Not your age. Men don't start building with their hands in their fifties," she said.

"People live longer these days."

"Probably because they aren't manual laborers."

"Then I'll die trying," I said. "Come with me. See me try."

She shook her head. You must be joking. Then an idea.

"I know what this is." She crossed her arms. "You're still mad about yesterday. Daniel, you got yourself thrown in jail. I didn't send you there."

"I don't care about that." I surprised myself. I really didn't care. "I'm trying to talk about something that matters, something real, a dream, my dream, your dream, other people's dreams, and why we forget who we are and what we are supposed to do."

"Because some things aren't worth remembering."

"You know that's wrong."

"Daniel, I get it. You're angry. You're acting out. Let's just forget about the concert. Mistakes were made, as they say."

I wasn't getting through to her.

Maybe if I touched her, she could feel the electricity crackling in my veins. The texture of what I was trying to say. She'd understand it was never about the concert.

I brushed against her fingers. Gentle at first. No response. Subtlety wasn't working. I pressed my hand into hers. This is real, I squeezed. Feel it.

Sharon pulled away.

"I need some whiskey." She waved at the waiter. "And you need … something."

Luckily, the waiter didn't see her.

I kept going. Probably a little too fast, but she needed to understand. A pulsating flutter, my book, my soon-to-be nonexistent *Practical Guide*, Evergreen failures and successes, none of it mattered, Elle, traffic, Jasmine, love, jealousy, pain. And then … hope.

"Okay, okay, but you have a good life, a comfortable life, an easy job." She indulged me, probably because the waiter wasn't coming over anytime soon. "Doing whatever it is you think you need to do. That's not what people do. You're being crazy."

"No," I said. "Doing what I keep doing is crazy. It's getting me nowhere. I'm telling you, I'm doing it. I'm going west."

"I'll be right here."

"You don't have to stay. Come with me."

And the toothy waiter was at our side. Sharon ordered a Whiskey Sour. "Make that a double," she said. "And a coffee for that one. Make it decaf."

Whatever I was saying apprently made Sharon think I needed sobering.

We sat in silence until the waiter brought our drinks.

She gulped hers while I stirred some cream into my coffee.

Out of nowhere, her eyes radiated warmth, and her hand was back on my knee. I tried to keep my coffee from spilling down my shirt as she squeezed there's got to be another way. A way for us to exist. Stay, Daniel. Stay with me. We can make our lives work here.

"Maybe take some time off. I know a therapist who will write you a letter. You can get a medical leave of absence."

I shook my head no.

"You'd have time to figure out what you need to do."

"I'm not going to be declared incompetent so I can sit back and make money. I can do that without the doctor's note at Evergreen every day for the rest of my miserable life."

"Come on, Daniel. You'd be playing the game and playing it well."

"Maybe I don't want to play the game anymore."

"Just take a week off, go on vacation. What do you have to lose? Come back and see if you still feel the same."

What? No.

"I'm not hedging my bets," I said. "I'm going west."

"Or you could wait and apply to other colleges. There are great schools on the West Coast. I'm sure between your book and that guide you're writing you could get another job, a better job."

"And be a controversial hire so I'd continue to do nothing. No, thank you."

"You could reinvent yourself."

"That's what I'm doing. Reinventing myself."

"Reinvent yourself as a professor," Sharon insisted.

No point responding to that idea. It was ridiculous. We were running out of time.

"Sharon, you're an artist. Greenwood isn't for you. Come with me. Use me to get out of here. Together, apart, it doesn't matter. But you need to get out of here, too. Be free."

"What are you talking about? I'm free. I'm here with you. No husband at my side."

"Real freedom," I said.

Sharon threw back more whiskey.

Her eyes lit up. Another solution. "You could buy a better house, one on my side of town. Get out of the Greenwood Ghetto. Life is happier, safer on the west side. They're talking about adding a gate, you know."

I shook my head. And wake up every morning, trapped, buried beneath the power-washed columns and colonial veneer, no, thank you. I'd rather live in a cemetery. At least with gravestones, eeriness accompanies death, decay, change, and memory.

"Maybe I could meet you out west." Sharon tried to compromise, an everyday occurrence in Greenwood and other planned communities across the United States. "I could meet you in Los Angeles, combine it with a trip to Disneyland for the girls and, in the meantime, you and I could still talk on the phone, chat online. It wouldn't be so bad."

"Maybe," I said before I thought it through. Then, "No. No meeting. No talking. No chatting. You're either mine or you're not."

Sharon's face reddened.

"Yours? You know I can't be yours. I can't just walk away. Not to be with you. You won't even have healthcare."

She told me about Brian and how he had ACL surgery a month

before.

"It would have cost forty-seven thousand dollars out of pocket without insurance," Sharon explained with a smile, happy to be retaining appropriate middle-class values. "What if you break a leg, need surgery on your knee? What will you do then? You're getting older."

She nodded her head slowly. Come on, Daniel. See the light. You know I'm right.

"Well, I guess I'll have to limp then." I shrugged. "But I'll tell you one thing: if I need ACL surgery, it will be because I used my knee climbing mountains or working, not because I jogged too much on the treadmill or I pedaled my three thousand dollar bike up too many of Greenwood's artificially created hills."

"Brian tore his skiing," Sharon said.

"Same difference."

"Not really."

I wasn't getting through to her. I was wasting time.

I needed to go, get out of there. Get home, talk with Zoe, quit Evergreen, begin packing. Or maybe I could leave everything behind. A fresh start with just the clothes on my back.

But … Sharon.

I looked around, hoping for a sign. The warm golds, hospitable browns, and well-placed, sociable oranges told me You've arrived. This right here is what makes life worth living.

And I knew it wasn't.

I stood up and hugged Sharon.

"Daniel," she murmured into my neck. "I am yours, you know, in the way I can be. Given the circumstances."

That voice. Sharon. The way she said my name. "Daniel, we can do this. Just like we did before." Soft. Vulnerable. Carnal.

"Stay," she said. "It used to be good, right? The first time. That's in us. We can do that again. You and me."

And for a moment, my life at Evergreen was perfect. I could write, work a half day a few days a week. Sharon and I could meet in the afternoons and enjoy each other. I could go home to my bachelor life, and Sharon could stay with her obligations. It wouldn't be the worst life. Some would say it sounded pretty darn good. If I wasn't fired, that is.

"I don't think so," I said.

"You're throwing away … love."

"Sharon, love doesn't look like this."

Her boy knew that. Funny it took me so long to catch up with a teenager.

She gripped onto my shoulders like she could squeeze the truth into me.

"You won't be happy," she said. "Out west, you'll still be the same person, just in a different place, away from all that you know, and then what will you have? Nothing but loneliness and depression. Even the dream that there could be something out west for you will be gone because you'll experience *the great unknown* and you'll know the truth: this right here is the best there is."

"Maybe," I said. "But you're right, I'll know the truth, what's real and what isn't. And that's worth the risk to me."

"There can be such a thing as too much risk."

"Not if you're alive. Not if there's hope." I knelt down beside her. I know. Cheesy as hell. But I was feeling it. Something about it felt like a proposal. Even though it wasn't. Not in the traditional sense.

"Get up," she growled.

I grabbed her hand. "Come with me. You can be who you've always wanted to be. You and me. Together, we can figure this out. We can exist where things can be messy if we just get away from this place."

"Shut up and get up. Stop insulting Greenwood. It's a fine place. A great place."

"But it's just that. A place. Nothing special."

"Stop being rude." She yanked at my sleeve. "And get off the floor."

"Come with me. What's the worst that could happen?"

Sharon's mouth opened. Then closed. Then opened again.

"What's wrong with you?" she managed. "Get up. Now."

Sharon pulled me to my feet, but I couldn't stop myself.

"Sharon, look at you. You're cheating on Brian again and again and somehow that's okay because it's Greenwood. As long as the grass on your lawn isn't three or more inches high, everyone's happy. But you're not happy, are you?"

Sharon gnashed her teeth and shoved me. Mid-shove she realized that the couple next to us was staring.

"Just go," she hissed. "Get out. Leave. No one needs you here."

Without saying a word, I dug two hundred dollar bills out of my wallet and plopped them on the table. That should cover it.

And I walked out of The Wood.

No "Come back here!"

No "Daniel! I've changed my mind!"

No "Don't walk away from me! Listen. Come back here!"

No crack in suburban propriety.

Just the sound of nondescript jazz music peeling away as I stepped out into the afternoon light.

CHAPTER TWENTY-NINE

My heart ached for Sharon as I got in my car and drove away. Unlike every other time we parted, I didn't yearn for who we were or what we could have been. Instead, wrenching sadness. This woman I knew, this woman I loved, refused to wake up from a nightmare. A nightmare I knew all too well.

It was as if she were a child, screaming and thrashing in her bed, and I ran in and said "Wake up! Wake up!" and she didn't. And then I started shaking her, a little at first and then a lot. "Wake up! Sharon, wake up!" but she squeezed her eyes shut because the nightmare was all she knew.

Except she wasn't a child. She was an adult. An adult who chose to live alone together with her husband, suturing wounds without thread.

Maybe one day Sharon would realize where she was. Maybe she would see that Greenwood's bubble was not only water-tight, but that she and Brian were running out of air, too. Maybe she'd walk up to the curved plastic border and tear a hole, thrust her hand outside, run her fingers through the wind and the rain and feel the sun beating down on her skin and realize there was more. Maybe that was what she was doing with the blog and the boyfriends. Or maybe that was what she told herself she was doing. Because the truth was neither the blog nor the boyfriends would get her where she needed to go.

But maybe she'd see beyond the free-from-want lifestyle. Or maybe Brian would. One day between the unending yard sales and the pool parties, they might look at each other and say, "We need something more." And maybe they'd set out together—or apart—but either way, maybe they'd shake themselves awake and break out of the climate-controlled sanctuary they created for themselves. It could happen.

Before I could spend too much time thinking about Sharon and who she could become, my phone dinged. Ding. Ding. Ding. Ding. Ding. Like a single-member church bell choir. Text message after text message all from Sharon. Ding. Ding. Ding.

I flipped open my phone. One message after the other, each doused in hatred.

The texts detailed just how much I was going to miss her, then question after question. Was I leaving her for someone else? What did she do wrong? Nothing, obviously. "You're the asshole who can't be satisfied," she wrote. Message after message mushrooming like a PMS-induced nuclear explosion, all evolving into "Fuck you, Daniel."

"You're going to fail," she wrote. "Fail at going west, whatever the fuck that means. You'll come crawling back to Evergreen, back to Greenwood, back to me, but I'll have moved on."

And a barrage. Too fast to read. Definitely too fast to respond to. Autocorrect making it more difficult. "What the duck were you thinking?!? Propelling like some asshole?!?"

And my phone rang. Dean Dyer's office.

I answered it, still hearing the din of Sharon's text messages in the background of the call. Ding. Ding. Ding. More messages.

"Doctor Conrad?" It was Tim. "Dean Dyer requests your presence at her office at five fifteen."

"No need for Dean Dyer to fire me or waste anyone's time setting up meetings and convincing me to resign. I'll do it right here and now. I quit."

"Oh, Doctor Conrad, you're such a kidder," Tim said. "See you at five fifteen."

Tim hung up the phone. Kind of surprising how you could tell someone "I quit," and have them just laugh in your face. I thought about calling Tim back, but I remembered that Dean Dyer did me a favor—or her husband did anyway—and if I was going to quit, I might as well go in and do it in person. No point spending the afternoon reading Sharon's rants, which only made me want to get up and do something. "I'm going to fuck up your little life again" came in while I was on the phone with Tim. "Call your publisher, tell the papers, tell anyone who will listen."

Which, let's be honest, sounded first-rate given that I didn't want to write that damn *Practical Guide,* and I didn't care who knew I was a fake. Expose away, Sharon.

The fact that she was cheating on her husband should be reason enough to leave well enough alone. But no. My maybe-not-entirely-fair realization that all women are insane? Sharon's desire to torch her own village—for the second time—so the heat could scald my skin was proof enough. A man would just leave well enough alone, shrug his shoulders, and say, "Eh, it didn't work out." I wasn't even sure if Sharon loved me—hell, I'm not even sure if she liked me or could tolerate me beyond a meeting here and there—but that didn't stop her from wanting to destroy my life. One more caustic text message: "Watch your back, Daniel."

So, I went to meet with another crazy woman—Dean Dyer—to get away from Sharon, the headmistress of text message vengeance, sure, but more to be a man and face my boss, even though everything up until that moment told me I'd leave the meeting more perplexed and disturbed than I thought possible. But knowing I was on the way out of Evergreen and fully aware that the next hour or more of my life could be taken over by Sharon corroding my character, I went to Dean Dyer's office. Hey, this could be fun, I thought, trying to make sense of illogicality, knowing that none of it mattered anymore. I could be the worst at some arbitrary Evergreen measurement of success. Or the best. It made no difference.

Not that it ever did.

But maybe I could talk with Dean Dyer, get to know her as a person, explain to her why I am the way I am. She could be herself. We could laugh together. Maybe I could show her what's wrong with Evergreen. Maybe she'd agree.

Meeting face-to-face was worth a shot. A shot in the crab bucket of craziness, which meant the pistol would backfire on me or ricochet off the bucket's metal rim in a freak, one-in-a-million accident resulting in me taking out my own eye.

If that was the case, maybe I could transition to "I quit" without much fanfare. Or maybe we could have an enlightening discussion. Either way, it would serve to distract me from Sharon and her rage dinging nonstop in my pocket, which was something. Even though I was running on fumes, energy cracked in my joints, hurling me forward.

I turned my phone off when I got to Dean Dyer's office.

Tim bopped along and told her I was there. Unexpectedly, she didn't make me wait.

"Doctor Conrad," Dean Dyer said, as Tim ushered me into her office. She remained seated and motioned for me to relax. "You look—"

I waved my hand to dismiss whatever she was saying. Either I looked good for a guy who spent the night in the slammer or my face looked worse than I thought from Cam's fists. It wasn't important.

"Fine. Let's start over. It's good to see you're up and out of prison relatively unscathed."

Normally, I would have said, "Jail, not prison." Made a big deal out of it. Then, just for kicks I might have made it seem like I had dropped the soap and the animal magnetism of my hindquarters drew inmates to me like starving children to a Happy Meal.

But I didn't feel like joking. There were real things to be said.

"Your husband really helped me out," I said. "I want to thank him, thank you."

She looked even more uncomfortable than if I had made a joke about Big Al and my derriere. Her chair creaked.

"I won't hear anything of it." She paused. "There's something I need to talk with you about, Doctor Conrad."

"I know," I said. "I'm done for. First the mess with the students protesting and now this whole punching a police officer situation, the Daniel Conrad deserves to die and whatnot will only be worse now. I get it. I punched the guy—"

"Allegedly," Dean Dyer interrupted. "A misunderstanding that caused him to slip and fall."

I was taken aback. Was Dean Dyer spinning my felony charge for me? Why?

"No, I really punched him," I said. Even though I didn't, or I don't recall doing it. Maybe more of a shove? Anyway, I wanted to shock Dean Dyer into being straight with me.

She raised her eyebrows. "Well," she said, "neither here nor there."

"It was downtown," I said. "He landed flat on the pavement. Poor guy."

She sighed. "Doctor Conrad, I brought you in to talk to you about something vitally important."

"Isn't the safety of our law enforcement officers vitally important?"

Maybe I was slipping. Pushing Dean Dyer like I used to. That tendency in of itself was reason to go west, to leave Evergreen and Greenwood—and just go. Patterns, precedents, presumptions about other people. I could break free and stay—maybe if I was a stronger man. Maybe if Evergreen was my dream.

But it wasn't.

"Of course, our law enforcement officers are vitally important to the safety of our community, our nation. They're risking their lives to protect us. I know that more than anyone," Dean Dyer spat before she could take a deep breath and collect herself.

Maybe her father or brother or mother or sister used to be a police officer. Maybe one of them died in the line of duty. If so, I wanted to tell her that I admired Officer Dyer. That was real work. Something worth celebrating. But I'm sure it wasn't that. Probably just Dean Dyer saying what people say. Nothing real.

"Let's get to it. You don't like being in the classroom. We can't have you in the classroom. You know this, right?"

I must not have replied fast enough.

Her voice shifted. Strong, goal oriented. "Let me cut to the chase. We've got an opportunity for you. A perfect opportunity, really."

A perfect opportunity to do what? To leave?

"You will be in charge of your own department."

"You want me to be Chair of the Psychology Department?"

"Well, no. It's a new department. So new, in fact, that there aren't any classes affiliated with it. No students. No colleagues, either. It'll just be you, really."

"Doesn't sound like much of a department."

"It will have all the power and prestige of a full department, but a department of one. And you'll be building it from the ground up, forming the department's goals, figuring out its mission statement, its goals."

She said goals twice.

My head throbbed.

"No," I said more to myself than to Dean Dyer.

"I know what you're thinking." Her voice dropped to a whisper. "Doctor Conrad, maybe I'm not being clear. That's your new job. You will have freedom to do whatever it is you do without impacting the institution as a whole. Without being bothered."

Without bothering anyone, she meant.

"Find someone else, someone more—"

"It's a position tailor-made for you."

And a tingling crept up my leg and settled into my side. I bounced my leg up and down to relieve the pins and needles.

"You know me," she said. "I'm a straight shooter. You know the issues we've been having with student success and completion?"

I must have nodded. Or maybe I didn't. I was flailing my leg around. Either way, Dean Dyer ploughed ahead with the conversation.

"Well, Evergreen just got a grant to address the issue. To come up with a plan. And you'll be heading it up, looking for solutions. You'd be our go-to guy."

I didn't feel like a go-to guy. I shimmied my pant leg up and touched my knee. Hot to the touch. Could I be … having a blood clot? A heart attack? A stroke? Was I—?

"You look concerned. Don't worry. You can't mess this up. We've been non-compliant for thirty years. What's another couple? It's a great job. Foolproof."

I saw a glimmer of whoever Dean Dyer was behind the paper-pusher she played at Evergreen day after day. She had to see that none of what she did mattered.

"Dean Dyer—Carol—tell me the truth. I'm a waste of space here. Someone you have to keep around, but you don't really want to."

Blank expression. The brief flicker of humanity, that wavering flash, that glint that suggested she was a person who understood, extinguished.

"I'm going to have to decline," I said, wondering if I was declining, in decline, or if the numbness was just a side effect of not doing, not moving fast enough.

I got to my feet.

She scribbled a number on a piece of paper. "Here."

And there it was, my new salary. A good deal more than I was making, and with even less oversight and less work.

For a moment, my dream of going west felt unrealistic. I wasn't an adolescent. I had responsibilities. Commitments. A career to think about. An adult would—

"Remember you don't have to do anything. You're just heading it up. We have statisticians. They'll crunch the numbers for you, write the reports. You'd just be our go-to guy."

No work, no more classes, no more students, a place to write, and a government salary with an increasing pension.

"Who could ask for anything more?" I said aloud despite myself.

Dean Dyer smiled. Success.

Adult life: balancing responsibilities, commitments, obligations with desire. I could put off my dream—

Then I remembered Zoe and how she shot daggers at me from the back of Frank's car. Pure disgust.

A flutter. Piercing my side. Crossing my chest.

"No," I said. "I can't."

"This job is good for you, Doctor Conrad. It's comfortable."

"Which is why it isn't good for me." I extended my hand.

"I don't understand."

"I have obligations." I allowed myself to take a deep breath. I would be okay. "To that kid of mine. And to myself. I've got to do something significant. This place is fine, but it's just that, fine. Not hot, not cold, just lukewarm."

"Is this some kind of joke?" Dean Dyer put her hands on her hips. "About the coldest week of the year?"

"No joke," I said. "You know how America was built on people taking risks, coming over here on ships smaller than the new Admin Building, leaving behind everyone and everything they knew, sacrificing for something bigger, something more important than themselves?"

She nodded slowly, no doubt wondering if she was agreeing to some anti-Native American sentiment.

"Well, I've been thinking about that American spirit and how it's evaporated from a place like this."

"Evergreen is a fine, American institution." She frowned.

"With a problem we haven't had to solve for thirty years," I said. "And all I'm saying is that men—and women—used to accomplish real things. Actual, tangible things. All I've been doing here is feeding some metaphorical monkey while I'm on the government dole, churning out crap I don't even believe in for people I don't even want to associate with."

"Take tonight and think about it," she said, "before you make any decisions. We need you, Doctor Conrad."

"No," I said. "That's what I'm talking about. Today, a guy can make an ass of himself, end up behind bars, tell his boss to fuck off, and there will be a second chance, a third chance even. I don't need second chances—or second second chances."

"No need to say anything right now."

"Consequences," I said. "That's what I need. What we need."

"Then you're in the wrong profession. The state's been trying to make us have consequences for thirty years. Those consequences have amounted to a memo here, talk of what we can possibly do, a threat of a small fine, but really—"

"That's why I'm doing this," I said.

For the second time, I stuck out my right hand.

I was steady. Resolved.

This time, Dean Dyer shook my hand.

"Please reconsider. We need you," Dean Dyer pressed.

"Don't lie," I said. "I'm an ass. You don't need me anymore than you need a second monkey on your back."

Dean Dyer smiled. "Thank you," she said.

We shook hands again.

I walked out of Dean Dyer's office, past Tim's desk and out into the Free Speech Zone. No one was there, of course. It was late on a Friday.

I could have paused. Stood in the middle. Looked around. If I'd found myself there yesterday, I would have shouted something.

Instead, I kept walking.

One stride faster than the last.

Past my office. Straight to my car.

Home to Zoe.

Nothing would stop us from being on the road before morning.

CHAPTER THIRTY

"It's done," I raised my hands above my head, triumphant.

"What's done?" Zoe sat cross-legged on the floor scribbling something in a tiny notebook. Weird girl. Her eyes widened. "Tell me you didn't kill anyone."

"No more Evergreen," I said. "And Jasmine's gone. And Sharon's gone, too. Everybody's gone."

"What did you do?" She frowned like she thought maybe, just maybe, I built a bomb and leveled the place. Not an impossible thought; it would be a way to succeed in taking out Sharon and Jasmine and all of Greenwood Planned Community with one detonator. Boom.

"Never mind," I said. "I'm free and I'm going to be a man. Just you and me on the open road, getting the hell away from this place."

"Wait, you're going to be a man? You are a man, aren't you?"

"A man biologically, yes. But spiritually? No."

"Sounds like progress."

I walked toward her. She recoiled.

"Whoa, what happened to you?"

I touched my face. My lip was bleeding and my left cheek felt swollen. I smiled.

"Life," I said. "But I'm better now."

Zoe frowned.

I couldn't help but say, "Be happy. Things are good!"

"It's just that … did you do something bad? Are you on the run?"

"No," I said. "Look alive. I quit my job. Broke up with everyone."

Zoe snorted. Yeah, yeah. Everyone.

"We're going places, you and me. Doing things."

"You worry me," she said. "It sounds like a lot of change all in one afternoon."

"Isn't this what you wanted? Me to stand up for something? To believe in something?"

"Sure, yes," she said. "I just … it's just that … are you okay?"

"Better than I've been in years. And your life—*our* life is going to keep getting better."

I walked over to her and sat, also cross-legged, at her side. "What do you want to do?" I asked.

"Tonight?"

Come on. Not tonight.

"No, I mean with your life."

I was hoping she'd say she wanted to become a therapist, a lawyer, or a doctor, and I'd say, "Done," like the benevolent, good guy father figure I wanted to be despite my lack of income. Maybe she'd say she wanted to take her degree and do some good for the world. In my head, Zoe would say "I want to be a pro bono lawyer, Daddy" and I'd say "You want to do something good for the world, Zoe. Then, I'm going to do something good for you" and plunk down the cash so she could do it. Not that she called me Daddy and not that I had the cash, but still.

"I'd like to go to art school."

"Art school?"

I strained to bury my disappointment.

"The Rhode Island Art Institute. I got in. Had to defer admission for this semester, but I'd like to go. If it was a perfect world and I could do anything I wanted, I'd go there in a heartbeat."

I must have sighed.

"Art school is legitimate."

A legitimate waste of money. Couldn't be her real dream. Not the practical, witty Zoe I knew. Art school. It sounded like something a child would fantasize about.

"No, really, who do you want to be? No joking around," I said.

She pursed her lips. "I want to go to the Rhode Island Art Institute. It's what I've always wanted."

Really?

"It's not easy to get in," she continued. "They reject ninety-three point two seven percent of their applicants. It's an honor to be accepted."

"And how much does this honor cost?"

"Forty-four nine and change."

"Forty-five thousand?"

"Forty-four nine and change."

"A year?"

She nodded.

Wow. Just wow. I was floored. Forty-five thousand a year.

Times four. That's a hundred and eighty thousand dollars. Zoe's dream. Nearly two hundred thousand. Panic set in. I wanted to give Zoe her dream. Be the person in her life who gave her something without expecting anything in return.

Maybe there was still time to call Dean Dyer back and ask for a second chance. That grant position must still be available. Unless she'd offered it to someone else. Probably Frank, the bastard. Maybe I could contact Tim and maybe he could get in touch with Dean Dyer and maybe she could say, "Sorry, Frank, I know we just offered you that cushy job, but Daniel Conrad needs it more, so sorry, Franky-boy, you're all out of luck." I'm sure Frank would take it in stride. "All yours, buddy," he'd say with the smugness of the bigger, better man. Could I do it? Could I go back to Evergreen for Zoe and give all those people the satisfaction—and give myself the dissatisfaction?

No.

But Zoe was looking at me.

"Okay," I said. "You're going next semester. I'll pay for it."

"What?"

"I'll figure it out," I said.

"No. You can't. You just quit your job."

"I'll figure something out," I said.

"No, you won't. I'm going to do it myself. Loans. Scholarships. I won't take your money."

"Let me do this," I said.

"No," Zoe said.

"I'll call the school and pay your bills."

"I'll tell them not to accept money from you."

I shook my head. "Why won't you let me help you?"

"You barely know me. You don't even know who I am."

"You're my kid," I said. "I may be a loser and an idiot, and you might wish that Frank was your father and not me, but I'm your dad."

Zoe smiled. "Frank," she said. "Why are you so fixated on Frank all the time?"

"Well, I doubt Frank would send you to that Rhode Island Institution."

"Probably not." She smirked. *Institute,* not an institution. "But then again, you shouldn't either."

"No," I said. "You're going to that damn school and you're going to let me help you do it."

Zoe smiled. "I'm going. It just might take me a bit to pull the money together, but I don't need your help. I can always go next year."

"Next semester," I said. "You can try to pay me back if you want. But let me help you start. Please."

"Then I'll pay you back with interest," she said.

I told Zoe to stop thinking so much and to throw on her fanciest clothes so we could go out on the town.

"There's a lot to celebrate," I said. "You as my daughter and me as your father for one. Also, there's the fact that you're going to that school of yours next semester."

Zoe beamed.

"I don't have anything to wear except some ratty old T-shirts and jeans," she said. "Is that okay?"

"What about Frank's dress?"

She laughed. "I still have that."

"Then throw it on, Pardner," I said.

"I look like a freak."

"Freak, artist, same difference. You better get used to it if you're going to art school."

She laughed and went into the bathroom to change.

"Bring anything you have on that institution of yours," I shouted after her.

"Institute, not institution! It's not a mental asylum!"

Zoe came out wearing the oversized dress.

"It's a perfect dress for a linebacker," Zoe said as I swept her out of the house and into my car.

We drove around to the fanciest restaurants we could find, all in Greenwood's Planned Community of Overpriced Complacency. As soon as we pulled into a parking lot, we stayed in the warmth of our car and watched the people walk in and out of the restaurant. Then, one of us would say "Too stuffy" or "Too hoi polloi" before we drove on, laughing because they all were the same: suburban safe. Not extraordinary enough to be *too* of anything in particular.

"People sure eat a lot in the suburbs," Zoe said when we came across our eighth restaurant in a quarter mile radius.

"Animal instinct," I said. "They're all afraid someone might come and burst their artificially created bubble, so they're eating, trying to stuff their faces, in case they get pushed out into the scary unknown of downtown Green County."

"Or maybe they're spiritually empty," Zoe said.

At what felt like the tenth restaurant parking lot, we settled on a steakhouse.

"You don't have to do this," she said. "Fast food's just as good."

"You think I can't afford it?" I winked. "We better eat here before my paychecks stop coming in. Pretty soon I'll have the stink of the unemployed. Then they won't seat me at these places anymore."

Inside, we ordered rib eyes and Zoe told me about The Rhode Island Art *Institute* over our appetizers. Despite her transient lifestyle, the girl had college brochure after college brochure with little tabs marking spots in the course catalogue with degree plans and potential classes she wanted to take.

She opened one of the brochures and pointed to pictures of the school and told me about how she wanted to get a B.F.A. in Furniture Design and a second degree in Jewelry and Metalsmithing. For once in my life, I didn't mock something as silly sounding as metalsmithing. I didn't question what she planned on doing with the degree: did she plan on living in a barn like some Amish person carving and cobbling things together? Wouldn't she get splinters whittling all that wood, or wouldn't she burn herself liquefying pieces of filigree in a forge? Instead, I just listened as Zoe told me everything she knew about Rhode Island.

"It's against the law to throw pickle juice on a trolley in Rhode Island," she said.

"What about pickles?"

"Very good question. Maybe it's fine as long as the pickles don't become pulverized into juice somehow."

Then she told me all about the school. Its rigor, its alumni, the professors she could learn under, which all sounded great.

"Oh, you'll love this," she said. "I can concentrate in Psychology, Sociology, Computer Science, or Business." Which I have to admit sounded like the only real thing there, probably because of my own career choices, which had gotten me nowhere fast.

"Don't study something you don't believe in," I said.

"But it might lead to a job."

"A job you don't want," I said. "Try doing what you want to do first."

Zoe told me her dream of opening a furniture shop. She showed me sketches of intricate folding tables, dressers, and cabinetry. Then she turned the conversation to me.

By this point, our steaks had arrived, so I was mid-chew when she asked me what I planned on doing with my life.

"I'll figure it out," I said.

In the glow of the steakhouse, Zoe asserted again that any money I tried to pay would be returned. "I'll draw up one of those loan charts and pay back every last penny with interest."

I told her I didn't want her money.

She insisted. I insisted back. I told her I'd win because I have more experience convincing women to do what I wanted them to do. "I'm Daniel Conrad, remember?"

"I'm definitely paying you back now," she said. "Why are you so gross sometimes?"

I thought through the numbers. I had that Porsche I probably shouldn't have bought and a house with a good forty-five grand of equity. If I could sell the house for a profit—maybe twenty more than I had paid for it, then that would put me at sixty-five. And then there was the Porsche. I was still paying on it. Maybe that would be a wash, but I'd have to get rid of it. Maybe the dealer would take it back? It had those scratches on it. I should fix those first.

"But you'll be happy?" Zoe asked.

"I'm already happier," I said. "Might be the company, but it's probably the Greenwood lifestyle. And this steak."

She laughed. "Let them eat steak!"

So I could count on sixty-five thousand or so, which would be enough to send Zoe to school for a year. That would give me enough time to go west, find something to do, cobble together enough to give her more. I didn't need much. Despite the warmth emanating from my plate and filling my belly, I didn't need the amenities Greenwood Planned Community provided. I could see myself living on an oilrig or working on a fishing boat or living in an apartment with a bunch of men, sleeping on the floor as we worked to make ends meet. It didn't matter. What mattered was Zoe and that silly dream of hers to make tables with secret compartments that looked like nothing I'd ever seen before probably because I wasn't the type of guy who bought expensive furniture. Still. Her ideas seemed unique and marketable.

"I doubt I'll ever be able to afford one of your tables," I said. "Promise me you'll send me one when you're famous."

"Well, that's one thing I can guarantee. You'll never need furniture," she said. "I'll send you so many pieces you'll get sick and tired of my work."

"Me? Get sick and tired of secret compartments? You know me, I've got to keep all my lies straight somehow. And since I'm only getting older, these little folding cabinets, nooks, and crannies will keep me organized."

"Maybe that's how I can market my furniture." Zoe perked up. "To shady old people!"

"As good of an idea as any."

Zoe got quiet for a second. "You sure you're not just running away from your problems?" she asked. "Like someone straight out of a psychology textbook?"

"I don't know. Maybe," I said. "I've taught Psych 101 more times than I can count. The whole textbook is probably etched in my brain, informing my actions. Chapter Thirteen, I believe, will help solve some of this. You want to see a mediocre slideshow on Freud's Ego Defense Mechanisms?"

"No, no, no." She snickered. "Seriously. Tell me."

"No running away," I said. "I'm running *to* something. Something bigger than Evergreen. Something bigger than Greenwood. Something bigger than me and my ego."

Zoe smiled. "That's the first thing you've said that's made any sense."

"Probably because it's the truth," I said.

The waitress came by with the dessert tray.

Zoe oohed and aahhed at the white peppermint bark cheesecake, the chocolate meringue with fresh berries, and the caramel apple mousse.

"You want to skip dessert?" Zoe asked.

"Give us one of each," I said to the waitress. "We're celebrating."

"Is it the young lady's birthday?" the waitress asked.

Zoe's eyes flashed. "Do you even know my birthday?"

"Do you know mine?"

"October?"

I shook my head.

Zoe then cattle-rattled, "January, February, March, April, May, June, July, August, September, October, November, December—first through thirty-first—am I right?"

I nodded.

Zoe clapped her hands. "I'm a genius!"

"So not a birthday then?" the waitress interrupted.

"No, a death day." Zoe grinned. "Daniel Conrad's dead. Long live Daniel Conrad."

And by the time the waitress returned with the larger-than-life plates of heaping chocolate, meringue, and gooey goodness, the hundred and eighty thousand dollars wasn't on my mind.

EPILOGUE

Okay, admit it. You thought I'd somehow go back on my word, figure out a way to weasel out of caring for Zoe after a good night's sleep. Maybe you doubted I could be that evil, but you thought I could be like everyone else. Maybe you assumed I'd find a way to fall back into bed with Sharon, or at the very least, maybe you thought I went back to Evergreen for one more semester.

Sorry to disappoint you.

Instead, I spent the next week building my new life. It took a week to tear my old life apart, another to come up with a plan for Zoe. I talked with Frank.

The bastard took the job Dean Dyer offered me and, now that he was making thirty-five thousand dollars more, he jumped at the chance to buy my Porsche, scratches and all.

"Time for that midlife crisis mobile," Frank said. "Now that I'm doubling down at Evergreen, I'll need something."

He paid too much for it. Zoe said he was just being nice.

Probably. He somehow succeeded in negotiating himself into more than the asking price, which meant he was being nice or he really is a fool.

"An extra five grand for the fact that this car was owned by *the* Daniel Conrad," he said. "Although, really, given all the women who hate you, I should knock ten off the price. My tires will be perpetually slashed."

Frank also threw in his old Civic, which Zoe says is another reason Frank's a good guy, which just might be. Although he is a hack for taking that job.

The last time I saw him, my better angels wanted to thank him. Thank him for being there for Zoe. For Jasmine even. Instead, when we exchanged keys, I just couldn't get it out.

"You're one shitty driver," I said instead. "And this is a nice car. High performance. Not a piece of junk. You'll need to watch the road more."

He laughed and patted me on the back.

Frank just might be a competent enough psychologist to know what I was trying to say.

The bastard.

"When you're ready to race, you know where to find me, buddy.

My new Porsche versus your new Civic. May the best man win."

Yeah, yeah. Yuk it up, Frank.

Thanks to Frank—there, I said it: thanks to Frank—I have an extra five thousand plus a beat-up old sedan I can use to drive Zoe to Rhode Island before I turn around and head home … to my new life … past Evergreen … west.

Which means I have more cash than I expected from the car after I paid it off. And then the house. Its proximity to campus combined with its location in the inferior end of the superior suburb of Greenwood means I can rent the thing out and make enough to pay the mortgage and Zoe's living expenses. Just a matter of finding the right renter.

Zoe says not to worry. God will provide. The first time she said it, I was shocked. Who believes in God anymore? But lately when she says it, I just say, "I'll believe it when I see it."

So now we have a renter ready to move in, and November is peeling away to late December, when Zoe and I can head out. Zoe to Rhode Island and me out west as far as Frank's Civic takes me. Of course, Zoe had to set her sights on a school as far east as humanly possible. Zoe says that's God's way of making my journey all the more difficult. Which makes sense. If anything controls the universe, it no doubt enjoys laughing at me, flopping around, making a mess of my life.

Who knows if I'll make it. The snow alone may block me in the Rockies. I just need one dense, winter storm and I'll be a Donner Party of one. With the possibility that I might find myself stranded, I originally planned to avoid driving back through Greenwood just in case Zoe's God wanted to continue the sick joke and have Frank's Civic break down in the middle of where I used to be. A town that doesn't know the old me would be better than the suburb that recognized and permitted the worst of who I was.

But no point avoiding Greenwood. If I'm stranded there for the rest of my life, I will be fine. Hell, I could work at Evergreen again or take up at the Greenwood Community Center teaching with AH-mazing Alan the poetry teacher. It doesn't matter. I have a dream—Zoe's dream—and that's enough to make me want to be different, even under the same circumstances.

Still, maybe, just maybe, Frank's Civic has more getup and go than I expect.

The best part is I know what I won't be doing. Wherever I find myself, I won't be the man I used to be.

Before we left town, I wrote three checks. One to my agent, Alexandra Morris, for the advance and the personal loan. One to Benny for triple his "salary." Then one to The Rhode Island Art Institute for Zoe. That one was technically an e-check, but it amounts to the same thing.

And with a total of six hundred and forty-three bucks in my pocket, no money in my bank account apart from what Zoe needs for tuition and living expenses, I loaded the last of our meager belongings into Frank's old Civic.

Zoe rushed across the icy grass and jumped in the driver's seat.

"Get in." She gestured to the passenger's seat. "Quick!"

I pushed the trunk shut and vaulted into the passenger's seat. Before I could get my belt on, let alone the door closed, Zoe peeled out of my street, lurching Frank's Civic enough to make me wonder if we left the transmission on the pavement.

"You know how to drive a stick, right?"

"Maybe."

"You're not giving me much confidence."

"Take a risk then," she said.

And we were on the interstate, driving east, away from everything we knew. Zoe stopped jerking the car. The road felt too smooth for a second. I glanced up.

Exit sign after exit signed beckoned. I took it upon myself to keep my head down and fiddle with Frank's CD player, which wasn't working.

"Last chance." Zoe gestured.

A bright sign: Exit now. Greenwood Planned Community. Family. Friends. Safety. A lure to well-developed discontentment for the old me.

"Nice try, kiddo," I said. "Not who I am anymore. Not what I want."

"What do you want?"

"To fix this thing." I yanked Frank's broken CD player out of the Civic's audio console and fiddled with a few loose wires. I had no idea what I was doing—making it worse, probably— but I tugged and click. The console powered on. Done. I hit play.

Earsplitting disco music reverberated off the speakers and rattled our bones.

Zoe tried to muffle her ears.

I toggled the volume down to a normal level. Still the synthesizers soared. That Frank. Of course he loved the worst music from the seventies.

Normally, I would have complained about other people's tastes, turned it into just how stupid everyone was, is, will be.

Not this time. This time I just started dancing. Right there in my seat. A little disco hustle.

"What are you doing?"

"Dancing."

"Is that what you call dancing?"

"Look at this move." I shuffled to her. "Bet you can't do that."

And, shaking her head, Zoe started to dance, too. A dance that was worse than mine if that was possible. Zoe wants me to include that she was driving, managing the clutch, shifting gears, and watching the road. Not to mention she had to keep at least one hand on the wheel. To which I say, "Excuses, excuses."

That's how we found ourselves leaving Evergreen and Greenwood's city limits behind. The airport and the old factories that once made Green County a booming testament to the immensity of American ingenuity were on the horizon. Even ragged and boarded up, the factories invited us to keep going, to keep trying.

So, me and that little girl of mine, together, we traded a mouthful of lies for a taste of hope. And we abandoned the material security of the familiar for the unfettered frenzy of a life we knew existed somewhere, even though neither of us had seen it or known anyone to get where we were trying to go. But we knew it was more than possible. That place existed.

"That's faith," Zoe said, somewhere on the interstate as the billboards told us we were going somewhere even though we were in the middle of nowhere. The disco music scarcely in my memory, just the sound of the bumpy road. A pothole here. A bit of gravel there.

Faith, sure. Let's just leave it at that.

Because that's the kind of guy I am. Daniel Conrad, letting a woman get the last word in a story I thought was all about me.

About the Author

Natasha Alvandi earned her Ph.D. from the University of Southern California in Victorian Literature in May 2011. She is a graduate of Rice University.

She taught English and writing for ten years at the University of Southern California and Lone Star College before she moved to Estes Park, Colorado.

When she isn't hiking mountains or volunteering at the library bookstore, she is pursuing a Master's in Counseling at the College of William and Mary.

This is her first novel.

For more information and to stay updated on the author, please visit www.natashaalvandi.com

ALL THINGS THAT MATTER PRESS

FOR MORE INFORMATION ON TITLES AVAILABLE FROM
ALL THINGS THAT MATTER PRESS, GO TO
http://allthingsthatmatterpress.com